LAST ONE SEEN

LAST ONE SEEN

A THRILLER

REBECCA KANNER

CROOKED
LANE

NEW YORK

Published in the United States by Crooked Lane Books, an imprint of The Quick Brown Fox & Company LLC.

Crooked Lane Books and its logo are trademarks of The Quick Brown Fox & Company LLC.

Library of Congress Catalog-in-Publication data available upon request.

ISBN (hardcover): 979-8-89242-128-7
ISBN (paperback): 979-8-89242-250-5
ISBN (ebook): 979-8-89242-129-4

Cover design by Heather VenHuizen

Printed in the United States.

www.crookedlanebooks.com

Crooked Lane Books
34 West 27th St., 10th Floor
New York, NY 10001

First Edition: September 2025

The authorized representative in the EU for product safety and compliance is eucomply OÜPärnu mnt 139b-14, 11317 Tallinn, Estonia, hello@eucompliancepartner.com, +33757690241

10 9 8 7 6 5 4 3 2 1

For Sarah

CHAPTER

1

Now

December 1, 2024

WE'RE SPEEDING NORTH. I don't know where we're going, other than away.

Eli is driving so fast, I feel like I'm being kidnapped. Or rescued. It's hard to tell. He told me I shot Justine and he's taking me where the police won't find me. He said, "Justine is gone, Hannah. Try not to think of her."

I'm hunched over in the passenger seat of his F-150, trying to hide my tears. I'm crying for him, for Justine, and for myself. I don't want to believe I killed her.

There are three people I suspect of killing her, and I'm only one of them.

I have to know: *Which of us pulled the trigger?*

Duncan, the director of the graduate writing program, is first on my list of suspects. He lurks at the edge of my nightmares. I can't shake the vision I have of him following me out of the party last night, just before Justine was killed. He follows at a distance he thinks is safe. He assumes I'm too drunk to see him. But I'm always on guard around him, because of what he did to me. I've seen the deadening in his eyes, the humanity seeping from his features and leaving something hard and impenetrable behind. He's capable of anything.

Eli is the second person on my list. I feel guilty for suspecting him. I love him and he loves me, but part of him remains unknowable. Everything he does is in service of some plan no one else knows about. He wants something, but I can't figure out what. Was falling in love with both Justine and me part of the plan, or a mistake? Was getting rid of one of us the only solution?

And finally, there's me. I can't trust myself. Not since I stopped taking my medication.

I can't remember exactly when or why I went off it; I was doing so well. Was I too broke to shell out the $200 a month for thirty tablets? Or did I want the highs the medication steals from me?

I took my last pill sometime this fall, and afterward, I no longer did things quietly. My run-ins with Justine weren't a secret. I'd become suspicious of her and who she claimed to be, but that wouldn't have driven me to murder. Only one thing could. She could have everything else: the money, the awards, everyone's respect and admiration. But Eli, I needed all to myself.

CHAPTER

2

Now

AROUND NOON WE stop at a hotel in Iowa. That's when I find out I'm "missing." I see it on the news before Eli changes the channel.

At first I don't recognize the missing girl in the photo. I only take note of her because of how quickly Eli leaps off the bed, his T-shirt straining against his back as he reaches his arm out, rocking the old hotel TV with the force of his hand as he makes the girl disappear from the screen.

Even in just the brief moment I saw the photo, I recognized the surroundings. The little bridge in the background. The trees along the Mississippi in the fall.

The girl in the photo is me. Hannah Silver. I'm the "twenty-six-year-old graduate student and aspiring writer who went missing yesterday evening."

I want to switch the channel back, but Eli is sitting close to the television now. Guarding it. He worries about me. Due to my past with Justine, when the police find her dead, they'll want to question me.

I'm not in a good state for questioning. Justine has driven me mad. She is my torturer and my muse, and her death hasn't changed that.

"Where are you going?" Eli asks when I stand up from the bed.

"The bathroom."

I don't usually close the door, but I don't want to give Eli any more reason to worry about me. I'm going to do something I want to keep secret: look into the mirror.

My eyes are dry and red, with dark hollows beneath them. My bones have started to show through my skin, skin so pale it's almost bluish. My cheeks, my only truly beautiful feature, the one that lifts me into the "pretty" category, are disappearing. But what makes me raise my hand to touch my face is the scar. The cover-up I applied last night has worn off. The scar is a circular mark with a trail, like a comet streaking from my cheek.

It doesn't matter, I tell myself. *I finally have Eli all to myself.*

I slowly pour water from a cup next to the sink into the toilet bowl so he'll think I came in here to pee. I flush, wait as long as it would take to pull up my pants, and return to him. To us, and our new life together.

CHAPTER 3

Then

April 2024, four months before graduate school, St. Louis

THE STARS FIRST aligned for Justine and me to meet the day I received an acceptance letter from Washington University in St. Louis. I'd gotten into their master of fine arts in writing program, but the letter also said that they could not offer me a stipend "at this time." I decided to see if I could change that.

I set up a visit to the university, then convinced another server to cover my shifts at The Hot Dish. I drove the eight hours from Minneapolis to St. Louis overnight, singing along with the radio whenever I could tune in something other than talk radio. I was going to be a *real* writer—not just someone who'd written one good short story for grad school applications. But only if I could secure the funding.

I arrived while it was still dark and watched the sunrise from my car before walking toward campus, elated, as if I were entering a fairy tale. I stopped at the base of two sets of stairs leading up to the first building. Brookings Hall loomed at the top of a wide, sloping hill—masculine and intimidating. It looked like a cross between a state capitol and a palace. It dared me to come closer.

I knew that if I belonged here, I would finally be somebody.

As I approached Brookings Hall, I was intoxicated by the beauty and bittersweet scent of the blossoming cherry trees. I took a deep breath of the fragrant air before passing under the Brookings archway and entering the English building.

Inside, the English department wasn't so splendid, except for the wide staircase, its thick, ornate wooden railings leading up to the second floor. I could feel, deep in my soul, that the staircase was magical. All the stories I could write seemed to loom above me, as hungry for me as I was for them.

I wrote in my head as I floated up the stairs. Instead of simply turning 180 degrees at the landing, I twirled and ascended higher. At the top, I found a reception area with a long table across from me, covered in a linen cloth. From my research, I knew graduate school programs in the liberal arts were half academic and half social, and that the socializing involved lots of wine. A faint smell of red wine still lingered. I could almost hear the echo of boisterous, drunken voices from all the department parties and guest lecturer receptions that had filled these halls.

On the left, I saw a hallway that was quite ordinary. I walked past rooms with professors' names and office hours handwritten on signs taped beside their doors. At the end of the hallway, I found a room with an airy energy.

Is this where the workshop takes place? I wondered. I sensed it wasn't. *Too ordinary.*

I turned around and walked the other way down the hallway, toward a dark, heavy oak door. It creaked as I pushed it open, revealing a huge lounge. No one was inside, yet the air vibrated with energy. *Big things happen here. This is where stories are workshopped.*

I didn't fully understand what workshopping was, only that it sparked ideas and shaped them into packages ready to be launched into the world. I sank into one of the couches and imagined my peers arrayed beside me. Together, we were fashioning a giant book, its pages flying in a loose circle around the room. We grabbed them out of the air, letting them dance in our hands.

I have to be here next year. I have to convince the director to fund me.

A sense of urgency surged through me, and I sprang off the couch. I rushed down the enchanted staircase and through the hallway to the English office. When I entered, the ancient secretary continued compiling some papers without looking up at me.

Does she even know I'm here? I wondered.

I stepped up to the desk, clearing my throat. "Hel—"

"What can I do for you?" she interrupted without looking up.

"I need to meet with the director."

Still without looking up, she said, "Do you have an appointment?"

"No, I was just hoping—"

"Have a seat."

I set up camp in the corner of the office with a book, my laptop, and a bottle of flavored coffee I'd gotten at a Kum & Go gas station along Route 218 in Iowa. It felt like I was waiting for something to happen—like a story about to begin. After two hours, I finally got called in to meet the director.

As soon as he opened his door and the secretary introduced him, my heart started to race. I stood up and walked toward him, standing as tall as I could and forcing myself to make eye contact. I extended my hand. "I'm Hannah Silver. Thanks for meeting with me."

"I'm Duncan, and I'm always happy to talk with prospective students," he replied, gesturing for me to come into his office. But instead of meeting my gaze, his eyes traveled down my body.

I launched into my pitch before I'd even sat down in the chair across from his huge, imposing mahogany desk. I told him how much I loved Washington University, and how dedicated I was to my writing. I offered to do whatever work I could to get funding. "I'd be willing to do anything, from secretarial work to giving campus tours," I said as he brushed some invisible lint from his tweed sport coat.

He nodded and thanked me for coming in. He hadn't even leaned back in his chair. "We'll take this all into consideration. And now, I'm afraid I have another appointment, but a few of our current MFA students would be happy to show you around."

Without the offer of a stipend, it was just window-shopping, but I couldn't resist. I had to see it all, even though it was still out of reach.

I'd thoroughly studied the website so I'd have intelligent things to say and wouldn't feel out of place. I followed behind the students, praising the "collegiate Gothic architecture." I told them it was modeled after the campuses of Cambridge and Oxford, adding that I adored it, especially the grotesques. Distorted, fantastical human and animal creatures perched on cornices, crouched above portals, and glared from the shadowy recesses of the Gothic archways. They were bizarre and beautiful, the way I sometimes felt since getting my scar. I saw mermaids and mermen, alongside traditional medieval grotesques with beaked heads. I said a silent prayer to a lion gargoyle as I watched water spouting from his mouth. It felt like some kind of omen. This place, with all its history and strangeness, was waiting for me. I couldn't help laughing aloud when we came to some owls judiciously studying Latin texts. I knew many of the grotesques had been there since the 1904 World's Fair, while the origins of the others were a mystery.

Everything I saw only made me fall deeper in love with Washington University. I wanted to go out for drinks with the current students and get some insider information on the department. I needed to know what my chances of receiving funding were. Had any of them also been left in limbo last spring? Was there anything they could do to help me?

It didn't take much to get them talking. The program was small—only five first-year students and five second-years—and we hit it off right away. As we sat tightly packed around a long table at Market Pub, I could feel it already: the confidence and power of belonging to a group. Phong, a first-year student, told me about Justine Updike, "a distant relative of the legendary writer John Updike. She can't decide if she wants in."

Claire, another first-year student, said, "Justine was accepted to ten MFA programs, but she won't commit to any of them. That means someone on the waiting list won't know if they're in until Justine finally makes up her mind." She turned to me, her heavily made-up eyes peeking from behind a wall of jet-black hair. "I'm glad you've already gotten in."

They told me all of this before anyone had even finished their first mug of Budweiser. Someone had poured me a glass before I could object, so I'd just said "thank you" and let it sit untouched in front of me. I knew better than to mix my mood stabilizer with alcohol. By taking my pill every night, getting enough sleep, and not drinking too much, I'd managed to avoid having an episode for over three years. Every time I saw my psychiatrist, he asked me two questions:

1. "Is there any chance you could be pregnant?"
2. "Have you been drinking?"

I'd been able to reply "No" to both questions every time he asked them.

I'd read the warning label on the pharmacy printout: *Alcohol can increase the nervous system side effects of Lamictal such as dizziness, drowsiness, and difficulty concentrating. Some people may also experience impairment in thinking and judgment. You should avoid the use of alcohol while being treated with Lamictal.*

My future looked bright, and I wasn't going to mess it up.

The consensus was that securing funding would simply be a matter of waiting it out. "The university has a nine-billion-dollar endowment," Claire said. "I'm sure they can spare a little for you."

The words "billion-dollar" were heartening. I was feeling pretty damn optimistic. I'd been accepted to a prestigious university, and it seemed like I would have plenty of friends. Claire made a toast in my honor. She was smiling so hard I could see a dimple in her left cheek. "To a happy, well-funded future!" she cried, and we all raised our mugs. I touched mine to my lips and set it down without taking a sip.

CHAPTER 4

Then

April 2024, four months before graduate school, Minneapolis and St. Louis

CLAIRE TEXTED ME the week after my visit: Apparently Wash U is still on Justine's radar. She's visiting Thursday. I'll let you know how it goes.

I was eager to get back on campus. I wanted to see Claire again, and I was curious about Justine. I got another server to cover my Thursday and Friday shifts and headed south.

When I met the MFAers at Market Pub, Justine hadn't arrived yet. Claire hugged me and said she was glad I was back. Everyone seemed genuinely happy to see me. I felt like I had finally found my people.

An hour later, Duncan, the director who'd barely had time to look me in the eye while I'd practically begged for funding, brought Justine to Market Pub himself. I knew it was her the moment she walked in the door. She had a retro celebrity aura about her. Twiggy-thin and wearing huge Chanel sunglasses, she commanded attention. When she took them off, Duncan stared at her as though he'd just witnessed a surprise striptease. She carelessly stuffed the sunglasses into her purse, as though they weren't worth hundreds of dollars.

Excitement was jerking the director around inside his skin as he walked her over to our table. He looked much more alive than when he'd spoken to me a week before.

"Allow me to introduce you to our current students," he said to Justine. He didn't even mention me. In fact, I don't even think he noticed me—or much of anything else. Justine's jeans looked painted on, and he was standing behind her.

I'd seen plenty of gaudy, expensive clothes on the wives of Minnesota Vikings or other newly rich women who came into The Hot Dish. Some of them tipped big, some stiffed me.

But Justine's jeans were different. They exuded a comfortable, take-it-for-granted sort of wealthy. Normally, I don't care about nice clothes, but she was wearing Balmain skinny jeans that I'd stalked on eBay for a year and a half. I used to get notifications on my phone whenever the price dropped, but it never fell far enough for me to bite. I guess that was their appeal, though. I wanted them because I'd never be able to afford them. Still, I'd clung to the hope that, through some late-night mistake by a fumble-fingered, drunken seller, they'd come down enough that I'd find my butt in a $1,500 swath of 98 percent cotton, 2 percent elastane.

Another student spoke up. "And Hannah, also a prospective student."

"Of course," the director replied, glancing at me for nearly an instant. "I didn't see you there."

A few seconds later my phone vibrated, and I saw I had a text from Claire: Maybe if his eyes weren't stuck in Justine's pants, his powers of observation would be better.

I hit "haha" and smiled at Claire across the table, but I couldn't really blame the director. There was a certain glow about Justine. She seemed to take up more space than she occupied. Her eyes were a stunning blue, and heavy-lidded enough to make her appear both seductive and distant. She had long brown hair and wore a black silk tank top without a bra. She didn't have anything to hide, it seemed. She hardly even had thighs. If she ever needed male attention, she could just send a picture of herself to the horny geeks at *The Chive* for their "Mind The Gap" feature.

But she didn't appear to need anyone's attention or approval. She simply said, "Hi. Pleased to meet you." She didn't seem *overly* pleased, though, which was part of her appeal. She knew the whole room was watching her, and it didn't affect her. Did her confidence come from her success as a writer, or from her looks?

I shifted uncomfortably on the bench, aware of the weight of my body and the scar on my face. I reached up to make sure the cover-up I'd applied was still there.

"Let's just get this out of the way," said Ben, a first year who looked more like an offensive lineman than a writer. "What's your relation to John?"

The director cut in. "That's not why she's here," he said. "She's an accomplished writer. She recently won *The Atlantic* student writing contest—a pretty impressive accomplishment for an undergrad."

I remembered Claire mentioning that Justine was a student at Columbia, but she hadn't said anything about the competition. I looked at the other students. They seemed just as surprised as I was.

Justine smiled, then dismissed Duncan by saying, "Thanks for bringing me. I'm sure I can find my way back to the Hildale House on my own."

I'd read that the Hildale House was usually reserved for visiting professors. What story could elevate a student to the same level as a professor? I wanted to read Justine's story as soon as possible.

The director practically bowed, his gaze still fixed on her, as he backed away toward the door. He didn't even notice a man he bumped into until the man told him to watch where the hell he was going.

Justine didn't answer Ben's question about her relation to John Updike, but that didn't stop him from sliding over to make room for her on the bench beside him. Apparently not enough room, though.

"Very flattering," she told him, "but I'm not that thin."

Ben blushed and scooted over even more, but Justine wasn't interested in sitting next to him. She walked around the table and gracefully stepped over the bench to sit between me and Amelia, a first year who I can only describe as extraordinarily ordinary; lank brown hair covered most of her face, which was pinched with tension.

Ben slid his beer across the table so it was in front of Justine. She barely glanced at it before ordering herself a vodka cranberry. Ben looked a little hurt, but she wasn't paying attention to him. She was looking at me.

"So, Hannah, where are you from?"

She remembered my name.

"Minneapolis," I said.

"Did you ever see Prince live?"

For a split second I considered lying to her and saying yes, but then I shook my head.

"I have a framed photo of a bridge lit up purple to commemorate his death," she said.

"The 35W bridge."

"Someday I want to walk across it dressed like Sheena Easton, blasting 'U Got the Look' at full volume from an old-school boom box."

I felt a twitch inside. A glimmer of what it felt like at the beginning of a manic episode, when the world abruptly went magic, and it seemed that anything was possible.

"That's the best idea I've heard in a long time," I said, my heart beating a little too fast for casual conversation. "I'm in."

"I thought you might be," she replied, winking at me as the server brought her vodka cranberry.

Did she really say that? I wondered. The playful look she gave me as she took her first sip confirmed she had.

She turned to the table and asked, "So, what happens in this place?"

"Market Pub?" Ben asked.

"Well, if you want to start small," she said, causing Ben to blush again. "But what I meant was, what happens in St. Louis?"

"Ah, STL," Ben said. "The 3-1-4."

"The 3-1-4?"

"The area code," he hurried to explain, dealing a fatal blow to his sex appeal. A guy who rushed to explain his quip wasn't going to end up with Justine.

The students told us about the touristy things we could do while we were in town: go up in The Arch, tour the Busch plant, and go to blues clubs.

After a while, the bar became too loud to talk to anyone except the person right beside you, and Justine leaned in closer to me. "So what about you? What do you write?"

I told her I was a server "for now" and that I was writing stories about a girl who walked alone at night. I didn't mention that my stories were based on my life or that the girl often ended up in frat houses and woke up there the next morning. I also didn't mention bipolar disorder, and that in fact the story I'd submitted to get into Washington University was about going manic.

When I asked her about herself and what she wrote, she sighed. "I'm getting so bored with myself and the story that won *The Atlantic* competition."

"I'm sure it must be annoying to constantly have to talk about your work," I said. (I didn't tell her it was also hard when *nobody* asked about your work.) I hoped she would choose Washington University over the other schools she was considering. Being near her felt like being near greatness, like there was only one degree of separation between me and success.

She smiled, lifting her vodka cranberry again. I couldn't help but notice the grace with which she moved, her fingers long and slender, manicured with simple, clear polish. "To drinking in good company," she said.

I hadn't realized Ben was eavesdropping, but he yelled to us so loudly the whole table turned to him. "We may or may not be good company, but we do enjoy drinking. Don't all great writers?"

We laughed. Modestly, except a bit louder than necessary. Though we'd never admit it, we were all desperate to fit in.

I clinked my glass against everyone else's and then touched it to my lips without drinking.

Justine stared at me over the rim of her glass. Her eyes were steady, focused. Soon the whole table seemed to be watching me.

I tipped my glass slightly farther back so it would look like I was taking a sip. My hand shook and I accidentally tipped my glass too far. Beer dribbled down my chin.

I closed my lips too late to keep a drop from slipping between them. I tasted the beer and felt it tingle on my tongue. I looked for a napkin to spit into, but there weren't any. As I swallowed, a memory of my last manic episode came rushing back. I involuntarily touched the scar on my cheek.

"Are you okay?" Claire asked.

"I'm fine. I just have to pee," I told her. I pushed away from the table and headed straight for the bathroom. I didn't actually have to go to the bathroom; I had to go to the mirror.

I was staring at my reflection, oblivious to all the people around me, when I heard Justine's voice. She was behind me, looking over my shoulder at my face. Her eyes were tracing the outline of my scar.

"How did you get it?" she asked.

It had all started with Jeremy.

CHAPTER

5

Summer 2020, Minneapolis

UNTIL JEREMY INTRUDED upon my life, I'd been managing my unruly energy fairly well—well enough, at least, that I hadn't ended up in a hospital or jail.

I'd always been prone to periods of risky behavior, especially when I was under stress. I ran away from home a dozen times before I was sixteen. But I always ended up coming back to make sure my mom was okay.

I was never sure how she would react to me. That uncertainty stirred up a panicky feeling in my chest, so I was always checking in with her, hoping she would be happy with me. If she was talkative and smiley, I felt better. If not, at least I knew where I stood with her, and I didn't have to feel uncertain anymore.

I wasn't aware of it at the time, but she had borderline personality disorder. Later, in therapy, I learned that I was obsessed with her approval because it was sporadic. The therapist explained that intermittent reinforcement—rewards given at unpredictable intervals—produces the greatest effort from the subject. I was also obsessed with her approval because my dad had suddenly disappeared when I was five. She wouldn't tell me what happened to him. Only that he'd "gone to another place."

One day, as I sat on the edge of her bed combing her hair, she said, "You know, your father deserted us." I was eight. After that, I looked at other families—families where the dad had stayed—and wondered how they were different from my mom and me. What was wrong with us?

When my mom was out of bed, she wasn't home. She was out at bars with various men. She took cold medicine or whatever the men gave her and stayed up for days.

I hated her for preferring the company of random men to me. But also, I understood. I was obsessed with guys, too. I wished I could be out with them all night like she was.

When I was eleven, I Googled my father. I wanted to find a picture of him so I could stare at it for some clue as to why he left. Had he made himself a new, better family?

Instead, I learned that he hadn't left us; he'd died in a car accident. He was the passenger in a car my mother had crashed into a tree while she was drunk. I asked my mother about it one day as she stood in the kitchen with her back to me, staring into a cupboard. I knew from checking the cupboard myself that it was empty except for a few cans of vegetable soup.

"Mom," I said, but she didn't turn around. I couldn't tell if she hadn't heard me or if she simply didn't care. "Why did you tell me dad left?" I asked. "Why didn't you tell me he died?"

She turned around and smacked me across the face. It hurt, but not as badly as when she stayed out all night.

By seventeen, I'd started staying out all night too. I didn't need any drugs to do it. I would get excited about something, usually a guy, and suddenly I didn't need sleep. I hardly even needed food.

I'd walk along frat row on University Avenue, hoping the guys on the balconies would see me and yell down to invite me in for a beer. It was never just one beer, and sometimes I woke up on the couch or in someone's bed not remembering what happened the night before. What I did remember, though, kept me coming back to the parties:

dancing in a crowd of college kids, guys competing for my attention, and people cheering as I chugged beer.

The only way I could sleep during that time was by drinking until I passed out.

I'd taken enough online quizzes to know that I had some sort of mood disorder. The jury was still out on whether it was generalized anxiety disorder, borderline, or bipolar. I always erased my browser history after taking the quizzes. I didn't want any evidence that I had psychiatric problems. I didn't want to be like my mother.

I managed to stumble my way through high school and college successfully enough to be in denial about my mood disorder.

Then came Jeremy.

He moved into the rundown house next to my apartment building in Minneapolis. I could see his nipple piercing through his wifebeater. If he had an easy smile, the piercing might have been sexy. But even from thirty yards away, I could tell he was as mean as they come. Or, at least, as mean as I knew of at the time.

I'd just been cut early from the dinner shift at The Hot Dish, where I'd been waiting tables since getting my BA in English the year before. I'd managed to find a parking spot right in front of my building. I was looking forward to putting my feet up and doing absolutely nothing with the same excitement as some people look forward to Christmas morning.

Jeremy was on the stoop with another guy who was also in a wifebeater. They were talking about some fight they'd watched. "After getting knocked out, that dude was down on the floor so long I thought he was dead," Jeremy said.

"That would have been so cool," the other guy replied.

Jeremy noticed me staring at him. I quickly looked away, but still, he called out to me, "Hey. What's on your shirt?"

I was wearing a sweatshirt I'd gotten the summer my mom sent me to Jewish summer camp. We weren't religious. She just wanted me out of the house. There was a Star of David on it and I was afraid that's what Jeremy was asking about.

I was so nervous I dropped my purse, and a lipstick went rolling down the street.

"Hey," he repeated, too loudly for me to ignore him. "Need any help?"

The way he said "help" turned my stomach. It sounded like he was proposing to do more than help me pick up my things. I turned to him and forced a smile.

"I've got it, thanks," I said.

"I don't think you do," he replied. He flexed his chest, and I could see his nipple piercing shift slightly beneath his wifebeater. When he smiled, the skin beside his eyes didn't move.

I laughed as though he'd made a joke and turned back toward my apartment building.

But as I walked away, the other guy said, "Shit, Jeremy. It looks like you're not going to get a piece of that."

"Yeah," Jeremy agreed. "She looks like one of those cold Jew-bitches who never gives it up."

Jew-bitches? People had said all sorts of anti-Semitic things around me, but only because they hadn't known I was Jewish or because they somehow didn't know that "Jew" shouldn't be used as a verb for getting the better of someone in a deal. This was different.

I had to get away from Jeremy and lock every door I could between us. The only creature I wanted near me was Lucy, my cat. She usually roamed the neighborhood while I was at work and magically appeared whenever I came home.

I was relieved when I heard Jeremy and the other guy laughing. It seemed like they were content to just snicker.

Before entering my building, I looked for Lucy and called her name, but she didn't come. She had many admirers in the neighborhood, including an older woman whose apartment she sometimes stayed at overnight. Exhausted and eager to put my feet up, I returned to my apartment without Lucy.

The next night, when Lucy still hadn't returned, I began to worry. I went around knocking on my neighbors' doors. The old lady hadn't seen Lucy. No one had, until I talked to a guy whose apartment smelled like weed. When I asked him if he'd seen Lucy, he said, "totally." I was afraid he was just really high and hadn't actually seen

Lucy. But then he walked deeper into his apartment and pointed out the window at Jeremy's house. "Isn't that her?"

I hadn't thought to look at Jeremy's house or I could have seen her from my own apartment window. I started frantically waving my hands, hoping Lucy would look up from the windowsill she was laying on and notice me. She stood up and I could see her little mouth moving, meowing, and she put a paw against the window as though she wanted to reach out to me.

I grabbed Lucy's cat carrier from my apartment and hurried over to my new neighbor's house. Using the flashlight app on my phone, I found the doorbell. Like everything else about the house, it looked old and abandoned. I pressed on it and waited.

No one answered, so I started pounding on the wooden door.

The door swung open so quickly that I stumbled forward, barely stopping my fist from hitting whoever had opened it. I could only faintly see his outline in front of me. He didn't turn on any lights. I could feel his presence as much as I could see it.

"Did you bring me a housewarming gift?" he asked. He remembered me. I couldn't see his expression, but his tone made me want to take a step back.

"My cat is missing," I said.

I heard fumbling and then a click as Jeremy lit a cigarette. The tip glowed brightly as he inhaled. He exhaled smoke into my face. "Yeah?"

"I think you accidentally took my cat."

He stepped toward me and stood in the doorway. I could see him now in the glow coming from the streetlight. He was in his boxers. Only boxers. I saw not only the mini-barbell nipple piercing and teardrop tattoo beside his eye, but another tattoo as well. His left pectoral was stamped with a large black swastika.

"Please just give her back, and I'll leave you alone." My voice wavered between pleading and demanding.

"I'll tell you what. You can come in here and look for her."

His tone was threatening. I knew better than to go in.

Lucy sometimes came when I called, so I yelled, "Lucy! L*uuuu*cy! Come here, Lucy."

Jeremy stepped out onto the stoop so we were only a few inches apart. He took a drag of his cigarette, and then, without stubbing it out, he tossed it past me, out onto the lawn.

"I don't have your fucking cat," he said.

"I saw her."

"You saw *my* cat. Anything that comes into my house is mine. Even if I drag it in."

He reached for my arm. I screamed and stumbled back off the stoop, dropping the cat carrier. I could hear him laughing as I ran back to my building.

When I called the police, the woman who answered told me that I'd need some evidence that Lucy was mine before I could report her stolen.

"But I don't have any evidence," I replied. "She's a stray I took in."

"I'm sorry," the woman said.

* * *

The next morning, I stood on the stoop of my building with my week's tips in a wad in my pocket, waiting for Jeremy to come out for a cigarette. I hoped he'd be easier to deal with in the daylight.

He emerged around 7:00 AM and lit a cigarette as he walked onto the stoop in baggy jeans, boots, and a wifebeater. He left his cigarette in his mouth, stuffed his lighter in his back pocket, and pulled a can of Rock Star from his front pocket.

As he cracked it open, I noticed marks I hadn't seen in the dim light of the streetlights—scratches along his arm.

"Hey," I called. He didn't respond. He just stared at me while he replaced the cigarette in his mouth with the can of Rock Star.

"I'd like to buy your cat," I said. I held up the wad of cash, fanning it out so he could see how much there was. He came over, and before I could take my hand back, he grabbed the money. He stuck it down the front of his pants. "Now someone is taking *your* money," he said, and then added, "*Jew.*"

"What are you talking about?" I cried. "I've never taken your money. You can't do this."

"I just did," he said. He raised his hands up and looked down at the bulge of money in his pants. "You want it?" he asked daringly.

I gazed around, searching for help. Across the street a man was coming out of his apartment building, so I waved and yelled, "Help!" He quickly looked down and continued to his car. I turned back to Jeremy. "I'll call the police," I said.

"Do you want me to kill my cat?"

I wished I were bigger than him so I could simply punch him in the face and take his keys. I could feel tears streaming down my cheeks.

"I have to get to work," he said. He took a single bill out of his pants and dropped it on the ground. "You're welcome."

I watched Jeremy pull out of his garage in a Killz Pest Control van. His comings and goings weren't going to be a secret. The van's engine sounded like it was dying of emphysema. A silhouette of an upside-down cockroach decorated the side door, which was dented from the inside. Black curtains covered all the windows, and both fenders had streaks of paint on them. I couldn't tell if the paint was from other cars, or road signs, or if it wasn't paint at all but blood.

I waited until his van disappeared from view before bending down and picking up the bill. It was a ten, and it was all I had left to my name.

That day at work, my friend Luke was bartending and he sneaked me a couple shots when I told him I was having a rough day. While refilling bread baskets and drinks and listening to snippets of conversations and the yelling in the kitchen, my fear for Lucy began to turn to anger. *How dare Jeremy take Lucy? How dare he do that to us?*

I could feel the power building inside me. My thoughts were going faster, sometimes repeating, sometimes scattering in different directions.

"Hey," Luke said when he found me in the break room, "Caddy is at one of your tables right now getting an earful." Caddy was the manager, someone I normally tried to appease. But how could I focus on Caddy when some asshole had Lucy? Luke continued, "They're complaining about the service."

I tried to explain to him what had happened to Lucy.

"You're talking too fast," he said. "I can't understand you, and I have to get back to the bar. Go home, get some sleep, and give me a call tomorrow." I wondered why he didn't want me contacting him at night. Was he dating someone? I'd never asked him because I didn't want to make our friendship awkward.

That evening when I pulled up outside my apartment building, cars were packed bumper to bumper on both sides of the street. A loose circle of men stood on the lawn outside my new neighbor's house. The streetlights illuminated the smoke rising from their cigarettes.

I either had to wait for a spot to open up or drive around looking for one and walk back. I couldn't wait. I found a spot two blocks away and hurried back, keeping my eyes straight ahead and putting on a sweatshirt. I pulled the hood up.

None of the men on the lawn acknowledged me as I approached, except a couple who looked me over.

I could hear a party going on inside the house. Jeremy opened the front door and called out, "The keg is ready. Go in the back door and down the stairs to the basement. Have your cash ready. Ten dollars for a cup. If I see anyone trying to sneak in their own cup, I'm going to bash their head in and put them six feet deep out here."

As the guys walked up the back stoop into the house, their boots clomped heavily on the steps. I followed, my heart rate climbing. Were there any other women in the house, or would I be the only one?

I entered a dimly lit kitchen. A few guys stood around talking. One of them was counting money. I got cold looks from a couple others. *You don't belong here* looks. No matter how old some guys get, they will always essentially be little boys in a tree house with a *No Girls Allowed* sign.

I couldn't find Lucy anywhere on the first floor. The window I'd seen her in from my neighbor's apartment was empty, and the shade was drawn. *Dammit,* I thought. *She must be in the basement.*

As I approached the basement door, I felt like I was in one of those scenes from a horror movie where I always want to call out, *Stop! Turn around! Don't be a fool!*

But I couldn't turn around. Lucy needed me.

A huge man with a bandanna over his head and a scorpion tattooed on his neck was selling red plastic cups. Another guy handed him a ten dollar bill and walked down the stairs. When I held my ten out to the big man, he didn't take it. I tried to pass by, but he put an arm in front of my chest. "You're in the wrong house," he said.

Looking at the scorpion, I thought, *Unfortunately, I'm sure I'm not.* Maybe he assumed I was too soft for this place. "I'm a friend of Jeremy's," I said. "Why else would I be at this sausage fest?"

He considered this for a moment, then, satisfied, he snorted and took his arm away. He grabbed the ten out of my hand. I almost didn't hear him mutter, "Flavor of the month" as I walked past him.

I stopped halfway down the stairs when the song "Blind" by Korn started blasting over the speakers. A few men started jumping up and down and deliberately colliding. I'd been to First Avenue too many times not to recognize the beginning of a mosh pit. I knew Lucy wouldn't want to be anywhere near all this noise. Maybe she was trapped.

Someone pushed me from behind and I stumbled to the bottom of the steps. I felt a hand on my arm. "I heard you talking to the guy upstairs about sausages," a man yelled in my ear.

I shook his arm off and moved away without looking at him. But he followed and swung me around to face him. I could see he was missing at least three teeth as he said, "I got a big one."

"Congratulations."

He grasped my wrist and drew it to the front of his pants. I felt the men around me closing in. "Wanna party with this?" he asked.

I couldn't break his hold on my wrist. I had to get away, and not just from him, but from the whole scene.

With my free hand I pretended to futilely feel around the crotch of his pants, as though I couldn't find what I was looking for. "With what?" I asked.

He swore and released my wrist.

A couple of men laughed. "She got you there, Toothy," one said.

I pushed a couple of guys out of my way and ran up the stairs.

Someone yelled, "Bitch," but no one stopped me as I hurried away through the kitchen. Instead of going out the back, I headed for the front door to avoid running into anyone else. As I opened it, I saw the cat carrier sitting on the porch.

"Lucy!" I cried, my heart lifting as I looked closer and saw her inside. She was too terrified to meow but her eyes were hopeful as she gazed back at me. I grabbed the carrier and ran back to my apartment. I locked the door and looked out the peephole to make sure no one had followed me.

CHAPTER

6

Then

JUSTINE'S QUESTION ECHOED against the hard surfaces of the bathroom. *How did you get it?* She was still staring over my shoulder into the mirror, waiting for me to answer.

"It's a long story," I told her, moving my hair so it covered the scar again.

Her hand appeared beside my face in the mirror and I felt her smoothing my hair away from my cheek and tucking it behind my ear. "I wouldn't have noticed it if you hadn't touched it," she said, "but if you want to hide it better, you just need more cover-up."

She took out a tiny vial of concealer and lightly dabbed it on the scar. I realized she was the first person I'd allowed to touch it.

A toilet flushed in the stall behind us. A woman came out, staring at us with wide eyes. Did she think Justine and I were lovers? Or was she staring at my scar?

"Let's get back," Justine said, "before we miss any juicy gossip."

"Okay, one minute," I said. I rinsed my mouth out, trying to forget that I'd accidentally taken a sip of beer.

As Justine led us back to the table, I felt like security for a celebrity. She absorbed everyone's stares, leaving me invisible. It was a relief. I didn't have to be self-conscious about my scar.

My stomach tightened when I saw my beer still sitting on the table. I'd hoped it had somehow disappeared.

"Are you sure you're okay?" Claire asked as I sat down.

I nodded.

"Was something wrong with your beer?" she pressed. "Was there something in it?"

"Yes," I replied, "alcohol. I'm not supposed to drink."

Claire swooped it off the table and handed it to the server. "Can we get a couple of waters here?" she asked.

I heard Justine's voice in my ear. "Please rescue me." Without turning her head, she glanced in Ben's direction to direct my gaze. Ben was staring at Justine, too drunk to hide his fascination.

"I'll read your palm for you," I told her.

We turned our chairs so we were facing each other. I didn't like turning away from Claire, but Justine needed me. *Thank you*, Justine mouthed.

I reached for her right hand, the one that offers insight into work life and how a person presents themselves to the world. I spread it open and studied her palm. Maybe I splayed it too far, or maybe there wasn't enough fat in her palm; the lines were too shallow to see in the dim light of the bar. But as I tilted it slightly, I did see something. Her heart line, the one that arcs upward toward the base of the middle finger, was long and curved. Her passions and desires drove her. Mine was long and curved, too.

Her life line was short though. Much shorter than mine. In fact, it was the shortest I'd seen. I guessed she was about my age, twenty-six, so if what I'd read online about palm reading was true, she'd die before me. *Way* before me.

My chest tightened. If she died young, it probably wouldn't be from natural causes. But that didn't seem like a good thing to tell her.

"Your life line is long," I said. Maybe I would have been more convincing if my voice hadn't wavered.

Her palm was starting to sweat. Her eyes were open wide enough now that when I glanced up, their absurd brightness startled me. I could see the faint outlines of her blue-colored contacts. This girl who was related to John Updike, who was the top pick of multiple MFA programs, who had the sort of thoughts that lead to winning *The Atlantic* student fiction contest, was going to die one day while I kept on living.

How odd.

I looked back down at her hand to hide my eyes and hopefully my thoughts.

She had hardly any love line, but a fat Mount of Venus. My love line wasn't as short, and my Mount of Venus wasn't as fleshy. I lightly pressed on hers, wondering if she was promiscuous or intensely sexual with one person.

It's none of my business, I told myself. I let go of her hand and became aware once again of the other students, the noise of the bar, and the smell of the street whenever someone opened the door. I reached for my water without meeting Justine's eyes. "I'm sorry," I said. "I wasn't able to see much in your palm."

She leaned in close. She smelled like the Chanel counter: a patch of violets slightly drunk on champagne. "Never apologize," she said. "It's weak and these people will sense it. Don't you see they're sizing us up?"

Us. I liked that. She was taking me under her wing.

"We'll all be fighting for every award," she continued, "whether it's here or somewhere else. So let's agree. No more suddenly getting up and running to the bathroom. No more 'I'm sorrys.'" She shoved her drink at me. "Have the rest of my vodka cranberry, and then smile like we're about to conquer the world."

I'd forgotten all about Claire, but she suddenly grabbed the drink and downed it. She slammed the empty glass back on the table while staring down Justine. "Thanks," she told her.

"It was for Hannah," Justine protested.

"Hannah doesn't drink," Claire said.

"Oh, I didn't know."

"Well, now you do," Claire said. She turned to me. "Do you want to get out of here?"

Justine grabbed my arm and shook her head no.

"I'm going to stay a little while longer," I told Claire.

Claire didn't say anything for a moment. I thought she was going to object, but then she simply said, "Enjoy." She gave a curt wave to the table and left.

Ben leaned across the table. "So, what do you write about?" he asked Justine.

I thought she was going to ignore him, but then she said, "Does the 'about' really matter?"

"Oh," he said. "Well, who do you like to read?"

"Russian writers, mostly."

"Tolstoy? Dostoevsky? Chekhov?"

"Yes."

"What's your favorite Dostoevsky novel?"

Instead of answering, she said, "You must know that graduate school isn't just about reading and writing."

I knew Justine was talking about connections, and I knew that if I wanted to be successful, I'd need the kind that made someone want to publish your story or invite you to a party where someone else might.

But I wasn't ready to think about that yet. I was afraid of what powerful people in the literary world might want from women. I'd read about the Bread Loaf Writers' Conference in *The New Yorker.* The article had nicknamed it "Bed Loaf" because of all the sex. Wedding bands just meant there was a story leading up to the lusty moment in which two people found each other. A past. "Material."

A shot had appeared in front of us. A guy at a table across the room raised his own shot glass to Justine. From what I could see, he was tan and had a nice jawline. Justine looked at him, tossed back the shot, and half-smiled at him.

I was afraid I was about to lose her attention for the rest of the night before finding out what I most wanted to know. "Do you think you'll come here next year?" I asked.

I wasn't sure if she'd heard me. Just as I was about to repeat my question, she turned back to me with a wistful smile. "I don't know," she said. "But if I do, we're going to bring this city to its knees."

We laughed, because we both knew we weren't really going to bring anyone to their knees. We were just writers, after all.

At bar time, when the manager flashed the lights, I noticed that my palm, especially where I'd held Justine's knuckles, was a different color than usual. Lighter. I ran my finger over it and the color faded. It was concealer, like she'd put on my cheek. Why did she wear concealer on her *hand?*

I knew. I'd felt teeth marks on her knuckles. They're called Russell's sign, and I understood exactly how she'd gotten them: she made herself throw up.

CHAPTER

7

Now

December 2024, northern Minnesota

THE DIRT ROAD ends before the cabin comes into view. We only know it's there because of the mailbox. Eli shuts off the engine, squeezes my knee, and says, "We're home." Then he pulls a bolt cutter from the back.

He heads down the snow-covered path to the cabin, and I stumble after him with a cooler and a few bags of dry food he got us at the grocery store on our way here. We have meat, cheese, rice, beans, oatmeal, pasta, snacks, and spices. He and I are truly settling in together.

As we get closer, I see that the cabin is neglected: boards are nailed over the windows, and the doormat has been chewed up by squirrels or some other sharp-toothed animal.

It's free for the taking.

I stand back as Eli cuts the padlock. He cautiously opens the door, looks around, and then motions for me to come in. The only evidence that any creature lives here is the mouse poop in the corners.

"Welcome to your new home," he says, his breath forming a little cloud of steam. He pulls a fake pink flower out of his pocket and presents it to me. It looks like the ones cashiers tape to pens to keep customers from stealing them.

"Awww, thank you." I reach to take it from his hand, but he tucks it behind my ear.

I imagine how ridiculous I must look in winter clothes with a flower behind my ear. "Am I a tropical beauty now?"

"Totally. Minus the tropical part."

Inside our new home, there's a bed with rough sheets and a plain down comforter, an oak table, two chairs, a rug, and a woodstove. We find a couple of blankets in the closet and drape them over our shoulders. It looks like we're wearing capes. What superheroes are we? Mystery Man and Blackout Girl?

I sweep the mouse poop out and move our few belongings and supplies into the cabin while Eli gathers wood. I huddle near him as he starts a fire in the woodstove. "Don't leave that meat out there," he tells me.

"Sorry," I say. I've fallen back into the habit of apologizing. It's strange that Justine will never again have the opportunity to correct me.

"We're not the only animals up here. There are wolves and bears out there," he says, gazing out the window at the vast snow-covered forest that surrounds us on three sides.

I peek out cautiously to make sure no wild animals are lurking before I go outside to pack some Ziploc bags with snow. I put the bags and the meat in the cooler and bring it inside.

I feel like a domestic goddess as I warm some baked beans in a pot I find hanging from a hook and slice up some beef jerky to add to it. Eli crushes some chips and throws them in. We're so hungry, it tastes like heaven.

"I have something for us," he says, lifting a box out of one of the grocery bags. It's an apple pie, which he sets on the stove for a few minutes, filling the whole cabin with the scent of dough, cinnamon, and sugar.

"Thank you," I tell him after swallowing the last bite of the huge slice he gave me.

He takes my hand. "From now on, I'm going to satisfy all your appetites."

The bed is firm, and I feel all of him more than I ever have before. We're north of all we've ever known. We're each other's everything now.

We've come all this way for me.

Afterward, we savor the heat we've generated. It feels as though our bodies are expanding like dough, filling in all the space between us. "Spooning saves lives," he says. We cling to each other beneath the covers as though our lives depend on it, which, now, they do.

CHAPTER 8

Then

THE TEETH MARKS on Justine's knuckles were my first hint that she wasn't as untroubled as she seemed. I thought also of her clear nail polish and discreetly expensive clothes. For someone who gave the impression of being naturally beautiful, she put a lot of effort into her appearance.

I followed her as she walked out of Market Pub. She glanced at the cars parked along the street. "Which of these is yours?"

My car was a mess. Snacks were scattered across the passenger seat, some of them in the form of crumbs. Worse, I had a sleeping bag in the backseat. I didn't want her to know I planned to sleep in my car if I was too tired to drive all the way back to Minneapolis that night. "The Hildale House is only a few blocks from here," I said. "I may as well just walk you back."

She gestured down at her shoes. Black heels that clearly weren't meant for walking.

I was about to say sorry for suggesting we walk, but I remembered in time not to apologize.

I drove her back to the Hildale House, wondering if we'd really see each other again. It felt like a perfect life was finally within my reach. I just had to get funding to make it happen. When I pulled up outside the Hildale House and put the car in park, Justine thanked me and squeezed my hand. My chest was swelling with the vision I had of us hitting it off the next year. I wanted her to know that I would be a good friend. I looked down at the teeth marks on her hand, then back up into her eyes. "Justine, if you ever need to talk about anything, I'm here for you."

She blinked a couple times.

"The marks on your hand, beneath the cover-up," I said. "I know they're from your teeth."

She snatched her hand back as though she'd just found out I had leprosy. Anger flashed in her eyes. I felt my stomach drop. I'd never forgive myself if I'd destroyed our bond.

"Thanks for the lift," she said. But her tone said, "Fuck you." She turned away and reached for the door handle.

Was she afraid I'd tell the others she was bulimic? "Don't worry," I tried to assure her, "you can trust me. I also have something I keep secret. I mean, I know that sounds contradictory." I was floundering, but I couldn't stop. "I hope I'm not upsetting you. I just want, I mean, I realize we might have something in common. I want you to know I understand."

She let go of the door handle and turned to look at me. "What secret?"

I only hesitated for an instant before telling her my secret, the secret that had given birth to all the others. "I have bipolar disorder. But don't worry, I haven't had an episode in years. As long as I take my medication and avoid drinking and drugs, I'm okay."

"An episode?" she asked.

I was relieved to see the anger leave her eyes. I wanted to restore the bond that had formed between us at Market Pub. "The mark on my cheek? It's from some trouble I got into during my last episode."

"Let me see it again," she said.

I pulled a Wet Ones from the pack I kept in the console and wiped Justine's cover-up off the scar on my cheek. I turned on the dome light. "It's a long, convoluted story, involving drugs and a biker gang," I said.

She gently touched the scar. It felt more intimate than anything I could remember. Certainly more intimate than any of the encounters I'd had with men.

"What did this?" she asked.

"A cigarette."

CHAPTER

9

Summer 2020, Minneapolis

THE MORNING AFTER rescuing Lucy, I walked the two blocks to retrieve my car from where I'd parked it the night before. As I approached, I saw Jeremy leaning against the driver's side door. I stopped. It was a bad sign that he recognized my car and had come all this way to confront me.

"I couldn't get into your apartment building," he said. I was standing ten feet from him, which felt way too close. He smiled cruelly. "And I wanted to give you something."

He stepped away from my car and raised a baseball bat.

As I turned to run, I heard a crash. I glanced back and saw that the driver's side window was cracked and Jeremy was already winding his arm back to swing at it again. This time his swing shattered the glass. My heart clenched in my chest. Afraid as I was, I couldn't just let him get away with this. I needed to catch what was happening on camera.

I ducked behind a parked car and reached into my pocket for my cell phone. It wasn't there. *Shit.*

I ran home and called 9-1-1 while looking out the peephole on my apartment door to make sure Jeremy hadn't followed me into my building. An officer from the Minneapolis Police Department showed up an hour later to take my report.

"Were there any witnesses?" he asked.

"I didn't see anyone else. I was too afraid of Jeremy to look around at anything else."

"We'll check with the residents in the area, see if they saw anything. Maybe someone has a camera that caught something."

"Thank you," I said, refilling the mug of coffee I'd given him. I hoped that my gratitude and politeness would make him like me and be thorough in his investigation.

"Did you and this Jeremy guy have a relationship?"

"No," I said, feeling disgust at even the thought of touching him in any way.

"I'm not trying to upset you. I just need to know as much as possible. Does Jeremy have some sort of grudge against you?"

I felt defensive, as though I'd done something wrong. "I'm Jewish," I replied.

The officer looked at me. "You think he has a problem with that?"

"He has a swastika tattooed on his chest."

"So he may have done some time. Guys get a lot of stupid tattoos in prison. I'll definitely run a background check on him."

Anxiety rose into my throat, making it hard to speak clearly as I told him, "He called me a Jew-bitch. He said, 'She looks like one of those cold Jew-bitches who never gives it up.'"

The officer took a deep breath. "Okay. Let's start from the beginning. When did you first meet Jeremy? I want to know everything that's happened from that moment to this one."

I told him about Jeremy moving in next door and taking my cat. I left out the part about going to a party at his house to retrieve her, and simply said I'd found Lucy on the porch.

"Did you call the police about him stealing your cat?" he asked, glancing around as if he didn't believe that I actually had a cat. He turned to look at the windowsill and Lucy looked condescendingly back at him. I was glad to see that her time at Jeremy's hadn't crushed her spirit.

"Yes," I replied. "I don't have any proof she's mine, though, so I was told you couldn't help me."

"I want to help you, Hannah. We're going to do everything we can."

"This should be investigated as a hate crime."

He nodded. "Yes, I agree. In the meantime, the best thing you can do is file a restraining order. Do you have friends or family you can stay with?"

That wasn't what I wanted him to be interested in. I didn't answer his question. Instead, over the high-pitched ringing that had just started in my ears, I asked, "Are you going to arrest Jeremy?"

"I don't know. I am going to question him."

The officer drove me to my car. My poor Corolla. I felt as though somehow I had let it down by not watching over it more carefully.

The officer added a few things to the police report, and then offered to drive me back to my apartment. "You may as well go home and start figuring out where you're going to go. I'm going to stick around and see if anyone got anything on camera."

"No," I said. "I'm not going back yet."

He tried to reason with me, but I told him all I wanted from him was for Jeremy to be arrested.

I didn't have any time to waste. I could feel it—the mania coming on. I didn't know what to call it then, but I knew the sensation of being taken over. Everything was on the table.

* * *

I went into work on my day off to ask Luke if I could borrow some money.

He came out from behind the bar and hugged me. "I'm worried about you," he said, handing me a small wad of tips.

"You won't have to be worried for long," I replied. My fear was fading, or perhaps it was just buried under the surge of manic energy, which hungered for action more than anything else.

I had a plan to get rid of Jeremy.

I drove to the nearest biker bar, exhilarated and annoyed by the wind whipping my face now that the driver's side window was gone.

A sign that said *The Establishment* hung over the door. The bar was dimly lit and small enough that I could see everyone inside, but it wasn't so small that a person couldn't discreetly trade a wad of cash for a baggie of meth. I was a bit more put together than the other customers, so I decided to tell whoever I tried to buy it from that I was a student.

I got a vodka tonic and sat at a table near the bathroom. Sitting still and watching to see who was dealing felt unbearable. I couldn't shake the urge to move. I kept catching myself tapping my foot or drumming my fingers on the table.

A man in a leather jacket sat alone at the bar, and people gave him a wide berth as they passed on their way to the bathroom. I couldn't see his expression, nor could I tell much from his clothing. His leather jacket didn't have any patches on it. The only thing that distinguished him from any other guy was how much the leather strained against his broad back.

During the first hour I was there, he went outside and came back three different times.

After the third time, I bellied up to the bar two stools away from him and ordered another vodka tonic. This was no place to pace myself. Without openly looking at him, I could see he had a skull tattooed on one hand and a tombstone on the other. He didn't say anything to me. He didn't even look at me.

I was inspired by my first interaction with Jeremy to "drop" my lipstick on the floor so it rolled toward the man's feet. I leaned *waaaaaaaaaaaaaaaay* over to get it, hopeful that he wouldn't be able to pass up the chance to look at my cleavage. I'd worn the least-modest shirt I possessed.

They say you can judge a person by their shoes. I smelled his freshly polished boots even through the rancid stench of old beer on the floor. I'd read that old shoes, when immaculately maintained, indicate that someone is conscientious. Is there such a thing as a conscientious meth dealer?

When I sat up, he was still looking straight ahead. He wasn't fidgety. He definitely wasn't his own best customer.

"Hey," I said.

He didn't respond.

"I like this place. It's my first time here."

He didn't even glance at me. Maybe he wasn't a fan of small talk. I decided to cut to the chase. "I'm a student at the University of

Minnesota, and I have finals coming up. I was wondering if you have anything to help me study for—"

"No."

"I have the cash." I opened my pocket so he could see the money, but he didn't even glance at it.

"Get in your car and get out of here," he said.

"What's wrong with my money?"

"I don't recognize it."

"I'm not a cop."

"You're not a student."

I stopped lying. He could see through it. "True. I'm a server."

Finally he looked at me. He had a scar on his cheek, a brief slash mark. It looked incomplete. I was glad I didn't have any scars or markings. I was a blank canvas. I could still be whoever I wanted to be.

"Do yourself a favor and get out of here," he said.

I felt my face flush. *Who the hell is he to tell me what to do?* "Fine. You're not the only game in town." I stood up but didn't go to the door. I had to know what I'd done wrong. "What is it about me that makes you not trust me?" I asked.

"I don't have what you're looking for. Go see that guy." He nodded toward a man sitting near the door.

I didn't understand what was going on, but I obeyed and went up to the guy by the door. As I approached, he frowned. Not wanting to admit I didn't know the name of the guy at the bar, I simply said, "I've been referred to you."

He had the red bulbous nose of an alcoholic and looked like he'd just barely survived a series of ass-whoopings. He gazed back at the guy at the bar and grumbled incoherently for a moment before standing up from the table and saying, "Alright then, come on." I suddenly realized who he was: the one who did the dirty work. The guy at the bar didn't want to risk selling to me, but this guy was going to whether he liked it or not.

Without another word, he headed outside. I followed him into the alley.

"Well?" he said irritably.

I pulled the cash out of my pocket and fanned it so he could count it. I kept a firm grip on it so he couldn't swipe it out of my hands like Jeremy had done.

"Okay," the guy said. He slipped me a little baggie and snatched the bills out of my hand.

"Thanks," I said, shoving the bag into my pocket.

"Get lost." He didn't need to say it twice. I was already turning back to the parking lot.

That's when I noticed a little man flanked by two enormous men who looked identical coming toward us.

"Joe," the little man called out.

My dealer, Joe, I guessed, swore under his breath, which felt like a very bad sign.

"I like your new old lady," the little man said, eyeing me up and down.

"She's not my old lady, David," Joe replied, "and she's on her way out." Fear had sobered him up so much he sounded like a different person. A very scared, very careful man.

David laughed as if Joe had made a joke. "We all know there's no way out."

A whisper came from behind me. "Run," Joe said. "Go."

I turned around and bolted down the alley. Footsteps sounded behind me and then someone grabbed me by the arm. His hand was a massive vice. It was one of the big guys. His black-gloved, meaty fingers squeezed almost my entire upper arm.

He spun me around.

"Let go!" I yelled, and bit his hand. He swore and grabbed me with his other hand. He dragged me back to the other side of the alley, and shoved me to the ground at David's feet.

"Here's the thing," David said, looking down at me. "Joe owes me money, more than we've found in his pockets. So now you're going to help him repay his debt."

One of the big guys yanked me to my feet and started searching my pockets, looking for the baggie. I squirmed to keep him from finding it. He was breathing heavily, exhaling the smell of chew and fried food into my face.

"She's just a high school kid," Joe lied. "Go easy on her."

"Well, she's no junkie," David said. He lowered his eyes to my cleavage. "But she's no high school kid."

"She has nothing to do with this."

David smiled mockingly. "Poor Joe. We seem to have a misunderstanding. I'm not officially a bank. I'm . . . *unregulated.* When you don't repay your debts, I take whatever I please."

The hand around my arm was like a Chinese finger trap. The more I tried to pull away, the tighter it gripped. This was the second time in two days that a man held me against my will. I wished I had something to even the score.

David reached out and pushed some hair behind my ear. I knew he wanted to see the fear on my face, so I tried to keep from crying.

A roar in the distance grew louder. Motorcycles. David heard them too. He turned to look in the direction the sound was coming from, then turned back to me. "Where'd you put it?"

"I don't have anything," I lied.

He smacked me across the face with the hand that held his cigarette.

Even through the pain, I could hear the tiny sizzling sound of cooking meat. The pain spread across my cheek

"You can let her go now," David said. The hand gripping my arm released me and I stumbled away.

The men walked past, toward their bikes. David went out of his way to shoulder me aside. "Student, my ass," he said.

"You shouldn't have come here," Joe yelled at me over the sound of engines revving.

I was in pain but still feeling the upward ascension toward mania. "*They* shouldn't have come here!" I yelled, spitting at their retreating figures.

On the way home, I put on gloves and bought drain cleaner, funnels, and other meth lab supplies, along with a burner phone. Then I got some cold medicine from the nearest Walgreens. The next day was garbage day, and I planned for Jeremy to celebrate it from jail.

While I waited for darkness, I iced my cheek and had a couple shots of vodka to dull the pain. The pain was no competition for the manic energy that had taken over my mind and body, and I wanted to keep it that way.

As soon as the sun set, I tiptoed around to the broken basement window of Jeremy's house. I wasn't surprised to see that he hadn't fixed it; he'd simply nailed a couple of boards haphazardly across the opening. I used a crowbar to pry one of the boards off, then ripped out the shade so people would be able to see in. After loosening the caps on a few bottles, I hurled everything I'd bought into his basement.

As I'd hoped, he heard the commotion. A light went on in the basement, and I saw him hurrying down the stairs. I sprinted to his front porch, emptied a bottle of ammonia in front of his door, and placed the baggie of meth on the chair from which he'd called me a Jew-bitch.

I hid in some shrubs across the street and called the police from a burner phone I'd gotten at the gas station. I gave them Jeremy's address. "The guy that lives there has been cooking meth and it smells like ammonia," I said and then hung up. I stomped on the phone and flung it down a sewer drain.

Once I was back in my apartment, I watched Jeremy through my window. He was stuffing things into a huge garbage bag and swearing so loudly I was sure everyone within earshot could hear. He dragged the bag out to his garbage can.

He'd just finished rolling his garbage can out to the street when the cops showed up.

Jeremy turned and ran back toward his house. When he reached his porch, he must have noticed the baggie, because though I couldn't see him anymore, I could hear him say, "Oh, shit. You've *got* to be kidding me."

Two officers stepped out of the squad car. One of them called, "Are you Jeremy Johnson?"

"None of your fucking business!" Jeremy shouted. "I know my rights!"

"What are you holding?" the officer asked, stepping onto Jeremy's porch.

"You know what the fuck I'm holding, because you planted it here! You guys have had it in for me since that bullshit domestic my ex pulled on me three years ago."

The other officer lifted the lid of Jeremy's garbage can and peered inside.

I was proud of myself because I knew what both officers were seeing: probable cause to arrest Jeremy.

Lucy started meowing, and I quickly closed the window and drew the shade. When I peeked out again, Jeremy was being led away in handcuffs. He ducked his head as he got into the squad car; I wondered how many times he'd been arrested.

* * *

The world felt electric. I was untouchable. I stepped outside, into the fresh, Jeremy-free space I'd created. The night whirled around me, and I was higher on my own mind than I'd ever been.

But by the next morning, I was spiraling. I hadn't slept at all. My brain was careening in a dozen directions at once. When I tried to nap, my heart started hammering in my chest.

Had Jeremy glared up at me after getting into the squad car?

I couldn't tell if it had actually happened or if I'd just imagined it.

I sat up and whipped around, making sure no one besides Lucy and me was in my apartment. I found her crouched in the closet. I tried to coax her out, but she just stared at me like I was crazy. Maybe I was. I needed more light. More safety. I shoved my bed against the wall and tried to rest, but I couldn't shake the feeling that someone was near.

I didn't sleep that night or for the next three. I was too busy fortifying my apartment and writing on the walls. The windows and doors were all barricaded with boards and furniture, and I'd scrawled instructions for myself on almost every available surface. What to do in case of various emergencies, the numbers of important places to call, and notes about the research I was doing online. I'd also created Facebook, Instagram, and Twitter accounts to sound the alarm about the dangers of modern society.

My phone kept ringing, but I was too busy to answer. Couldn't the caller just look at my social media?

On the fifth day after Jeremy was arrested, I heard banging on my door. I didn't answer, and the pounding eventually stopped. But a few minutes later, I heard a key slide into the lock and the door creak open. I grabbed the knife I was keeping in my pocket and raised my arm.

"Hannah!" my landlady cried. She looked around in shock for a moment before stepping back into the hallway and calling 9-1-1. When the ambulance came, I told her I wouldn't go unless she made sure no one erased all the important things I'd written on the walls.

"Okay, Hannah," she lied, "I'll make sure no one touches them."

* * *

The hospital psychiatrist was like a picture of Freud that had suddenly come to life. He stroked his beard as he studied my face. His gaze was so intense I had to look away. I glanced at the license from the American Board of Psychiatry and Neurology on the wall behind him. He had all the power in the room. Except that I wasn't going to stop talking for long enough to let him give me a diagnosis.

I told him that in the past I'd gone through periods in which I hadn't needed sleep because I was excited about something, such as walking frat row and getting invited inside for parties. I told him I had endless energy then. I felt amazing. Truly alive.

I didn't like how carefully he was watching me. He wasn't even trying to get a word in edgewise.

As I continued telling him how wonderful it felt to have so much energy, I realized I wasn't just talking incessantly because I didn't want to stop; I *couldn't*. My energy was waning. My rambling wasn't a superpower anymore. It was an exhausting weakness. I dug my nails into my palms so I could focus on the pain enough to stop talking. I forced myself to take a breath.

The psychiatrist looked intently at me over the rims of his glasses as he told me I had bipolar disorder. When I started to protest, he said, "Not needing sleep and feeling more energetic than usual are early signs of an episode. Even excitement that you interpret as good can be stressful. The parties you attended could have triggered a manic episode even if you hadn't consumed any alcohol. Drinking simply made it worse."

"Please, whatever you do, don't waste your time telling me not to drink. Lots of people drink and don't end up regretting it."

"People react differently to alcohol and other drugs. In someone with bipolar disorder, consuming any intoxicant is dangerous."

"Drinking helps me loosen up."

He explained that any change has the potential to cause mania, even if it feels good at first. "Many of my patients have told me that they initially feel an improvement in their mood. Mania can be seductive, but it leads people to do things they regret."

I looked away so he wouldn't see the shame on my face.

He continued, "You engaged in extremely risky behavior." I hadn't even told him about all I had done. I'd just told him I got the burn on my face by picking a fight at a biker bar. "If your landlady hadn't called an ambulance," he said, "there's no telling what could have happened."

"Can we skip the lecture?" I asked. "What solution do you propose?"

"Bipolar disorder is manageable with medication," he told me.

He prescribed a mood stabilizer and told me not to drink or do drugs. I also attended a couple of cognitive behavioral therapy sessions. The therapist and I pinpointed what triggered my episodes—mainly anxiety—and came up with a list of things I could do to manage it. I was also supposed to think more positively about my ability to cope with challenging situations.

The worst thing about getting my mind back to normal was the shame I felt about my behavior. I apologized to my landlady over and over.

She said as long as I paid to have the walls repainted, she wouldn't evict me. She even made me spaghetti and meatballs because I had hardly eaten for five days and she wanted to make sure I wasn't starving.

When I thanked her, she said, "Just promise me you'll take your medicine."

I held up my hand like I was solemnly swearing and said, "I promise."

Sometimes I regretted the promise, because even though my mania had led to the burn on my cheek, I missed the rush of energy and power I'd felt at the beginning of the episode.

Why couldn't I just keep what I liked about being bipolar, and medicate away the bad stuff? It seemed like a waste to medicate away *all* the magic.

CHAPTER 10

Then

April 2024, four months before graduate school, St. Louis

"Meth?" Justine asked. Her eyes were still big.

Instead of answering her, I said, "Sorry. I wasn't trying to make it about me." I turned off the dome light. "I just want you to know, if you ever need to talk to someone, I'm always available."

"I know," she said, winking at me. "Thanks."

She didn't correct me for saying "sorry," and she didn't try to dig further into my past. She squeezed my hand and then got out and walked up the steps to the house. In the glow of the streetlights, I could see that the soles of her shoes were red. Christian Louboutin. I'd never seen or heard of a pair of Louboutins that were less than $600. They made sense on her feet in a way that they wouldn't on mine. She had the easy confidence of the upper class. She was able to afford living in New York, and from her clothes I thought maybe she could afford Dubai. And yet she was here, in St. Louis, and I was certain we were going to be friends. I felt successful already. If guilt by association existed, shouldn't success by association also exist?

She waved to me and went inside. I already missed her and wanted to see her again.

I hadn't gotten a hotel room; I wanted to save money. But I didn't want her to know that. I pulled my car around the block and slept until the first light of day began to pour through the windshield.

* * *

In the morning sunlight I found a piece of folded notebook paper on the passenger seat of my car. Justine must have dropped it the night before. I picked it up and held it carefully in my hands. I could faintly see that there was writing inside, but I couldn't make out any of the words. Something had been spilled on it; the paper was tinged pink and wavy at one end.

I knew I should return it to Justine, but she hadn't given me her apartment number or telephone number.

What should I do with this?

As if of their own volition, my fingers slipped between the layers of the folded paper and pulled it open.

In print at the top of the page, I could make out the word: *Surfing.*

So many slashes crossed through the writing that only a few lines remained legible:

Body surfing a crowd of people to small to hold me. None of these arm's could hold all I contain. A bunch of easy marks. I might obscure just to see if I can.

I stared at the paper in shock. Had alcohol impaired Justine's grammar? Or maybe the writing wasn't Justine's.

Scribbles crowded the margins of the paper and arrows snaked in and around almost every sentence. The few words that didn't have slashes through them were smeared by whatever had spilled on the paper. I held it up to my nose and sniffed, even though I already knew the culprit. Hard alcohol. Vodka cranberry. The paper was hers.

I decided not to tell anybody about it. From all the slash marks and notes, I could see that she struggled with writing. Was "Surfing" the beginning of a short story she was writing for workshop?

I had to get back to Minneapolis in time for the dinner shift, so I decided I'd just take a picture of the writing and message it to Justine once I found her on socials.

Claire texted me a couple of hours into my drive back to Minneapolis: Did you find out if she's coming?

When I stopped at a gas station, I replied: No, just that we'll bring the city to its knees if she does.

She replied right away: So she's still holding onto the offer of a stipend? What are you going to do?

I looked at my phone. I wanted to text back *What?* But I already knew. Justine was the reason the school didn't know if I would get funding or not. She was the only student who was offered a stipend and hadn't confirmed whether she would attend. I was first on the waiting list.

I couldn't have it all. I couldn't have two years with Justine *and* funding.

When I was done filling my tank, I got back in my car and rested my head on the steering wheel. The horn sounded, startling me and the clerk who was changing the water in the window washing station beside me.

"Everything okay?" he asked.

"Yeah," I said. "Sorry. I'm totally fine." I started the engine, put the car in drive, and took off like I was being chased. I hoped that if I drove fast enough, I could leave Claire's news behind.

CHAPTER 11

Now

December 2024, northern Minnesota

We're finally happy. We're finally a couple. When Eli wakes up each morning, he starts the woodstove. I get out of bed too, because without his warmth, or that of the stove, I would freeze. I clean up the cabin while he gathers wood, and then we bed like honeymooners who've waited until marriage.

The mice, the cold, the threat of wolves—they're all worth it.

Now there's nothing superfluous to worry about. Here we can only concentrate on one thing: survival. No thinking of school or the people in my graduate program. No worrying about who's gossiping about me, or rolling their eyes when I'm not looking, or trying to steal my boyfriend.

The only kink in my happiness is that sometimes Eli doesn't respond when I say his name, the name he's told me is his. At night, when he's asleep, I whisper different ones, to see if any of them are actually his. I look for a twitch, a movement beneath his eyelids.

Aaron. Anders. Andrew. Benjamin. Bill. Bob. Clark. Dan.

Nothing.

I have to be careful; he wakes up easily.

I write all the names I try on the cardboard from a box of Kraft Macaroni & Cheese that I hide under the mattress. *Ethan. Eugene. Evan. Ezra. Felix. Fred.*

I put an asterisk by a few. He tightened his jaw when I whispered, "Felix."

Usually I face him when I quietly say the names. But when it's really cold I stay curled like a spoon and try not to move my jaw too much when I whisper. His cheek is pressed against mine and I don't want to wake him.

* * *

His body jerks one night when I whisper, "Justin." Then his arms tighten around me. It feels good. Some things never stop feeling good. Alcohol, drugs, they lose something over time. People need more and more until their livers are shot or they overdose. But being squeezed by this beautiful man, feeling his body suddenly pressed more tightly to mine, will always do it for me. I move against him. But when he kisses my neck, I can't mistake the name he moans into my ear. "Justine," he says. "Justine."

It scares me, but it doesn't turn me off. What would it feel like to be the real Justine—to be perfect in every way?

I come thinking I am her, posing for a photographer with a perfect smile—one that isn't too grateful or too big. A real writer's smile.

But then, suddenly, I'm angry. What's more humiliating than having your boyfriend say another woman's name? Is he even my boyfriend? I untangle myself from him right before he climaxes.

"Justine?" he asks, his voice full of anguish as he comes into nothing. No, not nothing. He comes into the absence of her.

I don't know how many nights they spent together, only that it was enough so when he's not fully awake, he thinks it's her next to him.

I wait for him to say something. There's nothing he can say to fix this, but I want him to try. When he doesn't, I reach out and grab his hand. I put it to my face. To my nose, which is bigger than hers, and my cheek, which is scarred instead of smooth. He draws his hand away, which hurts me even more than I'm hurt already, and makes me want to hurt him back.

"Don't you remember?" I say. "She's dead."

He takes a jagged breath and then there's silence.

For the first night since arriving at the cabin, we don't huddle together for warmth. The wet spot has split our bed in half. I shiver from the cold, and I shiver because she's here with us, despite everything I've done to get Eli all to myself.

CHAPTER 12

Then

May 2024, three months before graduate school, Minneapolis

I GREW INCREASINGLY NERVOUS about funding as the school year drew closer. I didn't have Justine's number. I had to find her on socials. I'd deleted the social media accounts I'd had during my last manic episode three years earlier, so I had to make new ones.

When Luke saw me creating an Instagram account during my break, he said, "Are you sure you want to be back online? It's dangerous out there." He was worried about me because I'd told him I had a little slip in St. Louis and had tasted beer.

"I have to find someone," I said. I showed him Justine's profile picture. She stood at the top of a mountain I couldn't identify, even after I read through the comments. I liked that Luke didn't seem impressed by her; his gaze didn't linger on the screen.

"I need a good profile photo," I told him. I hated pictures of myself; I didn't have a single one saved to my phone. "Do you have any old pictures of me?"

He sat on the couch beside me and looked through his phone. He had a picture of me from Halloween in a pirate costume that was at least one size too small.

Luke tapped on the photo, then smiled at me.

"That one?" I asked. "Does that look like someone whose stories you'd want to read?"

"Yeah," he said, "definitely."

I felt a little flutter in my stomach. I wondered again if he was dating anyone. I pushed lightly on his arm and said, "Come on. Seriously."

He smiled. "Yeah, this isn't profile picture material. It screams 'Hot and Insecure.'"

"Um, thanks?"

We didn't find a good picture of me. "Let's just take one now," Luke said, holding his phone up in front of my face. "I'll photoshop it to make sure you look your best. Now turn your head a little to the side."

"To hide my scar?" I challenged him.

"No one looks good straight on," he said. "Not even me."

Luke followed me and messaged some of his own followers to follow suit. Before I went back to work, he gave me one last bit of instruction: "Don't message this Justine girl until you have at least a hundred followers."

CHAPTER

13

Then

When I logged into my Instagram account the next day, I had fifty-three followers. Close enough, I decided, and messaged Justine: Hey, I have "Surfing." Is this the start of a new award-winning story? I want to get it back to you. BTW, I enjoyed meeting you in "The 3-1-4." Let me know when you decide where you're going next year.

Because she hadn't followed me yet, it went into her Message Request folder, which I knew most people didn't check.

So I logged into my X account and followed her there. Because she didn't follow me back, I couldn't private message her. I could only tweet her.

I didn't want her to know I was trying to figure out if I'd get a stipend. I tweeted: @Justine: Can you DM me or followback? I have "Surfing." I want to return it. BTW, will you be bringing St. Louis to its knees next year or what?

Five seconds after sending it, I realized the tone might have been off. The "or what" sounded aggressive. And my X profile itself was off. I only had two followers, one without a picture, and one whose picture was a teddy bear.

I Googled "#followback X" and followed the first three hundred accounts listed. Just as I was beginning to feel pathetic, I got a notification that Luke had tweeted: @HannahSilver97: Welcome to the Xverse. Now I can see you whenever I want and I don't even have to tip.

Claire followed me back on Instagram the next day. Justine didn't.

CHAPTER 14

Then

I GOT THE NEWS on the graduate school blog: "The MFA program is honored to welcome Justine Updike into the program next fall. In addition to her stipend, Justine will receive a $45,000 Olin Fellowship for Women in Graduate Study."

Shortly after, I got the email that I wouldn't be funded. I could feel the panic starting in my chest.

I got out a Worry Exploration worksheet that a therapist had given me. It was supposed to help me see when I was "catastrophizing." *What are you worried about? Are there clues your worry won't come true?* I couldn't focus. I crumpled up the worksheet and tossed it in the trash.

I was upset that I wouldn't have the money to go to graduate school, but I also felt like a bad friend because I couldn't just be happy for Justine. I decided to congratulate her over X and remind her that I had "Surfing." Or at least, I tried to. The little ball that goes round and round while something is posting kept going round and round, until I got an error message. I tried to repost it a few times, but the same thing kept happening.

* * *

A couple hours later, I got a notification that someone whose handle was @9inchStilettos had responded to my tweet:

You smell like drama and a headache

I was so stunned I pinched my arm to make sure I was awake. Why would this stranger lash out at me for congratulating Justine? When I released my fingers, my skin was red. I wasn't dreaming.

I replied: ?!?!?!?!?!

Someone whose handle was @PoisenPosies chimed in: #youdon't havetogohomebutyoucantstayhere

And then I started receiving multiple notifications from X. I looked at Justine's profile and saw that I'd tweeted congrats five times.

Someone whose handle was @BenJammin tweeted: There's a glass of shut the fuck up on the table, why don't you try it @HannahSilver97?

I tweeted: Are these your friends, @JustineUpdike? I can see why you want to move.

@BeenThereDonut: Oh, you're clever and condescending on the internet!? I bet that confidence translates well into the real world.

I tweeted @Justine: Call off your monkeys! Please DM me so we can talk

Someone else piled on: @HannahSilver97, Your hysteria is exhausting even from a distance. Aren't you tired of yourself yet? We are.

I kept receiving notifications. I felt like I was being punched in the gut over and over again.

What the hell was happening? I couldn't make sense of it.

I called Claire, but she didn't answer. I had the urge to leave a message, and as soon as I hung up, I had the urge to call back. But I did neither.

I wished my mother was like the ones on television, and I could call her for advice and reassurance that everything would be okay. I already knew her solution to every problem, though: pills, which kept her either out at the bars or in bed, depending on if she was taking uppers or downers.

That day at work, Luke noticed I was on edge. I handed him my phone so he could see what happened on X.

He flinched as he read the exchange, but when he looked back at me, his eyes were steady. "You've dealt with people worse than this at the restaurant. If you can handle the women who come in and yell at you because there's sugar, eggs, dairy, or whatever the hell they're allergic to on our menu, you can handle these twitches." He turned my phone off and handed it to me. "Go put this in your purse and forget about it."

CHAPTER

15

Then

But I couldn't forget about it. At 3:00 AM, I tweeted @Justine: Your secret is safe with me. Why aren't I safe with you?

Not long after, when I went to her profile, a message appeared saying I couldn't view her account. She'd blocked me.

I went to the nearest gym and got a day pass. I knew that if I didn't put my extra energy somewhere I was going to go manic.

I pounded the step mill. I started to feel self-conscious in my old leggings and Target brand sports bra. The other people at the gym were wearing Under Armour, Lululemon, Nike and Adidas.

As I left the club, I once again felt the pecuniary chasm between everyone else at the gym and me. I walked past three Audis, a BMW, and a half dozen upscale SUVs to get to my car. Other than me, the people at my gym appeared to have money. *Extra* money.

A box of Quest bars and some shiny energy drinks shone up at me from the passenger seat of a Mercedes parked beside my Corolla.

I suddenly had an idea.

* * *

At Walmart, I got the generic equivalent of Spanx and a tank top that put my waitressing muscles on full display. I shimmied black skinny jeans up my legs and over my hips before slipping into five-inch heels. Despite the workout I'd just done at the gym, I could feel my superpower coming on: mania. It would help me get the money I needed to go to graduate school. I bought all the cheap protein and energy drinks I could and printed a sign that read, 'Lean Machine Energy, formulated specifically to fuel machine-based gym workouts.'

I set up camp near the cardio machines, where people sweat the most and look the most miserable. I knew what it felt like to be on the endlessly revolving staircase of the stepmill machine. It felt like you were just one more step away from an existential crisis because you were working so hard and going nowhere.

I get to be these people's salvation, I thought, *and my own.*

Men who were splashing into pools of their own sweat with each step beckoned me over with such desperate enthusiasm that it was hard not to run as I brought them their drinks. A woman with a stomach cramp handed me a ten dollar bill and didn't take the five in change I made for her.

Soon a little line formed. Half an hour later, management finally noticed me and kicked me out. So I went to the first level of the parking ramp. When the maintenance man told me I had to leave, I flirted with him and gave him an energy drink so he'd let me stay.

I kept going to Walmart and then a different gym each day. I cut my mood stabilizer dose in half. I was excited by all the cash I was amassing. I was only sleeping about four hours a night. I knew I should start taking my mood stabilizer as prescribed again, but I also knew that if I did, I might not have the energy or confidence to keep selling "Lean Machine Energy" where I wasn't supposed to. I promised myself that as soon as I'd made enough to go to graduate school, I'd titrate back up to the full dose of Lamictal.

By my twenty-fifth day as a saleswoman, I'd reached my goal.

As I took the Lamictal tablet from the bottle that night, I already grieved the manic energy that had enabled me to do something I wouldn't ordinarily do. I thought nostalgically of a manic episode from my teens when I'd stayed up for three days straight repainting my mom's apartment and going to every thrift store in the Twin Cities so I could find cheap furniture, lamps, tables, and art to completely redecorate it.

I reached up and touched the scar on my face to remember why I had to take my mood stabilizer. I threw the pill into my mouth and swallowed it.

Washington University, here I come.

CHAPTER

16

Then

August 2024, one week before graduate school, St. Louis

"We've arrived," I told Lucy once we were in our new apartment. She was hiding under the bed while I went back and forth to the car for boxes.

"Need a hand?" called a man who was shuffling down the alley toward me, tapping a cane along the ground in front of him.

"Thanks, but I've got it," I told the blind man, wondering how he would lend a hand if I'd said yes.

He stopped and nodded in the direction of my car. "You need that engine looked at. I heard the valves when you pulled in. You should go down on McPherson Ave and let Harvey look at it. He'll fix it right up."

"I didn't hear anything," I said, then admitted, "I wasn't paying attention to anything except getting here."

"Welcome to the neighborhood, little sister," the man said, handing me a business card before continuing past me. "If you do go to Harvey's shop, tell them Leroy sent you."

I hoped he didn't also have a heightened sense of smell. I was sure I stunk. I didn't know if I was sweating from the humidity or from nerves. The first workshop was next Wednesday.

I used my free time to apply for a couple of work-when-you-want cleaning jobs, and I found a plasma center where I could donate twice a week.

A few days before school started, I saw Justine at the university bookstore. She'd unblocked me on X a couple of months earlier, but she hadn't responded to the message I'd sent asking if we could talk. I gave up my place in the checkout line to go meet her. She'd just walked in wearing her Chanel sunglasses and a scarf. "Hey, Hannah," she said as she approached, as though nothing strange had happened between us.

"Hey! I'm so glad we ran into each other," I told her, silently adding *since you've completely ignored my message for the past couple months.* "How have you been?"

"Good. You?" she said. But she didn't stop walking.

I turned around and followed her. "I need to talk to you. I also want to give you back some writing you left in my car. I think it's called 'Surfing'?" I watched her face for some reaction. She kept walking. "I didn't know I'd see you here," I said, still following her, "so I left it at home. But I have a picture on my phone. I can text it to you if you want to give me your number."

"Sure," she replied without looking at me. "But not right now. Where did you find *Lord of Misrule*?"

She was holding a piece of paper in her right hand, the hand with the teeth marks. It was a voucher. Her scholarship included books.

"Let me show you," I said.

Even with the aromas of bookbinding glue and old paper, I could smell her Chanel Paris-Riviera as I walked her to the little corner where the modern literature was in several piles marked *NEW* and *OLD* on a dusty shelf.

"Have you found an apartment?" I asked when we were in the checkout line. She still hadn't taken off her sunglasses or scarf. She tightly grasped her book voucher. She had more than the seven books we had been assigned, and she hadn't chosen used copies. I felt a pang of jealousy.

CHAPTER

17

Now

December 22, 2024, northern Minnesota

THE WET SPOT Eli and I created grows between us each night, along with my anger. They feed off the silence, pushing us to opposite edges of the mattress. I realize, in the coldest, darkest part of the night, that Justine is lying between us. To get to Eli again, I would have to touch her, and I know I've touched her enough. Just touching her hand brought me so much trouble.

She's even more present now than she was when she was alive.

She doesn't stay in bed. During the day she is with us, warming herself at the stove, looking at my hand when Eli and I play cards, sitting with us at the table during our silent meals. But she always returns to bed in the evening before we do. She waits for us.

I ask her: *Who killed you?*

But she doesn't answer.

Are you here for revenge?

Silence.

Eli will not admit to anything. Not sleeping with her, not even saying her name.

But I know I heard it: *Justine.* I hear it over and over now, the way his voice was full of emotion, more emotion than when he says my name. In my thoughts, I put our names side by side and mine is so much less. Why did I expect he would choose me if given the chance? Perhaps I didn't want him to have the chance. Perhaps I killed her.

I want to call Luke and tell him everything. I miss him terribly. He's always given me the benefit of the doubt. He would reassure me that I'm not a murderer. I wish I had my cell phone, though perhaps it wouldn't do me any good. There are no cell towers here.

"You're acting strange, Hannah," Eli says. The way he says my name hurts. Everything hurts now in this new world where he wants Justine more, even when she's dead. "Your nightmare—"

"It wasn't a nightmare. You said her name."

"You're confused."

"Do you think I'm having auditory hallucinations?" I say sarcastically. My certainty is beginning to waver, though. My mother sometimes heard things no one said and saw things that weren't there. At breakfast one morning when I was still small enough to need an old phone book on my chair to eat at the table, my mother told me, "Last night the house was picked up in a tornado. I've been up all night. Will you check out the window to see if we've landed yet?"

Another time, after she told me my father had left us, she woke me up in the middle of the night. "Your father is dancing with a beautiful senorita in the living room," she said. "Go see him now before he leaves again." She followed after me as I went to see him. As I looked into the empty room, she whispered into my ear, "Your father is the only man I ever, *truly*, slow danced with."

Now, with Eli telling me I imagined him saying "Justine," I wonder if my mother really told me those things or if I imagined them. *Was she crazy, or am I?*

I wake up sometimes hearing my voice screaming her name. "*Justiiiiiiiiiiiine,*" I scream. But my lips are sealed. The scream is coming out of the past, from the night she disappeared.

I know I was there. I see how she looked at me first in anger and then with her eyes widening in fear. I liked the fear. I can still feel the jolt of power in my chest, and how I wanted to enlarge it.

CHAPTER 18

Then

As Justine and I stood in the checkout line, I struggled to push down the wave of jealousy that was washing over me. Of course Washington University had given Justine a book voucher. The university wanted the best, and it made sense that they were willing to pay for it. I willed myself to be happy for her.

"Yes, I have found an apartment," she said, briefly glancing at me before returning her gaze to farther ahead in the checkout line. It was the first time she'd looked directly at me that day. "It's near the North Loop."

"Nice. You're close to campus and the bar scene." Rent was cheaper in St. Louis than Minneapolis, but I still couldn't afford that kind of convenience.

I noticed that Justine wasn't carrying a purse or holding any keys. After I paid for my books, we stopped at a table in an adjoining student recreation area to exchange phone numbers. I texted her the photo of "Surfing."

"Really, Hannah?" she said as she looked at the picture.

"Isn't it yours?"

She laughed. "Good one. But I'm guessing it's *your* writing."

"No," I said vehemently, shaking my head.

She wasn't paying attention to me. She put her phone back in her purse and picked up her books. "Bye, Hannah," she said as she started to walk away.

I shouldn't have pressed her about "Surfing." I quickly asked, "Can I give you a ride?" I wanted to ask her face to face what had happened on X. "I'm parked on the corner of Forsyth and Skinker."

It was only a few minutes' walk from the bookstore, but the heat and dew point made it so humid that walking felt more like swimming. "I usually read e-books," she said. "I'm only now realizing how heavy literature is."

I offered to take her books. I was already holding seven with no problem, but I'd carried heavy trays of food on the fingertips of one hand. Plus, I had at least thirty pounds on her. I squatted so she could easily slide her books onto my pile.

"But now you can hardly see where you're going," she said as I peered around the side of the pile to navigate my way to the car. "Oh wait, I have an idea. Let's make it so you can't see where you're going *at all*. We'll play a trust game. Stand still."

It felt like some kind of test. A test of trust? Courage?

"I really need to talk to you," I said.

"We'll talk after."

"After what?"

Instead of answering, she took off her sash belt and blindfolded me.

Being blindfolded brought back memories, except that when I'd played the game as a child, I'd had a hand free to hold onto the person guiding me.

As though reading my mind, she said, "I've got you." She placed her hand lightly on the back of my elbow. I let her guide me, trying not to hesitate before each step. I wanted to restore our bond.

After a moment, I decided it definitely didn't feel like we were headed to my car. I intermittently heard noise from restaurants and bars as doors opened and closed on one side of us. We were on a crowded sidewalk.

"Okay," she said, "just a couple more steps." I felt the whoosh of a door opening. She led me into a noisy room and said, "Set the books down on the table in front of you." She took the blindfold off. "We can talk here."

The bar wasn't sad during the day like the one at The Hot Dish. People didn't seem to be drinking to get drunk, and they weren't drinking alone. They were engaged in discussions; the drinks seemed secondary.

Justine stuffed her sunglasses and scarf into her purse. She ordered us a couple of vodka cranberries.

"I actually don't drink," I told her and the server.

"Oh, that's right," she said, and ordered me a nonalcoholic beer. When the server walked away, she asked, "Is drinking off-limits because of your bipolar disorder?"

A familiar feeling of shame from my days of waking up in strange beds caused my face to flush. "Basically," I said.

"What is it like?"

"Not drinking?"

"No. Bipolar disorder."

My chest tightened. "Is this research for your writing? Am I going to be the unwitting subject of a Justine Updike story?"

"Don't flatter yourself," she said, winking. "I really only ever write about myself."

I smiled. "Me too."

"We're just two normal fiction writers," she said, and we both laughed.

But still, I felt uneasy. Either of us could have been mentally taking notes for a future story. Was I going to write a story about a beautiful graduate student with teeth marks on the back of her hand? Was she going to write about a bipolar girl who bought meth? We were like two scorpions trapped in a jar.

After our drinks arrived, Justine continued her prodding. "So, are you going to tell me about bipolar disorder, or do I have to ask Siri what it's like?"

Instead of answering her question, I asked, "What happened on X? Why didn't you respond to all the nasty tweets? Why did you block me?"

"You're a writer. Stuff should happen to you."

I straightened up in my seat so our eyes were level. "Stuff already has happened to me."

"New stuff. The best writers are the people who've suffered the most." Before I could get mad, she said, "I'm just kidding. As for social media, I don't pay much attention to any of it. I temporarily blocked you so you wouldn't keep arguing with my other followers."

"But you must have seen the bullying. Why didn't you block *them* instead of *me?*"

"None of it matters, Hannah. You can't be so sensitive."

"If I weren't sensitive, I wouldn't be a writer."

Her face clouded. She'd heard what I hadn't said aloud: *If you're not sensitive, why do you write?*

But then her eyes filled with sympathy. She tilted her head and said gently, "Even before you told me you were bipolar, I knew something was going on with you. You don't trust anyone, not even yourself."

Was that true? Was I being too suspicious of Justine? Of myself?

"It's okay," Justine said. "I don't trust many people either." She reached across the table and squeezed my hand. "I'm sorry you have to live with bipolar disorder."

"It may be a disorder," I replied defensively, "but it's also a superpower."

She laughed as if I was kidding.

I didn't want her to laugh. "It's better than a drink," I said, gesturing at her vodka cranberry. "It's an ecstasy of spinning out of control. But first it makes you invincible."

"What's the wildest thing you're ever done while manic?"

We seemed to be tiptoeing near frenemy territory, so I didn't tell her about going to Jeremy's house or the biker bar. I told her about how I got the money for graduate school by selling "Lean Machine Energy" at the gym.

"Wow, you ripped off unsuspecting gym rats?"

"I didn't rip them off. People wanted something to make their workouts easier, and that's what I sold them."

"But you changed the name so you could get more money."

"They got what they wanted—motivation to work out. It was a bargain." I looked at the time on my phone. I was working a cleaning shift in less than an hour. "We need to get going," I told her, throwing some cash on the table to cover our drinks.

"Thanks. I'll buy next time," she said as we left.

She got into the passenger seat of my Corolla as though she was lowering herself into the vestibule of hell. She started fiddling with the temperature controls. I wondered if she'd ever been in an economy car before. "We're better off with the windows open," I told her. "The air conditioning takes a while to work."

She frowned. I resisted the urge to apologize. "I live just a few blocks from the Pageant," she said.

"Nice," I said. The Pageant was the main concert venue near campus.

She shrugged. "It's okay."

When I pulled up outside her apartment building, I idled, hoping she'd invite me inside. "It's so cute," I said. "I love brownstones, and that arched doorway makes it look like you live in a fairy tale."

"If you love brownstones, you should have seen the one I lived in in Manhattan. It was beautiful inside and out. The ceilings were so high I never felt claustrophobic like I do in this one. It had crown molding and a real fireplace."

I pictured her there, writing, with just the sounds of wood crackling and the clacking from her typing. I wanted to be there too.

"The word 'charming' is thrown around a lot," she continued, "but that place *owned* the word. What I like most about *this* place," she gestured to her apartment building, "are those hideous boxes bulging out of the windows."

"It doesn't look hideous to me. I don't have a window air conditioning unit yet," I told her, in the hope she'd invite me in.

As though hearing my thoughts, she said, "I'd invite you in for a drink, but I have a gentleman caller on his way over."

Gentleman caller? I wanted to ask if it was the guy who sent her a drink when we were at Market Pub. But her hand was already on the door handle.

She attempted to unbuckle her seatbelt, but it was stuck.

I leaned across her and jiggled the buckle until it sprung open.

After she got out, before she slammed the door, I saw the titles of the extra books she'd bought. Collections of short stories by two of our professors.

"Let me know what you think," I said, nodding at them.

"I think they're brilliant, and you should too," she replied. "That's my career advice to you. Thanks for the lift."

CHAPTER 19

Then

Saturday, August 24, 2024

As soon as I walked through the door on the night of the first alumni-sponsored party, I saw Justine. I was surprised; I'd assumed she'd be fashionably late. Her back was to me and before I could approach her, Claire came over and gave me a little hug.

"Do you see why I'm never late?" Claire asked, gesturing around at the oak floor, leather furniture, and recently painted walls that were tastefully adorned with art. "We need to relish every moment we can in these charming mini-mansions. As MFA students, we're officially on track to be starving artists."

While Claire got me a ginger ale, my eyes roved over the souvenirs on the mantel and shelves: a Venetian mask with a golden crown, and then something more beautiful than anything I'd ever seen before. Even more beautiful than Justine—the man from Market Pub who had sent Justine a drink. I hadn't gotten a good look at him that night, but now my eyes were gobbling him up.

He was standing in a circle of English PhD candidates, a drink in his hand, a small smile on his face. He was as dark as a white man could be. Jeans just tight enough to denote confidence, loose enough that there was no desperation in the seams. Perhaps he'd spent long moments on his hair, used hairspray you can only get at a salon. But he didn't seem to need anyone's approval. Unlike the people around him, he was confident enough not to laugh too loud or too long at anyone's jokes. He was attentive without being on the balls of his feet.

Was he cocky?

I never liked cockiness. Not because it's unattractive in itself, but because rarely has any man had the stuff to back it up. It's like a little dog's bark. But as I watched the stranger, I was certain he wasn't faking anything. He was completely calm, with an aura of knowingness about him. He seemed like someone who could block a punch without appearing to have seen it coming.

When everyone else laughed at someone's joke, he turned partway toward me and our eyes met. He raised his glass ever so slightly. Claire had put a ginger ale in my hand and when I raised it too eagerly some spilled over the rim. He smiled a full smile, not just the little amused smile he'd had on before. I wiped my hand on my skirt and looked away, embarrassed. When I looked back, someone was blocking my view of him.

"What were you looking at?" Justine asked.

A small fury reared its head within me. Did Justine have to have *everything*? The brownstone, the clothes, the winning story, the money, *and* this beautiful man?

"Hannah is getting a lay of the land," Claire said from where she'd sat down beside me. "I was just about to explain the major players to her." I wanted to ask about the beautiful man, but Justine was still blocking my view of him.

"This party is pretty standard," Claire said. She gestured at an attractive man who was wearing a sport coat and jeans. "There's Professor M, the young, hip professor who wants to seem cool. He'll be leading the workshop Wednesday. He says things professors aren't supposed to say and laughs too quickly at everyone's jokes." She nodded toward another man. His sport coat had a burn from a cigarette or cigar on one sleeve and looked damp. "And then there's Barkley Newhouse, who was a famous writer in the seventies and is now a fall-down drunk but has tenure, so they keep picking him up and propping him at the front of the nonfiction classes."

I'd studied Professor Newhouse online, but I almost didn't recognize him in person. He looked like a cross between the photo of him on the Wash U website and an extremely elderly Incredible Hulk. His drinking was legendary. He was a former Fulbright Scholar, graduate of Yale and Oxford, and huge fan of whatever nearby liquor was strongest. He'd taught at the University of Iowa for a few years before coming to Washington University.

"Come on," Claire said. "I'll introduce you."

She pulled me through the little crowd around the ancient professor. The only person I recognized was Ben, who nodded hello to me. Professor Newhouse was telling everyone about the best blues bars in St. Louis. When he paused, Claire said, "This is Hannah, a new first year."

He studied me less than a second before asking, "What do you write, Hannah?"

"Fiction." *Or close enough*, I thought.

"You'll take my nonfiction class in any case."

"Everyone takes Professor Newhouse's class," Ben said.

"Nonfiction just isn't my thing," I replied.

"Give me a moment with this one," Newhouse told the little crowd.

Claire squeezed my arm and followed the other MFAers to the mini-bar. Professor Newhouse looked hard at me. "Hannah, I want you to take my course. It's a rite of passage for anyone who wants a degree from this program. Everyone who gets an MFA here has my fingerprints on their thesis."

Since he taught nonfiction, there was absolutely nothing he could say to entice me to take his course. "I wouldn't be any good at nonfiction," I said. I decided to add something playful so he wouldn't hate me. "I love to lie."

"We all do. The best liars make you believe the lies."

I laughed half-heartedly. Enough to be polite, but not enough to encourage him to continue.

"Are you brave enough to stand behind your lies," he continued, "and call them memoir?"

I wanted to get away from him, but he was the first professor I'd met at Wash U and I didn't want to make a bad first impression. "I'm sure your class is wonderful, Professor Newhouse. But I don't want to write memoir, or anything resembling it."

"That's disappointing, because it looks like you have a story to tell." He stared pointedly at my cheek where I thought I'd applied enough foundation to cover my scar. "You could tell the story as it happened, or as you wish it happened. It doesn't matter, so long as you tell it."

I turned partway away from him, so he couldn't look at the scar as I asked, "Wouldn't it be a bit arrogant to think that, at twenty-six, I have enough experience and insight to make myself the focus of my writing?"

"Most writers are arrogant. It helps."

Before I could stop the words from leaving my mouth, I asked, "Have you read Justine's story that won *The Atlantic* student fiction writing contest?"

He chuckled. "I started it. I put it down because I already knew the ending."

"How? How did you know the end of Justine's story without finishing it?"

"I didn't say I didn't finish it."

"Yes, you did."

Suddenly I felt an arm around my shoulders. Justine squeezed me tightly. "I heard my name. Are you guys gossiping about me?" she asked.

I took a step back and bumped into a woman standing behind me. It was Amelia, the woman who'd sat on the other side of Justine at Market Pub.

"Sorry," I said. "I didn't see you there." She barely met my eye. She was either shy or feeling guilty for listening over my shoulder. She was like a nervous mouse who doesn't want to be noticed but is hungry for the crumbs people might drop.

"Amelia," she said. She pushed her long, unkempt hair over her shoulder and shook my hand like she'd never done it before, pumping too hard.

"Jesus," Newhouse said, "can't you afford razors on your stipend, Amelia? Your legs look like a gorilla's."

Amelia twitched a little. Her mouth opened as if she was about to say something, but instead she took a sip of her drink. She looked into her glass, as though she wished she could dive in and disappear. I imagined the humiliation she must feel.

"Hippies are the least interesting of all the uninteresting creatures," Newhouse said, "and the worst-smelling."

I was done worrying about making a bad first impression. "I'd think you might appreciate the reminder of the seventies," I said to Professor Newhouse. "Weren't they your heyday?"

He smiled as if that was exactly the effect he wanted to produce in me. Amelia looked at my face like she didn't know what to make of it. I'd like to have been able to describe her gaze as "grateful," but "nervous" was more accurate.

"Hannah and I are getting a drink," Justine said. I let her take my elbow and guide me to the bar.

I reached for a bottle of tonic water, but Justine swatted my hand. "Only the best for you tonight." I wanted to apologize for talking about her, but before I could, she disappeared into the kitchen and came out with two glasses. "Dessert in a bottle," she told me.

"I don't drink alcohol," I reminded her.

"Not even on special occasions?" she asked, then winked. I was glad she remembered that I didn't drink. "Here you are." She handed me a glass of the dessert drink.

I couldn't help puckering my lips after the first gulp.

"You'll get used to the sweetness," she told me.

"Are you sure there's not alcohol in this?"

"Oh, shit. I'm not sure."

I ran to the kitchen. There was an open bottle of Inniskillin Icewine. I smelled it. I turned back to Justine, who had followed me into the kitchen. "It says 'Icewine' right on the bottle. How did you not notice that?"

"I'm sorry, Hannah. I really am. But if you really didn't want to drink, wouldn't you have read the bottle before drinking? I think you wanted real wine."

Did I?

"Look on the bright side. It's good for your career. I saved you from being the most hated person in the graduate program."

"Hated for what?"

"Teetotaling. Being the death of the party."

I was so upset I picked up the bottle of icewine and turned it upside down. She stepped back and looked down at the growing puddle we were standing in, then smiled back up at me. "See, now you're acting like a real writer!"

I was still holding the bottle in my hand but I was no longer pouring from it. I wanted to smash it against the counter. I drew my arm back.

"Do it," she said.

That stopped my hand. I didn't want to do anything she told me to anymore. I set the bottle down on the counter.

"This is the best I've seen you," Justine said. "The most writerly. Do you think it's a coincidence that all the great writers are drinkers? They do crazy things. Like you used to."

I hadn't even told her the worst things I'd done.

"Do you think Hemingway ever deprived himself of a drink?" she asked.

"I don't want to end up like Hemingway. He killed himself with a shotgun."

She tilted her head. "Wouldn't it be worth it? Wouldn't you rather go out the way he did than disappear forever?"

I thought for a moment before replying: "I *want* the option to disappear forever. That's why I don't write nonfiction."

"You write fiction because you're afraid."

"Afraid of what?"

"You tell me."

I was so overwhelmed for a moment that I couldn't speak. I started to tell her, "I don't kno—"

But she interrupted. "Whatever it is, don't worry about it tonight. You've already given up your sobriety for today, so let's make the most of it."

"I don't think—"

"Stop! Stop thinking so fucking much! You're giving me a headache. And what about *your* head? It's going to explode if you don't give it a rest. Take a break from worrying for the rest of the night. Tomorrow you can go back to being stuck in your head, but tonight let's be *here*.'" She held out her smooth, manicured hand. I wasn't sure I should take it. "Be here with me," she said.

Ben came into the kitchen and said, "Hey, what are we toasting?"

Justine replied, "Hannah!" She smiled and took the bottle from me. "*All* of Hannah, good and bad." She tipped the bottle up to her lips and took a couple of gulps. She wiped her mouth with the back of her hand and then held the bottle out to me.

She hadn't seemed like someone who would drink directly from the bottle or wipe her mouth with the back of her hand. *Am I a special (wonderful, horrible) occasion to her like she is to me?*

"Stop giving me those puppy dog eyes already, Hannah, and drink," she said. She was irritated. More irritated than I'd ever heard her before.

I didn't want to lose her. I took the bottle from her hand. "Fuck it," I said, and then toasted: "To me!" When I tipped the bottle up and the wine hit my tongue there was an instant where I had a flashback of being hooked up to a keg, everyone around me cheering as though I were doing something amazing.

* * *

At some point we began exploring the room like we were alone at a museum. When we got to the Venetian mask, Justine dared me to take it off the wall and put it on.

"You first," I told her.

"I have another idea," she said. "There are initials on the golden urn on the mantel. Without looking at it, just by feel, tell me what they are."

"You want me to feel up an urn that's probably full of someone's ashes?"

"Or put on the mask," she said. "You decide."

There was no way I was putting on the mask. "If I try to figure out the initials on the urn, can I read your *Atlantic* student fiction winning story?"

She hesitated, then said, "Only if you get them right."

And so, I made my way toward the mantel, avoiding eye contact with Professor Newhouse or anyone else. I couldn't help bumping into someone who seemed to appear in my path out of nowhere. Or maybe I just didn't notice him because he was so slight. He seemed to get smaller as I looked at him. Even through a few glasses of wine I could clearly see his anxiety. It was the director. "Hi, Duncan," I said, holding out my hand.

Why wasn't he mingling, working the room? What had happened to him? He looked at my hand like he didn't know what to do and then weakly grasped it.

"Well, nice to see you," I said, and continued on to the mantel.

I closed my eyes and examined the urn with my fingertips. Then I went back to Justine and told her, "The initials are WHG."

"Have some more wine and try again," she said, handing me her own glass.

As I wandered back to the mantel, Claire grabbed my arm. "I think it's time to get you home, Hannah."

"I can't go yet. I'm doing something."

"Are you sure?"

"I'll tell you more soon."

The rest of the evening passed in a blur. Amelia kept trying to talk to Justine, but Justine ignored her until later in the evening when I saw them talking with their heads so close together they looked like a two-headed monster. As I approached, they stopped talking. Their heads separated and they looked at me with guilt and hunger.

Or had I just imagined that?

When they wandered outside, I followed. Justine called back to me, "I'll be inside in a minute, Hannah. I'm just having a little tête-à-tête with Amelia."

I went back in and noticed the stranger again. He was still standing in a little circle of PhDs. I hadn't seen him and Justine interact at all, so I was beginning to doubt that they were together. He was fair game.

An alumnus came over and started talking to me, but I have no idea what about. I found it hard to think about anything but the stranger.

Later, when everyone was buzzing and I was standing in a half circle that had formed around the old professor, I felt the stranger's gaze again. I turned to meet his eyes. His gaze was sharper than it had been before. He'd been thinking of me too.

I wanted to stay the same as he looked at me. I tried not to fidget, or breathe faster, or look away and then quickly back to make sure his eyes were still on me. His gaze became a statement: *I want you*. And then, by raising one eyebrow, a question. A question to which he knew there was only one answer: *Yes, I'm going home with you*.

But I didn't go quickly. The time between his question and my answer would be the buildup that would make everything that came after better. I didn't want to be easy. Easy = easily forgotten. I'd stay a little longer.

I moved out of the little half circle around Professor Newhouse and went to stand over the guacamole. I peered into the mess of crackers undone from their careful display. All the while I was thinking of the stranger, feeling his gaze on me.

Suddenly, the old professor started coughing so loudly it broke the trance the stranger had put me in.

I pushed through the people gathered around and asked, "Are you okay?"

"A little less so every day," he replied.

I couldn't help it, I hugged the old professor. It was clumsy with him sitting in an easy chair and me leaning over him. His cheek was scratchy and his hands weakly grasped at my arms. I silently swore off drinking. I didn't want to end up as weak as the professor.

"Now get out of here," he said, "before people start to talk."

When I straightened up, I started to panic. I'd been distracted from the stranger for a moment, and now I could feel it—he was no longer looking at me. I looked back at him and followed his gaze to see where it had landed.

Justine. She was back. I studied her to see her as the stranger did. Her long brown hair was lying over one shoulder, leaving the other bare besides the thin strap that framed her décolletage. I was certain there wasn't a bra between her erect nipples and the tan cotton of her dress.

If she started to move, I'd never get the stranger's gaze back; she walked like warm honey spilling from a jar. She leaned away from the overeager guy in front of her, searching for an out. I was afraid she'd look straight into the stranger's eyes. He'd silently ask her the same question, and her gaze would respond, *Yes, let's leave right now.*

I set my glass down near the guacamole and hurried to the door. As I opened it, I noticed the stranger watching me. Justine came and put her hand on his shoulder. Though he was staring at me, I knew he was going home with her.

* * *

In the morning, I woke up to find Lucy looking at me with great disappointment. I'd forgotten to feed her the night before. She meowed indignantly until I got out of bed and plopped a can of Fancy Feast into her bowl. The sucking sound it made as it left the can made me want to vomit.

My head was pounding and I thought I couldn't possibly feel any worse, but then I got a text from Claire.

CHAPTER 20

Then

Sunday, August 25, 2024

DID YOU HEAR?

I replied: Hear what?

The phone rang and Claire's name popped up on my screen. She didn't even give me a chance to say hello.

"Remember that urn?" she asked.

"Urn?"

"From the party. At the alumni's house."

"The one with someone's initials on it?"

"Yeah," she said, "that one."

"What about it?"

"It's missing."

"Missing?"

"Gone."

"What happened to it?"

"I don't know," she replied. "The alumni think someone must have taken it."

"Who?"

"No one knows."

I squeezed the phone to my ear. Maybe I could squeeze more information out of it. But Claire didn't say anything else.

"Okay, thanks for telling me," I said.

Along with forgetting to feed Lucy the night before, I was sure I'd forgotten to take my Lamictal. As soon as Claire and I hung up, I went to the bathroom medicine cabinet and gulped down a pill.

Then I went outside to look for my car. It was right in front of my building, blocking a handicap ramp. As I got in to move it, I wondered what my blood alcohol level was.

I drove it into the alley so I could look through it without worrying about anyone watching me. I searched it top to bottom—under the doormats, in the trunk, in every compartment.

"What's going on, little sister?" someone asked.

I turned and saw Leroy coming toward me, cane swinging in front of him.

I don't know why I was so forthright with him. "I was worried I'd stolen something."

He smiled knowingly. "It's okay as long as you stole it from someone who can afford another one. Some of us have to hustle a little. Like what I said about your car . . . I heard the engine and told you to go to Harvey's shop. They give me a kickback when I refer people."

I tell him I never took my car in. "I'm too cheap to get my car repaired just because of a little noise. And I know a bit about hustling."

He laughed and said, "I sensed you might."

I drove my car back onto the main street and parked in front of my building. Back inside my apartment, I searched top to bottom, until I was satisfied the urn wasn't there. I was so relieved I sank down onto the floor and cried. I vowed to take my medicine every night and not get drunk anymore.

But even as I made the vow, I wasn't sure I could keep it. In the grander scheme of things, nothing truly terrible had happened. My car was home safe, I hadn't stolen the urn, and Lucy would eventually forgive me for forgetting to feed her.

CHAPTER

21

Then

JUSTINE CAME OVER that afternoon with groceries.

"Wow, you didn't have to get all this for me," I said.

"It's hangover food," she replied, setting bananas and a box of saltines on the counter. "You were really messed up last night."

As she put some coconut water in the refrigerator, I asked, "What were the letters?"

"Which letters?"

"The ones on the urn."

She turned to me and shrugged. "I can't remember," she said, her ridiculously white teeth flashing brightly in the darkness of my apartment. "All I know is that you got them wrong."

"I wish we hadn't played that game. Now all those people saw me touching an urn that's gone missing."

"Oh, you heard," Justine said. "I wasn't planning to tell you because it was probably just a drunken prank. I'm sure the thief will feel bad about it once they sober up." She clapped her hands together. "Now, let's get you out of here for a while. Ben is waiting outside. Claire, Amelia, and Phong too."

"They've just been sitting outside the whole time?"

"We're worth waiting for."

"Let me throw some makeup on and we can go," I said. My hands were shaky as I applied cover-up and foundation to my face. Even under the makeup my skin looked pale.

* * *

I saw Ben's pickup as soon as we exited my building. Amelia and Phong were sitting in the bed, sweating profusely. Claire was in the passenger seat inside the cab.

"Claire is kind of a vampire, so we let her sit inside," Phong said.

"I was sitting up front with them," Justine nodded at the cab where Claire and Ben had turned around to wave at me. "But I'll hang out in back with you."

"Isn't it illegal to ride in the back of a pickup?" I asked. I was nervous about the police. Even though I hadn't found the urn in my apartment, I felt like I'd done something wrong. I didn't want to draw any attention to myself.

Phong laughed. "You definitely haven't lived in St. Louis long. The police have better things to do."

I didn't say what I was thinking: *They have plenty to do in Minneapolis, too, but they still find time to pull people over.*

I sat down beside Amelia. I noticed she'd shaved her legs. I hoped Professor Newhouse hadn't gotten to her. I smiled at her and her mouth wavered, as though her lips were trying to smile but couldn't quite make it.

Justine put her head in my lap and her feet on Phong's lap.

"Now, where were we?" Phong asked Justine and slid her sandals off. "The right one, right?" He started massaging her foot.

I looked down at the faint smile on her face and saw my own reflection in her huge sunglasses. My expression was strained.

"Where are we going?" I asked, hoping we were on our way to a pub even though I knew I shouldn't drink. *I'll stick to beer, and I'll only have a couple.*

"Kaldi's," Justine said.

I hoped it was a bar, but I didn't want to ask. No one needed to know how much I wanted a drink.

We hit a bump and Justine winced. "I'm too bony for this," she said, pulling her foot from Phong's hands and sitting up so her head no longer rested on my lap. She banged on the back window to the cab, and Ben slammed on the brakes so hard I nearly crashed into the window. Justine hopped out and moved to sit in front beside Claire.

"Are you feeling better?" Phong asked me.

"What do you mean?"

"Justine told us you haven't been quite right lately."

I wanted to ask exactly what she said, but I didn't want to seem overly worried. "I'm fine, thanks."

To my dismay, the pickup came to a stop at a coffee shop. People were sitting outside in a little enclosed area, sipping lattes and iced coffees. I'd forgotten my purse, so I turned to Justine. "Can you get me a glass of water? I'll find us a table."

I stepped over the enclosure and grabbed chairs to put around the sole unoccupied table. It was only big enough for three people to sit comfortably.

I looked at Instagram while I waited. The first thing in my feed was a picture Justine had used to check in at Kaldi's. It was a photo of two lattes pushed together. The #latteart was exquisite. I imagined only a twenty dollar tip or Justine's beauty could compel a person to spend so much time creating a milk-picture of David Bowie and another of a little boy carrying a huge heart. When the barista painted the little boy in milk, was it a proposition, something he was too shy to say aloud? Or merely something he wanted to say differently than so many other men who came before him—men who held their hearts to Justine with nothing but words?

I took a screenshot of the picture and texted it to Luke, teasing:
Baristas > Bartenders?

"Here," Justine said, plonking a water down on the table. I realized she was standing over me. She was looking at my screen. "Find anything interesting?"

Ben came up beside Justine and laughed down at me. "Is Justine's Instagram your screen saver?" he asked. "We heard about how you were all over her X account."

Had Justine told everyone about me congratulating her over X and getting torn apart by her followers? Had she told them she blocked me?

I forced a playful smile onto my face as I gazed up at them. "The suspense of not knowing what you guys were ordering was killing me, so I checked Justine's Instagram."

"A picture doesn't do these lattes justice," Justine replied, and stepped back so Claire could set them on the table.

Amelia came out of Kaldi's and looked at the lattes jealously. She set her glass of ice water on the table next to them, establishing that she'd be sitting next to Justine.

"Thanks for holding down the fort for us, Hannah," Claire said.

It was miserably hot, but still, I felt a bit better when we were all crowded around the little table. I was part of a group, the group I'd wanted to be a part of since I'd found out that a Master of Fine Arts in Creative Writing existed. I was sitting between Claire and Justine, the women I hoped were going to be my new best friends.

I heard my phone ding with a text. I opened it, and there was a picture of Luke holding a puppy. He'd texted: Hot guy with a puppy > Everything.

I felt a little flutter in my stomach. I hit the heart reaction but then immediately took it back by hitting "haha." It would be stupid to finally get up the courage to ask Luke if he was single now that we were five hundred miles apart.

"Holly shit," Justine said, leaning in closer to admire the picture. "Who's that?"

I quickly turned my phone over so she couldn't look at Luke any longer. I didn't want to give her any information about him. "Just a bartender where I used to work."

"Sure," Justine said teasingly.

Ben set down his drink and reached over the table to where I hid my phone in my lap. "Let me see."

"No, my battery is low," I lied, sliding my phone into my purse. "Tell us about the workshop."

"You think we're going to let you change the topic that fast?" Ben asked. I was certain he just wanted to see the photo because of

Justine's reaction to it. He wanted to figure out how he could make her say "holy shit" too.

"Leave her alone," Justine told Ben. "Hannah doesn't want everyone lusting over one of her boyfriends."

"I don't have any boyfriends," I said, and stopped myself from clapping back at Justine: *What about you? Have you run into the guy who sent you the shot the night we met? Were you able to pay him back?* She probably hadn't meant to cause the little blush of shame I felt at the implication that I was promiscuous.

"I'll teach you about workshop, Hannah," Ben said. "Show us the picture of the guy who isn't your boyfriend, and I'll show you how it's done."

I wasn't going to let Ben verbally tear apart a photo of Luke just to make himself feel better.

"Never mind," I said. "I can wait until workshop to learn about it."

Ben laughed. "Workshop isn't only going to be on Wednesdays."

"What do you mean?" Justine asked.

"The thing about workshop is that it doesn't *stay* in workshop." Ben was basking in her attention. He was speaking more loudly than he needed to. "There's no escape. No off switch. We don't hang out with anyone else; we hate everyone, and they hate us. The poets are fractured and weird. The English Masters and PhDs compare us to the greats and think we're fakes and wannabes. They believe all the best literature has already been written and we're just mucking up the literary canon."

We laughed nervously. I wasn't sure if we were laughing at the other students or ourselves.

"But we don't think their opinions are worth anything," Ben added. "We workshop the shit out of them and find them lacking. We pretty much find everything lacking."

"So it's a defense mechanism?" Justine said.

"Maybe," Ben replied. "But it's also just really fucking fun. The problem is, it's impossible to shut off 'workshop mode.' Enjoy your mind right now, before it goes into workshop mode."

"Workshop mode?" I asked, even though I already knew. I'd been in 'workshop mode' with myself for as long as I could remember, trying to figure out what was wrong with me so I could fix it.

Claire cut in, "Workshop mode is a permanent and irreversible condition where you can't look at anything without trying to put together an eloquent critique of it."

"Not *anything*?" I asked. "What about . . . each other?"

"Each other *especially*," Ben said.

Justine smiled. "Show us."

"That wouldn't be fair at this point," Ben replied. "We'll wait until you guys know how to workshop so you can defend yourselves."

"Careful," Justine said, "I might workshop you back. I'm a quick study." She winked at me. "And Hannah is too."

C H A P T E R

22

Then

Wednesday, September 4, 2024, graduate school, the first workshop

When I walked into workshop, I noticed that the furniture on one side of the room had been rearranged into a rectangle, consisting of two overstuffed couches and two easy chairs. Justine sat in one of the chairs, and the professor sat in the other. They were like a queen and king at opposite ends of an invisible table. Perhaps Justine had deliberately chosen to sit where Ben couldn't drool over her as he usually did. He was sitting at the end of one of the couches, as close to her as he could. I took a seat on the other couch across from him, also near Justine.

Three rays of sunlight from the high lancet windows shone into the center of the rectangle. I looked at my outfit in the bright light. I wasn't sure if we were supposed to dress up for workshop. I'd worn a short-sleeved silk shirt and my nicest pair of jeans. Justine was going with the athleisure look: a white tank top, cashmere and linen track pants that probably cost a couple hundred dollars, and flip-flops that she let slide off her feet. Her toenails were a muted shade of pink. I saw the remnants of corns and bunions before she tucked her feet under her legs. She must have been an athlete of some kind before going to Columbia.

"All right!" the professor said, smiling eagerly. His smile reminded me of something Claire said about him recently: "He's young and seems way too agreeable to be a very good writer. I mean, why does he need us to like him? If he was a good writer, we'd like him for allowing us to breathe his air."

He clapped his hands together. "So! Let's get the formal business out of the way. First, you don't have to call me Professor, but if you can't help it, just call me 'Professor M.' Otherwise, I answer to James. Second, break out your calendars and see what dates work for you to bring in stories. We'll workshop two stories each week." He was holding the sign-up sheet in his hand, and we were all watching it like hawks eyeing the last mouse in the field. "One of you has already expressed a preference, so we'll start the sign-up sheet there. Pass the sheet to Justine."

Everyone's eyes were glued to the sign-up sheet as it was handed down to Justine. She took it between her immaculate fingers and quickly signed it. Had she decided to go first? Last? She passed it to Ben, who took it with a grateful nod. I was going to be the last one to sign up.

Claire raised an eyebrow when the sheet got to her. She tilted it so I could see it. Justine signed up to go last, and no one else had signed up for that day. Claire texted me: Cowards.

I hit the "haha" emoji, but I was a coward too. I didn't want to go on the same day as Justine.

By the time the sheet got to me, though, I didn't have a choice. I had to sign up to have my story workshopped on the same day as Justine's.

"No big deal," Claire told me when we left workshop. "You're going to be great."

I wondered again about the piece of paper Justine had left in my car. She'd claimed it wasn't hers, but I didn't believe her. Writing was probably hard for her, and therefore her process was slow. That's why she'd signed up for the last workshop slot available. I'd just been unfortunate enough to have to sign up for the same date. Our writing would be going toe-to-toe.

C H A P T E R

23

Then

September 2024

I LOVED BEING A graduate student. I'd finally found other people who loved discussing everything under the sun. We "workshopped" not only literature, but also the facades of shops and restaurants, trying to decide which we might enter. We discussed the gait of a passing dog and the architectural design of a seminary that all of us found intimidating, but not so intimidating that we didn't sprawl on its lawn to discuss Breece D'J Pancake, an author who'd committed suicide at twenty-six (the age I happened to be, though I didn't mention it) while in a graduate creative writing program. We imagined what he might have written if he'd lived a little longer.

One night after workshop, armed with coupons that Andrew, a first-year MFA student like me, had found in a newspaper at a coffee shop, we headed to Steak 'n Shake. Andrew was three years younger than I was, and much trendier. He was short and skinny, with glasses nearly as big as his head. If there was a deal anywhere within a ten-mile radius, he'd find it. Instead of paying the usual $5.99 to get a grilled cheese and fries delivered to our dirty table in a plastic red basket, four of us ("limit of four per coupon, please") only had to pay $4.39 each. It was greasy spoon chic.

"This is heaven," I said.

"The floor in heaven is surprisingly sticky," Phong observed, not unhappily. Our shoes sounded like Band-Aids being ripped off as we left the restaurant.

From there we went to a sex shop in a nearby suburb. The clerk glared at us from behind the counter as we wandered up and down the aisles, workshopping. Our laughter was riotous, echoing through every corner of the store.

Most of us agreed that one of the movie titles, *Barely Legal,* was elegant in its simplicity, that it demonstrated a mysterious, alluring restraint by whoever was in charge of titling such things.

Phong summed it up for us. "The contrast between the graphic content of pornography, and the nearly, *nearly* subtle title, adds a whole new tone and layer of meaning to *Barely Legal Butt Babes IV.*"

* * *

One day, after workshop, I told Claire, "I was made to be a graduate student. I finally feel like I've arrived. There's no place I'd rather be."

Justine overheard me and said, "That sounds like something we should all toast!"

"Where are we going tonight?" Andrew asked.

"No need to make any big decisions," Ben replied. "Let's start at Market Pub and see where the night takes us."

We went to a few bars, but I managed to only have a couple beers.

At the end of the night, Ben decided to drop us off in the opposite order he'd picked us up in.

"You're the first one to be dropped off," Phong said to me. "You know what that means."

Did it mean they were going to talk about me as soon as I wasn't there to defend myself?

"Party at Hannah's!" Ben said.

I shook my head. "My apartment is a mess."

"We have something we can't do in public," Ben explained. "We always do it at the apartment of whoever gets dropped off first, to make sure no one misses out."

I started to repeat that my apartment was a mess, but Justine didn't let me finish. "*All* our apartments are a mess," she said, even though I was certain her apartment was perfect.

I decided not to argue. I was grateful to be part of the group, and I didn't want to jeopardize that. Hopefully no one would care that my apartment wasn't fancy and I hadn't cleaned it recently.

Our footfalls reverberated down the hallway of my building as I led us to my apartment. It sounded like a stampede. I unlocked the door. Ben, Amelia, Phong, Claire, Justine, and Andrew followed me inside.

Andrew looked through the cupboard for glasses.

"I only have four," I told him. "I'm sor—" I looked at Justine and didn't say "sorry." Justine pulled a bottle of vodka out of her purse.

Amelia said she had to use the bathroom. She looked uncomfortable, even more so than usual. I hurried to point the way down the hall.

Ben rolled a joint and everyone came to sit in a circle around him. He looked to Justine. "Should we wait for Amelia?"

Justine laughed as if Ben must be joking. He lit up and passed the joint to Justine without taking a hit. Claire rolled her eyes.

When it got to me, I asked, "This isn't a strain that causes paranoia, is it?" Ben said no, but I still only took a small hit.

Andrew put on some music and we brutally workshopped it until Andrew asked what we wanted to hear.

"I want to hear 'Lavender Haze,'" Amelia said.

"I bet you do," Ben said, looking from her to Justine.

What is Ben trying to say? Does Amelia have a crush on Justine? Or is Ben projecting?

"Shut up," Justine said to Ben. "You're high."

"Isn't that the point?" he asked. He noticed Lucy under the couch. He took a hit and blew smoke at her.

I grabbed the joint from him as though I was going to take a hit. Instead, I stubbed it out on his boot and handed it back to him. "Thanks for stopping over. Now I need to write."

Ben giggled. "I didn't know you were such a crazy cat lady, Hannah. Is your cat getting drug tested or something? For fuck's sake, let him enjoy his nine lives a little."

"*Her* nine lives. You need to go."

When everyone left, Justine said she didn't need a ride from Ben and stayed behind.

She waited until everyone's footsteps had faded off down the hall, and then asked, "Remember when you read my palm?" Before I could respond, she said, "Tell me what you really saw."

I allowed myself a drink while I thought about what to say. It would be cruel to tell her she had a short life line. I said only, "I saw that you're passionate."

"Okay, don't tell me." She winked.

"Is there something you're worried about?"

"Actually, I'm a little bit worried about you." When I protested that there was no reason to worry about me, she said, "Don't talk about me anymore, Hannah. I heard you ask Professor Newhouse about my story."

I'd hoped she somehow hadn't remembered or cared too much about my discussion with Professor Newhouse. "I'm sorry," I said, without agreeing not to talk about her anymore; I knew I would still do anything to read her story. "And don't set me up again."

"What are you talking about?" she asked.

"Because of our 'Guess the Letters' game at the first party, people think I stole the urn that went missing."

"Don't try to put your behavior on *me*. You were stumbling around acting like an idiot. You can't hold your liquor."

"So then why did you bring vodka to my apartment?"

Justine sighed. "I'm going to hit the road, Hannah. I just wanted to check in to see how you're doing."

"It's getting dark. I'll give you a ride home."

She shook her head.

"You shouldn't be out alone."

"I've already got a ride," she said.

"Ben?" I asked. "Is he coming back for you?"

"God, no," she said.

"Who?"

"No one you know."

After she left, I stood staring at the door. Was the person giving her a ride going to be the reason she died young?

I looked out the window and saw her walking down the street away from my building. She turned the corner at the end of the block.

She hadn't walked off in the direction of her apartment.

I ran outside and around the corner just in time to see her get into a Ford F-150. The windows were up, but still I saw her mouth moving, opening wide to yell at the driver. He leaned back away from her. I watched them argue until it started to rain and I couldn't see inside the truck anymore.

I stayed where I was, watching to see what direction the truck would go. But it didn't go anywhere. The door opened and Justine stumbled out. I rushed after her, but the curb seemed to jump up at me out of nowhere. I lay on the ground feeling like the world was spinning too fast. I had to stop drinking. I *would* stop drinking, I vowed.

"Are you okay?" someone asked.

Even though we'd never spoken, I knew it was the stranger. He crouched beside me so our eyes were level. I was aware that my writing was too full of the words "dark" and "beautiful." But as I looked at him, I knew that all along, I'd been describing this man. His eyes were dark, his hair was dark, and his skin was sparkling in the rain. I wouldn't have believed he was real if not for a single crack in his veneer: a shaving nick on his neck.

"Are you okay?" he repeated. His breath was 100 proof vodka. It's a lie that you can't smell vodka. I could smell it from across a crowded room. I could smell it from ten treatment centers away. I felt more intoxicated as I breathed him in.

I no longer cared about Justine, or anything else that wasn't this man who seemed to have emerged directly from my dreams. He reached his hands halfway across the small space between us. I remembered the advice about kissing I'd read as a girl: lean halfway toward your date and let him come the rest of the way. The stranger had opened a door and was inviting me to walk through it.

When I hesitated, he didn't draw his hands back. His desire was on the table. His eyes were piercing. I looked down at his hands, how steady and unwavering they were.

There were only two things that could overcome my shyness: alcohol and lust, and I'd sworn off alcohol. Well, sort of. I put my hands in his. His fingers were strong and slim, and I wanted to pour all of myself into them.

He didn't pull me up, he *lifted* me up. I had an English major. I thought like this. Everything was symbolic and I decided that is what he truly wished to do—get me back on my feet.

Once we were standing, he took off his jacket and draped it around my shoulders. It was warm and smelled good, masculine, even in the rain. Aftershave, cologne and warm skin. He moved to the street side of the sidewalk.

"Do you want to come up?" I asked him.

He took my hand and we rushed together through the rain. When we reached my apartment, I stumbled in ahead of him.

I looked in my refrigerator for something to give him to drink. "I don't need a drink," he said.

The sound of him locking the door behind us made my heart pound in the same lusty way it did when I heard a belt buckle in the dark. Soon his hands were on my back, my neck, combing my hair, pulling gently on the snarls close to my neck. I let my head fall to the side to expose more of my skin, inviting him to kiss my neck. I leaned back against him, pressed my hips back against his.

And then his hands were on my skirt, yanking it up.

I should have been thinking of him, of us, but instead I thought, *Justine.* Not even this beautiful man could make me forget about her for long.

"Too fast," I said and shook him off.

He stepped back. "Okay. Tell me what you want."

I pulled my skirt down and turned to look at him. I didn't mention Justine in case she'd told him about me and the argument we'd just had. "Talking, a little intellectual foreplay, then some actual foreplay."

"What do you want to talk about?" he asked.

"I want to talk about how at the alumni party you looked like a man with the confidence to go slow."

My insult was successful; he took another step back. "Confidence makes men go slow?"

"Not all men. Only the best ones. They don't rush ahead like teenagers who are afraid they'll lose their chance."

"Then isn't it the opposite for confident women? They're not afraid to do what they obviously want to?"

"There are worse things than being afraid."

"Then why do you act so tough? Why don't you ever smile?"

He was asking too many questions. I'd had enough. "This night is over," I told him.

I opened the music app on my phone and blasted "Closing Time": "You don't have to go home, but you can't stay here." I set my phone just outside my bedroom door and locked myself in. Through the music, I listened to his movements in the apartment. The creak of the floor as he made his way to the bathroom, the faint sound of the medicine cabinet opening. He walked back through the living room to the apartment door, undid the lock, and his footsteps faded down the hall.

I ran to check the medicine cabinet to see if he'd stolen anything. Nothing was missing. I locked my apartment door and crawled into bed.

As I took my mood stabilizer, I prayed that Justine wouldn't find out that I'd brought the stranger home.

CHAPTER

24

Now

I CAN'T STOP THINKING about Justine, and how much emotion was in Eli's voice when he said her name. *Justine.* I can't stop hearing it over and over again, and I can't forgive him. Not if he won't admit to it, which he won't. "You're the only woman for me, Hannah," he says. "I can't live without you. And you can't live without me."

Is he threatening me? His eyes are darker than usual, I can't read them.

Though we have to huddle together for warmth, we are as far apart as two people pressed together can be. Perhaps he fears me as much as I fear him.

CHAPTER

25

Then

AFTER THE STRANGER left, I tossed and turned. I wasn't only awake because I was worrying that Justine would find out I took her (ex?) boyfriend home. The inside of my head didn't feel right.

I didn't sleep well the next two nights either. By Saturday, I had the worst headache of my life. I didn't know what was wrong. My thoughts were moving too quickly to grasp. I didn't even know if I was actually having thoughts. It felt like something was happening in my head, but I couldn't figure out what. And it wasn't just my head. My whole body tingled. The noises outside my apartment were so loud they rattled my brain. Engines as loud as buzz saws zipped past, and tires screeched so piercingly it felt like they were ripping through my synapses.

I was nauseous and dizzy. I couldn't force myself to eat, except when I was overcome by hunger. Then I stumbled to the refrigerator to drink from the ketchup bottle. But when I popped it open, the smell was overwhelming. I gagged before I even tasted it. I didn't want it anywhere near me. I staggered out to the dumpster to throw it away. Bad idea. The rotten egg stench of the dumpster hit me before I even opened the lid. And the colors outside. They were so bright they burned my eyes; the grass was so green I couldn't look at it directly, and the sunshine felt like it was setting me on fire.

Though the pavement wavered beneath me, I managed to make it back to my apartment. I crawled into bed. Despite the heat, I pulled my sheet over me.

The buzzer jolted me upright. Who could it be? I decided not to buzz in whoever it was. But then the buzzer rang again, and again.

I was so aggravated I buzzed the person in without even knowing who it was, so I could tell them they were rude and needed to find something else to do besides piss me off.

When I heard footsteps approaching down the hall to my apartment, I threw open my door to confront the person. My anger faded and was replaced with guilt when I saw Justine coming toward me in a little black dress, sling-back heels, and a big smile. I hoped she hadn't found out I took the stranger home. I hoped he was as discreet as he seemed. Amelia followed behind Justine in a similar outfit. Heavy footsteps plodded after them. Ben was coming up the stairs.

"You didn't think we were going to let you spend Saturday night alone, did you?" he called to me. Justine and Amelia's heels clicked against the wood floor as they entered. Ben clomped in behind them. "You better get ready fast," he said. "I'm already starting to sweat from the tropical climate in here."

"Ready for what?" I asked, though I realized what he meant as the words left my mouth.

"The party."

"I'm not feeling well."

"Of course you're not feeling well," Ben said. "No one could possibly feel good in a tiny, one-hundred degree box."

"I think it's only seventy-five right n—"

"Quit standing there and get your shoes on!" Justine said, playfully pushing me toward the closet.

"I have such a bad headache. I don't think I'd be much fun at the party."

"We're not letting you miss it," Justine said.

When I still hesitated, Ben said, "Hurry up. My antiperspirant is melting down my arm."

I slipped on some black flip-flops, hoping they were formal enough that I wouldn't stand out at the party.

When we got outside and I saw Ben's pickup, I instinctually headed for the open bed to sit with Andrew and Phong. "Nope," Justine said. She stepped in front of Amelia to block her from getting in the front. "Hannah, you can ride up front with Ben and me. Amelia, you sit in back."

Amelia pressed her lips together and did as she was told.

When we walked into the party, I noticed people looking at me funny. Or was I just paranoid?

Claire took one look at me and brought me directly to the kitchen. "Light or dark roast?" she asked. I shrugged. She put a K-Cup into the Keurig machine and leaned back against the counter while we waited for it to brew. "Are you okay?" she asked.

"No," I said. I started laughing and couldn't stop. Something was coming loose inside me.

"So this is where all the fun is," Barkley Newhouse said, entering the kitchen and going directly for a bottle of wine on the counter beside Claire. "But why do I smell coffee?"

"Hannah's mixing things up a bit tonight," Claire said.

"Ah, I see," Barkley said. He looked at me thoughtfully. "I've actually been meaning to talk to Hannah," he told Claire. "You can rejoin the soiree for a while."

I didn't want to make Claire babysit any longer. "I'm good," I told her.

"Okay, you know where to find me if you need me," she said.

When the Keurig was done excreting coffee into the mug, Barkley poured a little Bailey's cream into it and held it out to me. He saw that my outstretched hand was shaking, and he set the mug on the counter.

"I think you'd be doing better if you took my class," he said.

I picked up the mug and took a sip. Even just the smell of it was energizing. "How so?" I asked.

"It would help you see what you're not admitting to yourself." He went to the doorway to the living room. "Come here," he beckoned.

He pointed, not inconspicuously, at the other first-years. "Look at them. They've walked in off the playground and expect they'll continue getting recess every day. They've only seen the street from afar. They know nothing about anything."

I started to object, but he continued, "I wish I were younger. I'd put on a mask and threaten the girls and wallop the boys until they finally had something to write about. I'd stalk each of them separately."

Phong saw us looking at him and raised his glass as if we could clink from across the room. Barkley scowled and waved at him to move out of the way. Phong shrugged and stepped to the side.

Barkley squinted at Justine. "That elfin one might already have something to say. Whatever it is, though, she didn't say it in her award-winning story. What a crock of stolen sentiment."

"Why didn't you like it?"

"It felt a little . . . familiar." He lifted one brow, and stared hard to make sure I got it.

I remembered him saying he knew how it ended without finishing it. "Familiar, as in ordinary?"

"No. Now, perhaps, it might seem ordinary. But it wasn't when I saw it for the first time."

My heart started to pound. I could no longer hold back the thought that had been burbling at the edge of my consciousness for the last month: *Did Justine take the money that should have been given to me?*

"When was that?" I tried to sound casual, but I was slightly breathless.

"Oh," he said, clearly satisfied to have my rapt attention. "There's no use mentioning it. No one wants to admit the emperor is naked after marching in his parade."

"Who could she possibly plagiarize without getting caught?" I challenged.

"Careful with the *p* word. Even with tenure, I know when to keep my mouth shut."

"Then why did you mention it?"

"So when she tells you you're worthless, you don't believe it."

"She's my best friend. I can't imagine her telling me I'm worthless," I said.

"She already has. She's telling everybody, just not with words."

"What are you talking about?"

"She brought you here like this," he said, gesturing at my face.

"Like what?"

"Open your phone's camera and see for yourself."

I gasped at my reflection. My scar was glaring out from my cheek and my eyes didn't look right. There were bags beneath them and yellow crusts gathered in the corners.

Why hadn't Justine told me to do something about my face before we left my apartment?

"Get used to seeing her back," he said, "and watching your own."

I wanted to go home. I stumbled over to the circle of my peers and nearly crashed into Ben as I tried to whisper in his ear. I gave up aiming for his ear or whispering. "I need to go home," I yelled.

Justine grabbed me and walked me away from the circle. "We just got here," she said, guiding me down the hall to a bedroom. "Rest in here for a little while, and then we'll get you home."

That's all I remember about the night.

Or did I just imagine everything?

I woke up Sunday morning in my own bed. I felt like shit. Had someone slipped something into my drink?

Was last night just a nightmare?

But when Claire texted me to see if I was okay, I knew I hadn't dreamed up going to the party. I responded: Yes. Thanks for babysitting me.

She sent another text: So far it's just a rumor, but I've heard some things went missing last night.

Not again. I dropped the phone and buried my head under my sheet. I was stuck in a nightmare and couldn't escape. My mind wouldn't let me.

CHAPTER 26

Then

On Monday, I called my psychiatrist's office. It usually took weeks to get an appointment, but there'd been a cancellation. I just wanted to talk to him over the phone, but the doctor's office insisted on a video visit.

I had the urge to look good for the meeting, but why? The doctor should see that my medication wasn't working. Still, I washed my face, combed my hair, and put on a clean shirt.

I told the doctor about the last five days, and how my head didn't feel right.

"You're still taking the hundred fifty milligrams of Lamictal?" he asked.

"Every night."

"It worked for you in the past, so I don't want to take you off it. Let's try increasing your dose to two hundred milligrams a night."

"But I don't think it's helping."

"If you'd like to try something else, we can. But we'll need to taper you off the Lamictal slowly. Otherwise, there's a risk you could have a seizure. It will take five weeks to safely stop it. In the meantime, we can introduce another medication and see how you respond."

I wanted to make sure I'd heard correctly. "Seizure?"

"Yes, going off Lamictal too quickly can cause seizures. But the more common side effects of stopping it suddenly are headaches, fatigue, an inability to focus, and even suicidal ideation."

Through the pounding in my head, an alarm was sounding. The side effects he'd described were the ones I'd been having. Something was wrong with the pills I'd been taking. I needed new ones. "I don't want to go off it," I said. "Let's try increasing it."

"I'm glad to hear you say that. It worked so well for you in the past that I think it would be a mistake to give up on it without seeing if adjusting your dose helps. We'll increase it slowly to prevent side effects."

"Will you call it in right away?"

"I will, Hannah, as soon as we're done here." It felt like he was talking aggravatingly slowly. "I'll prescribe you twenty-five milligram tablets, just as I did when we were working up to the hundred and fifty milligram dose. The twenty-five milligram looks different from the hundred and fifty milligram."

As soon as we hung up, I stumbled to the bathroom. I opened the bottle and looked at the pills. They were blank. They didn't have any inscription on them whatsoever.

I knew something was wrong. Prescription pills always have some kind of identification.

Could the manufacturer have messed up this batch? Or were these something else completely? And if so, what the hell had I been taking?

That night, as soon as my pharmacy texted me that my prescription was ready, I ordered an Uber. I didn't feel like I could drive straight, and I wasn't going to wait twenty-four hours for my meds to be delivered.

I couldn't help tapping my feet as I waited in line at the pharmacy. I felt like I was going to explode. The pharmacist looked at me more carefully than I liked, or maybe I was just paranoid. I rushed back out to the parking lot, clutching my prescription.

"Look out!" my Uber driver shouted out the window at me, laying on the horn. I heard the squeal of tires as another car slammed on its brakes. I turned to see a red car with an angry man in the driver's seat.

"Oh my god, you saved my life!" I told the Uber driver as I got in. *And now these pills are going to save it again.*

As soon as the driver stopped the car outside my building, I jumped out and raced inside. I locked my apartment door behind me, opened the bottle, and carefully examined one of the pills. It had an inscription on it.

Since I was pretty sure I hadn't been taking Lamictal for the last several days, I had to titrate up again. I popped the 25-milligram tablet.

* * *

The next day, I felt a little better. I knew I could get through any leftover withdrawal symptoms. What worried me more was going manic. I had to be careful not to get too excited about anything, because that could trigger an episode.

I read the meditations my therapist recommended, but when I still felt anxious that afternoon, I decided to go to Target and buy an exercise mat. After an hour of yoga in the tropical heat of my apartment, I collapsed into a puddle of my own sweat.

CHAPTER

27

Then

On Wednesday, I walked to workshop. I was nervous to be around people when I was still feeling so unstable.

Justine had saved me a spot next to her, on the couch closest to her easy chair. As soon as I sat down, she let her Prada sandal slip off her foot and nudged me with her toe. She saw me look at her foot and quickly tucked it up underneath her, but not before I noticed a bunion. "Are you good?" she asked.

"Yes," I told her, and stopped myself from saying any more. One sign of going manic is talking too much and too fast, and I would not appear manic if I could help it.

"You look like you're still not feeling well."

I smiled with what I hoped was calm confidence, but I could feel the strain in my face.

Professor M's smile also looked strained. "Let's get some ugly business out of the way before we turn to your brilliant stories. The department has asked all of us to look into what happened to the urn.

"If any of you have any information, please let me know. The alumni are very supportive of the department. We have a special relationship with them."

I didn't want to draw attention to myself, but I had to know. "Excuse me, Professor M," I said. "Who, um, is in the urn?"

"Oh!" he said. "I forgot that not everyone knows. William H. Gass. The writer and philosopher who taught here for thirty years. He died several years ago."

I didn't remember much about the night, but I remembered telling Justine the initials were WHG. I'd been right. Why had she told me to try again?

"Does anybody have any other questions before we get to workshopping?" he asked.

No one said anything. I looked at Justine. She seemed to be paying attention to Professor M, but as I kept staring at her, I was sure she felt my gaze. She was purposely ignoring me.

"I need to talk to you," I told Justine after class. We were standing in a little circle with Ben, Claire, Andrew, and Amelia. "Can you come over tonight?"

She nodded yes. Neither of us wanted to have this discussion in front of anyone. I asked Ben to drop me off at home. He looked disappointed. "You're not going to come out with us?"

"Not tonight," I said.

Amelia, Andrew, Phong, and I climbed into the bed of the truck and Justine sat in the cab with Ben. Claire looked back and forth between us for a few seconds and then hopped up and sat next to me.

I hung onto the side of the truck bed as Ben pulled away from the curb and accelerated. "Can you believe someone stole that urn?" Amelia asked.

"No," Claire said, "it was hideous."

"I thought the urn and its disappearance demonstrated the futility of trying to hold onto that which has passed," Andrew replied.

"How much do you think it's worth?" Amelia asked.

"You can't put a price on such things," Andrew replied. "But if you could, probably five dollars."

"No," Claire said. "It was brass. So probably more like a hundred."

"But who else would want it?" Amelia asked. "Who else has the initials WHG?"

Claire found Amelia annoying, and it showed in her voice as she told her, "The initials could be filed off or the urn could have been melted down into a gaudy necklace. Haven't you ever watched . . ." she was trying to think of an example of a show, but before she could, Andrew broke in, "television."

"I'm sorry," Amelia replied. "I don't think like a criminal."

"Or a writer," Claire muttered.

Amelia looked like she'd just been slapped. But no one noticed her except for me.

"The urn wasn't stolen for profit," Andrew said. "The thief is probably someone who's angry at the department or the dead writer and wanted to make a statement. Maybe a disgruntled student."

"I've never heard anyone say anything bad about Bill Gass," Phong said.

When we got to my apartment building, I rapped on the cab window. Ben and Justine turned to look at me. I tried to keep my tone light, which was hard since my jaw had been clenched since Professor M mentioned the urn. I nodded at Justine and told Ben, "Don't keep her too long."

"I'll only keep her as long as she lets me," Ben teased. I'm sure Justine didn't like that, but she didn't object.

"See you soon," I told her.

CHAPTER 28

Then

When the buzzer went off later that night, I put the final touches on my apartment before opening the door for Justine.

She had a to-go cup in her hand. "For you," she said. Even before I took the lid off, I could smell it.

"A Long Island iced tea," she said.

"Thanks," I said, forcing a smile.

"Are you feeling any better?" she asked. "You seemed really off in workshop."

"I'm great." Truthfully, I was still feeling like I was on the edge of going manic, but as long as I stayed calm, hopefully I could keep from losing my shit while I titrated back up to my full dose.

"I'm so happy to hear it." Her blue eyes were sharp as she gazed at me. "I have to utilize your facility," she said, as I'd assumed she would. "And then I'm all ears about whatever you wanted to talk about."

"Of course. Just so you know, the light isn't working. There's an electrical problem."

"I think I'll be okay." She winked as she added, "There are some things I can do in the dark."

"I'm sure there are plenty," I said.

I took a seat on the couch as though I was going to patiently wait for her. After I heard her lock the bathroom door, I tiptoed through the hallway slowly so the floorboards wouldn't creak. My heart was in my throat as I listened through the door.

Before she'd come over, I'd gone to the store and bought orange paint. When I'd returned home, I'd emptied my prescription bottle into a Ziploc baggie that I put in the trunk of my car for safekeeping. Then I'd put some aspirin in the bottle, hung white towels in the bathroom, and waited.

When the buzzer had gone off a few minutes before, I'd put orange paint around the bottle, carefully placed it back in the medicine cabinet, and unscrewed the light bulb.

Now, through the bathroom door, I heard Justine open the medicine cabinet. "Fuck," she muttered. I heard the pills shaking inside the bottle like the beads in a maraca, and then I heard the clack of the bottle hitting the tile.

It was a heartbreaking sound. I'd suspected she'd tampered with my pills, but I'd hoped I was wrong.

A little, concentrated glow of light was suddenly visible under the door. She must have been using her iPhone flashlight. She swore quietly, and then not so quietly. I heard the faucet.

"The paint is waterproof," I told her through the door. The faucet went silent, and the door swung open. I hoped she would look sheepish and ashamed, but instead she looked furious. For the first time, I saw a vein popping out on her forehead. "Sorry, I have to go," she said.

"Why did you replace my prescription with something else?" I asked her. I wanted her to apologize and somehow explain herself, so we could go back to being friends. "I could have had a seizure."

She tilted her head, as though she was concerned. "You've really lost it, Hannah."

"No, I haven't, even though you wanted me to. *Why*, Justine? I trusted you."

The concern on her face faded and was replaced by scorn. "Don't try to blame me for anything. You were broken long before I came along."

"Maybe, but I always put myself back together."

"*You* didn't put yourself back together. A doctor and some pills did it for you."

"A doctor prescribed my medication, but I'm the one who has to fight through my pride and all the stigma of having a mental illness to take it every night."

For a moment she didn't know how to respond. Then she went for the jugular: "And how do you like taking your pill and going to bed alone every night? Don't you miss all the guys?"

Had she read the story I'd submitted with my application for graduate school? And why was she so cruel? "You have no idea what it's like to be me," I said.

"You're right. I've never had to take a pill to keep from waking up in a frat house wondering where my underwear is."

Shame washed over me. I was afraid I'd start to ugly cry, and she'd see that she'd hit a nerve. "Get out," I told her.

She pushed past me, getting orange paint on my arm and the doorknob as she left.

Even after she was gone, my heart felt like it was in my throat. I was breathing so hard and fast I couldn't get the breath all the way past my heart and into my lungs. I opened my laptop and started writing a story about a woman who steals another woman's pills.

"You haven't broken me, Justine," I said the next morning as I put the last touches on my story. My anger felt like a surge of power. "You've unleashed me."

CHAPTER 29

Then

That Wednesday, Ben's story was up for workshop.

There were only two rules of workshop:

1. The writer doesn't speak during workshop. (The story must speak for itself.)
2. The writer isn't referred to by name during the discussion, and is only referred to as "the author."

We spoke as if the author wasn't there.

Ben was sweating even before class began. His story was atrocious, by far the worst thing I'd ever read. But I knew that wasn't why he was nervous. The story was personal. It was about a man who loves a "mysterious" woman named "Josephine." She's "a beauty with fawn-like limbs and huge blue eyes that can see into and through a man's soul." Her mouth is "a perfect bow" that he wants to "gently, and then not so gently, untie." But the most mysterious thing about her is that she doesn't love the narrator back. He suspects her of having a secret lover, who she hides from the narrator because she doesn't want to hurt him. The reason she doesn't want to hurt him is that she secretly loves him back. She's just afraid to admit it to herself. When the protagonist tells her he loves her, she tells him he wouldn't love her if he knew who she really was. He says, "There's nothing you could tell me that would make me stop loving you." She wants to believe him, but she's too afraid. Her agony becomes unbearable. She ends it with a fifth of Jack and a gunshot to the head.

Only someone in love would have the bad judgment to turn this story in.

But I didn't think the large contingent of workshoppers who didn't have their own vehicles would say anything about it. Ben's truck was like a school bus during the day and a party bus in the evening. The only other person besides me who owned a vehicle was a quiet woman who never went out with us after class.

"So! Let's start with Ben's story," the professor said. "What did people like about it?"

Phong called it, "Intriguing."

"Say more about that," the professor said.

"It's an unromantic romance. A sort of postmodern love story."

"I agree," Amelia said. "If the author shortens it, he could submit it to 'Modern Love.'"

"It reads like a modern *Great Gatsby*," someone added.

I could see Andrew making a face. Was it possible he was thinking of actually critiquing the story of the guy who was his ride around town? He couldn't help himself: "A *Great Gatsby* without the great or the Gatsby?"

Phong nodded slowly. "I would like the story even more if the narrator didn't focus so much on Josephine, but rather, on his own feelings toward her. It would be more interesting if he had some insight into his own psyche instead of fixating on the surface-level story, which has already been done so many times and far more masterfully."

Ben's face flushed. I was afraid he was too angry to speak. We waited in silence to see what Justine would say about the character "Josephine."

She didn't address Phong's comment. She simply said, "A gun isn't a very female way to kill yourself. Women are more likely to use pills."

Amelia nodded. "I agree. And how many women drink Jack Daniels?"

Professor M jumped in with the same question he asked every workshop, but this time it hit differently: "What is the writer trying to do with this piece?"

No one wanted to say it aloud: Ben was pleading with Justine to openly return his love. And now there was no turning back—no pretending he wasn't pining for her—because he'd put it in writing. We'd all printed it out and marked it up with our comments.

Andrew said, "I don't think the writer knows what he's trying to do."

Ben was seething. He didn't comment during the discussion of the second story we workshopped. As soon as class ended, he took off instead of bringing everyone out to dinner.

"Need a ride?" I asked Claire.

"I'd love one."

"I should ask everyone else, too," I said.

"They'll be fine," Claire replied. "Everyone except you and Ben lives close to campus."

I was thinking of Justine. *Keep your friends close and your enemies closer.* If she walked home with the other MFA students, would she talk about me? Would she tell them I'm bipolar?

"Justine!" I yelled as she walked away across the quad. She didn't turn back right away. She waited for me to yell again. "Justine! Do you want a ride home?"

"No thanks," she said. I watched Amelia, Phong, and Andrew race to catch up to her.

CHAPTER

30

Then

"Let's go to Steak 'n Shake," Claire said to me. It felt a little strange to go without Andrew's coupons, as though it was a restaurant you went to just because you liked the food, not because it was ironic

"Yes," I said, "I'd love to."

"So what did you think of Ben's story?" I asked her in my car on our way to dinner. She and I had both been quiet in workshop.

"I'm reminded of the Elizabeth Bishop quote about J.D. Salinger: 'It took me days to go through it, gingerly, a page at a time, and blushing with embarrassment for him every ridiculous sentence of the way.'"

I laughed. "Yeah, it would have been less humiliating to just ask Justine out directly. Why did he have to put it in bad writing?"

"He was upset about the 'secret lover' he mentioned in his story. I think he realized Justine was 'cheating' on him, driver-wise, when she stopped asking him to take her grocery shopping. He knew someone else must be taking her."

"Why didn't he just assume it was me?"

"He saw her in this other guy's pickup."

Pickup? I knew immediately who the other guy was: the stranger.

"He told you?" I asked.

"He called me. Crying. Ben thinks he and Justine are destined to be together, but some 'secret lover' is screwing up their destiny."

After we'd eaten our steak burgers and fries, Claire picked up our red plastic baskets and brought them to the trash. She dumped the remaining fries into the slot and then threw the baskets on top. "Let's wash this down with a cocktail and an O'Doul's."

"Let's," I said.

It was humid, but we decided to sit on the patio at Market Pub anyway. I wanted to enjoy summer a little longer. If I were still in Minneapolis, it would already be too cold to sit outside. Claire told me to grab a table while she went in to get our drinks at the bar.

I entered the noise and bustling energy of the other patrons and plonked myself down at the only empty table. As soon as I sat down, I noticed Justine, Andrew, Amelia, Phong, and Ben at a table on the other side of the patio. Had they made up already? Had Ben begged Justine to forget about the story? Was he denying it was about her?

I couldn't get up from my table, or someone else might take it. I waved at the other MFA students, but no one looked my way. Finally, Amelia noticed me, but instead of waving back, she turned to Justine. I saw her lips moving. Justine twisted around to look at me, then turned back to her table, shaking her head.

When Claire returned with our drinks, I gestured at the table Justine was sitting at with the other MFA students. "Justine is ignoring me," I said. "What's going on with her?"

"Probably the same thing that's been going on with her ever since I met her. She sucks. Why do you still worry about her?"

"That's a good question." Could I explain to Claire that my mom had borderline personality disorder and the intermittent reward of her approval was addicting? I felt the same sort of panic in my chest when I was uncertain of Justine's attitude toward me as I'd felt with my mom.

"I mean, is she really someone you want to be friends with?" Claire probed. "Isn't there a 'point of no return' in terms of how badly you'll let someone treat you?"

"I can't stop trying to figure out what's going on between Justine and me," I told her. "We have a real connection. It just isn't consistent."

"Is it real?" Claire asked.

"It's magical."

"Magic isn't real."

"It is to me. I feel like anything is possible around her. Maybe she'll become a famous writer. Maybe I will too."

"You can be successful whether she likes you or not."

I just shook my head. I wasn't so sure.

Claire's tone softened. "Justine is just passive-aggressively bringing everyone to heel as usual. Don't let her get to you. Don't be like Ben. I think he wants to kneel down in front of her, but the table is in the way."

As if he'd somehow heard his name across the crowded patio, Ben smiled at us, then stood up and started looking for extra chairs to bring over to their table.

"Should we go over there?" I asked.

Claire shrugged and grabbed her cocktail off the table. "I suppose."

Justine pushed one of the chairs back so it was slightly behind the circle of chairs. "Which one do you want?" Claire asked me.

Amelia leaned across the table. "You sit here, Claire," she said, hitting the table in front of the closer chair with more strength than I knew she possessed.

"Go for it," I told Claire.

"Hey, Claire," Justine said.

"So you guys made up?" Claire asked Justine and Ben.

Ben's smile expanded so it was nearly taking up his whole face.

"We just had a simple misunderstanding. *Someone*," Justine said, her eyes flicking over to me and then away as though the sight of me repelled her, "has been giving me a lot of unwanted attention, so I was sensitive about Ben's story. We all were." Amelia and Phong nodded in agreement.

I pinched my arm, hoping this was just a nightmare I could wake up from. "I'm the one getting unwanted attention, Justine. Or did you think I *wanted* you to come to my apartment and mess with my pills?"

"You've lured me to your apartment for the last time," Justine said. "I'm not interested in you and your bipolar delusions any longer. I tried to help you, but you're already too far gone."

Claire placed a hand on my arm and quietly said, "Let's get out of here."

But I couldn't leave. Not with Justine spreading lies about me. "You're just angry I proved you were tampering with my pills," I said.

"Hannah," she said, exasperated, as if we'd had this same discussion a million times before. "I was just making sure you were *taking* your pills. I was sad to see the bottle was full. I know people with mental illness don't like to take their medications, but it's obvious you really need—"

I interrupted her lie. "What did you do with the pills you stole from my apartment?"

Justine sighed and dropped her head into her hands for a second before looking up at me. "Why would *I* take a mood stabilizer? I'm not the one who's bipolar. You told me you think you write better when you go off your meds, and you've been pretty crazy lately, so I was checking—"

"Shut up, you dreadful twat," Claire said. She pulled me away from the shocked faces of our fellow MFAers, past the other patrons who I noticed were looking at me, and all the way to my car.

Before getting into the passenger seat, Claire did her whole cocktail like a shot and then said, "Time to blow this pop stand."

When I pulled up outside Claire's apartment building, she squeezed my shoulder.

"Don't let that spoiled bitch ruin things for you. You're here to get a degree, and she can't stop you. Just focus on that."

I was afraid Justine *could* stop me, though. The things she'd said made me seem unstable and dangerous. If the writing program started to believe I was harassing her, they'd kick me out.

I needed to fix the situation.

I needed some proof of what had happened when she came to my apartment.

“Thanks,” I told Claire. “I’m looking forward to turning my story in soon.” Exposing Justine as a fraud was the only way to keep people from believing the lies she’d told about me. I had to put her on the spot. And I had an idea. My future depended on pulling it off, and I’d have to feel a little reckless to carry through with it. I skipped my pill.

CHAPTER

31

Then

AT THE NEXT Saturday night department party, I felt self-conscious as soon as I walked in. I was nervous about my plan. I'd rehearsed the night in my head dozens of times, but my head was a dangerous place because I'd skipped my medicine the last three nights. I wasn't sure I could trust anything that went on in there.

I was walking toward the bar when I heard a little huff. I turned to see Amelia looking at me with indignation. She was wearing the sort of simple dress Justine usually wore, and the same Prada sandals. She'd lost weight and was still shaving her legs.

"Hi, Amelia," I said. "How are you?"

"You know, Hannah, everyone is sick of your shit."

"What are you talking about?"

"It's weird how you were with Justine."

"No, it's weird how she was with me. She stole my pills."

"She told everyone how creepy you were the first time she met you," Amelia said. "You came up with an excuse to touch her. I mean, pretending to be some sort of gypsy palm reader is a stretch. She told us how you talked to her about her sex drive."

I was so shocked, I couldn't even think of how to respond before she said, "Just stay away from her." She walked away like she was Scarlett O'Hara and she'd just made some dramatic pronouncement.

I stood there for a moment, shaking. Could I pull myself together enough to carry out my plan? I headed to the bar for the one cocktail I'd allow myself—not just for the liquid courage, but because I needed a cherry stem.

When I returned to the living room with my drink, I saw that Justine had arrived. She was standing in a circle of fans in an LBD that was probably a child's size ten. Why was she always the center of attention, even though she was rarely the one talking?

I wasn't going to just let her stand around looking fabulous. But first I decided to return to the bar for a little more liquid courage. I wanted to loosen the tight feeling in my chest.

When I started to feel a buzz, I wandered over to the little circle around Justine. "How is your story coming?" I asked.

"Good," she said, in a tone that indicated the discussion was over.

I raised my voice. "Is it anything like the one that won *The Atlantic* student fiction writing competition?"

"You'll just have to wait and see," she said. I would think that the hardest thing to fake is being relaxed. How did she do it? Her lips weren't reaching up or down at the corners; they were a perfectly sealed bow.

"'Wait and see'? Like how we have to wait for *The Atlantic* story?"

"Hannah," she said slowly, as though English weren't my first language, "we've already been over this. The *Atlantic* isn't publishing the winners. The prize is a thousand dollars and bragging rights."

Professor Newhouse was right. The story wasn't hers. "If you really wanted to brag it up," I said, "wouldn't you pass a copy around?"

"I did pass a copy around. To the ten schools I got into." She turned her back to me.

"Justine," I said loudly. "Let's make a deal." I hold up the cherry stem from my cocktail. "If I can tie this in a knot in my mouth, you'll show all of us your *Atlantic* story."

The other MFA students were interested—eyebrows slightly raised, quiet, eager for what came next. Justine turned back to me enough to see what I was holding. "If not," I said, "I'll never ask to see it again."

"I don't care whether you ask to see it or not," she said, her jaw tight. "I want the focus in workshop to be on my current work. I don't want to be on a pedestal. I want to be workshopped as hard as everyone else."

I'd rattled her. She no longer looked relaxed. "The best way to get off the pedestal is to let us see the story," I said.

Amelia gestured at me and announced, "Hannah's obviously drunk. Besides, no one but a porn queen can tie a cherry stem in a knot with their tongue."

No one but a porn queen? How about a waitress? The Cherry Stem Knot was a trick I used to get bigger tips. "You'd be surprised at how many wild and crazy things are possible, Amelia."

My sarcasm wasn't lost on her. "Do it, then," she said. "Try to tie the stem into a knot."

I set my purse down on a couch and turned to the other MFA students. "If I tie this in a knot, will you agree Justine should share the winning story with us?"

A couple of them nodded nearly imperceptibly. Phong glanced nervously at Justine to gauge her reaction. "Hannah's not going to be able to do it anyway," he said, "so what the hell? It'll be entertaining to watch her try." But he and I both knew he was hoping the stem came out in a knot.

I was prepared. I'd bent the stem a few times before asking Justine how her story was coming along, making sure it was long and soft. I held the stem up to show everyone it wasn't in a knot yet. "Justine is going to show us her winning story if I can tie this in a knot with my tongue," I yelled to the entire room. The conversations around our circle quieted. People were starting to look at me.

Justine forced a laugh. "This is ridiculous," she said. "I'm heading out."

Still holding the stem above my head, I announced, "You can see the cherry stem is intact and there's no knot."

People started pushing closer for a better look. I pretended I was back at The Hot Dish, and a huge table of drunk guys who were full of cash for the strip club later were looking for a little excitement with their meal. "We've got it all here," I used to joke with them. "Dinner and a show."

This crowd wouldn't be as easy, but I was going to work them with everything I had. I looked up and opened my mouth wide. I lowered the stem onto my tongue, and then moved it around my mouth to get it wet and pliable. I exaggerated every movement. Out of the corner of my eye, I saw that Justine hadn't left yet. She was sitting on the couch, staring down at her phone, pretending nothing important was happening around her.

Some people watched me skeptically, but most looked like they hadn't been so thoroughly entertained in ages.

Still exaggerating my movements, I bent the stem around the tip of my tongue and took it between my front teeth. I bit down gently, crossing the two ends. Then I used the tip of my tongue to push one end into the loop I'd made.

I smiled, pulled the knotted stem from my tongue, and held it up like I was presenting Simba at the end of *The Lion King*.

The crowd clapped wildly.

Victory.

People pushed closer to get a better look at the stem. One man tried to take it from my hand.

I pointed to Justine, who was staring at me from the couch. "I think I speak for everyone when I say we're excited to read your story. Do you have it on your phone, or are you bringing us a paper copy?"

Justine pushed through the crowd and headed for the door. Amelia went after her.

She could run, but she couldn't hide. The murmurs had already started.

"This is *The Atlantic* student fiction story we're asking to see?" a man in a corduroy blazer and dark jeans asked the woman beside him. I liked that he'd said "we."

"Yes," she replied.

"Isn't it already available?"

"I don't know," she said. "Hopefully, we'll find out."

* * *

That night, before I passed out, I took a picture of the knotted cherry stem and texted it to Luke.

He responded: Nice. You've still got it.

I knew that by "it" he just meant my serving skills, but it was a sexy text in any case. I felt a sudden wave of nostalgia for Luke, Minneapolis, and The Hot Dish. I missed coming home from work every night with a wad of cash. Donating plasma and the occasional cleaning gig weren't proving to be very lucrative. I texted Luke: Just out of curiosity, how much $ did you make tonight?

He texted back: I don't know. I haven't counted it yet.

What could possibly be keeping him from counting his cash? Was he with someone?

Before I could ask, I passed out.

CHAPTER

32

Then

Sunday afternoon, Claire texted: I no longer want to have anything to do with you.

I was so shocked that for a moment I couldn't respond. I felt the walls crumbling in on me. Claire was the one person in St. Louis who'd had faith in me. I replied: What? Why?

She responded right away: You know why.

My hands started to shake. It took me a moment to text her back: No, I really don't.

She responded: Because you lie and make scenes and stalk people.

That didn't make sense. Claire had never believed Justine's lies about me. Justine must have gotten to Claire somehow and changed her mind.

I texted Justine: What did you tell Claire?

My phone rang and lit up with "Justine."

I answered, "Hi, Justine. I hope you're calling to apologize."

There was a pause, then a voice that didn't sound like Justine's, said, "Hannah?"

"Who is this?" I asked.

A sigh full of sadness. "You really are obsessed with Justine." It definitely wasn't Justine's voice. It was Claire's.

"Oh, Claire! Sorry. It said 'Justine' when you called."

"Why would it say 'Justine'?"

"Someone must have switched your contact info with Justine's in my phone. I didn't expect you to call, considering the texts you've been sending me. But now I realize they weren't from you."

She was silent for a moment. "Hannah, I know you don't want to hear this. But you need to stay away from Justine. I don't think she's good for you. And I think you better call your doctor."

"I had to call him two Mondays ago because I wasn't feeling right. I figured out Justine replaced my mood stabilizer with something else."

"Do you have any proof?"

"No, but I know she did. I painted the prescription bottle orange and invited her over while it was still wet to see if she'd mess with it again."

Claire didn't say anything.

I continued, "You should have seen her! She had orange paint on her hand and she got some on me and on the doorknob."

"Hannah, if you don't promise me that you'll call your doctor, I'm going to request that the police do a wellness check on you."

I was eager to get off the phone with her so I could text her a picture of the doorknob with the orange paint on it right away. "Okay," I said.

I took a picture and immediately sent it to Claire, who was "Justine" in my contacts. Then I got nervous and looked at the picture on my phone. The orange was hardly visible.

I studied the wall again to make sure it was there and I didn't just dream this all up. I texted her again: Sorry, bad picture. You'll have to see it in person.

No response.

Anxiety was starting to grasp at my breath. My hands were shaking.

I swallowed my mood stabilizer and made myself some chamomile tea, but I was afraid it was already too late. I looked at myself in the mirror. My eyes were wide and my gaze was wild.

Oh, shit. I thought. *Here we go.*

CHAPTER 33

Then

I WENT TO WORKSHOP the next Wednesday like always, even though it wasn't like always. I didn't know if I had friends anymore. I held my head up high as I entered the deceptively cushy room. It suddenly went quiet. The people I'd hung out with only a couple of weeks ago looked at me as though from a great distance. I felt like I was entering an arena. Justine gave me a warning look as I approached a seat near her, so I took the only other empty spot, which was on the couch between Ben and Amelia. Amelia had lost more weight, and she was wearing stretch pants and a tank top identical to Justine's.

"Hey," I said to Claire before sitting down.

She was sitting on the other side of Ben. "Hey, Hannah," she replied. But I didn't like the way she looked at me. Her eyes were full of pity. Amelia shifted away from me on the long couch.

Ben nodded at me. I nodded back, trying not to look as grateful as I was for his friendly acknowledgment.

When class began, I was hyperaware, noticing every movement anyone made, and watching them give each other looks. Or was I being paranoid?

I took out my pen and looked down at my notebook. "How is everyone doing?" Professor M asked. I didn't look up. I didn't want to see people giving each other looks anymore. I tuned out everything but my writing.

"How are you, Hannah?" Professor M asked, jolting me out of my writing trance.

I forced myself to look up.

Justine was trying to affect a serious and concerned expression, but I could tell by her eyes that she was smirking.

"I'm doing well," I said.

"Okay, just checking," Professor M said. "You're awfully quiet."

It's a feat to be quiet when you're on the edge of a manic episode. I didn't want to start talking because I couldn't predict what I'd say, but I was sure I wouldn't be able to stop.

I shrugged and offered a smile. He smiled back at me, and then, thankfully, began the workshop.

It was a relief to look back down at my notebook.

I wrote the whole time, not paying attention to anything going on around me. I didn't look up until the notebook was full. Everyone was gone but the professor.

"I'm looking forward to your story, Hannah," he said, then gestured to my notebook. "Or will it be a novel?"

I noticed for the first time that I liked his face. He had happy crinkles around his eyes and dimples that showed when he was smiling. I felt a little spark of lust. He winked and said, "We'd better get going. We don't want to intimidate the maintenance crew."

He held the door of the workshop room for me. "Thank you," I told him, resisting the urge to start talking to prolong our interaction. But when I got to the door that led out of the building, I turned around. I wanted to ask him about himself and how he realized he wanted to be a writer. But there was nobody there. The hallway was empty.

CHAPTER 34

Then

SHOPPING WAS SO pleasurable it felt like I was hooked up to an IV of oxytocin. My clothes no longer fit right. They fit my body but not my spirit. I tried on whole stores and bought half of one on my credit card. I was on fire as I strutted through DSW Designer Shoe Warehouse in five-inch heels, and while snapping selfies in little dresses I tried on in the fitting rooms of Macy's, and as I stuffed seven pairs of undies in my purse at Victoria's Secret while pretending to be studying the *5 for $30* sign.

The world was a playground and I wanted to play my heart out.

I'd known since the first episode that my real life was in the mania. That's when I was truly alive. All the rest of life was a dull impressionist painting, like being trapped in a Monet, trying to make it back to a Jackson Pollock.

Saturday night, I took a couple shots before heading to the party. I was going to show everyone I was strong and not afraid of being alone.

But when I arrived, I thought maybe I didn't want to be alone. Men fluoresced through the room. How had I gone so long without companionship and romance? Each man was a world of possibility.

Duncan stood at the edge of a group of alumni shifting his weight from foot to foot as if deciding which one to take off from. As director of the writing program, I would've expected him to have made it farther into the room. *Shouldn't he be schmoozing up alumni?* His social awkwardness didn't diminish his appeal. In his tweed sport coat and pants of indeterminate material, he looked like a sexy nerd.

Professor M was wearing his classic professor garb, as usual. Even the corduroy patches on the elbows of his suit jacket looked sexy to me. I'd never noticed how piercing his hazel eyes were before. Was there flirtation in his gaze?

"No notebook tonight?" he asked me.

"I've run out of paper. Do you have any I could borrow?"

"Not on me. Come see me during office hours."

Was that a come-on? "What if I can't wait that long?" I asked playfully, but he had already moved on to talk with some other academics.

I didn't trust myself to be normal, so I kept my lips sealed while I eavesdropped on other people's conversations. I hated that one student threw out the term "middle brow" and then everyone started using it. *Did graduate school make these people pretentious, or did they go to graduate school because they were already pretentious?*

That's all I remember about the first part of the evening. I'd consumed more alcohol than I had planned to and, at some point, realized I needed to leave.

Apparently, I hadn't gotten very far.

I came to on the sidewalk, staring up at the distorted faces of alumni, professors, and students pressed against the window. A streetlight shone on me like a spotlight. I realized: *I'm on a stage.* I was lit up not only by the glow of the streetlight, but also by the hungry gazes of everyone inside, all desperate to see me.

But where were Claire, Justine, and the other MFAers? I hadn't seen them all night.

It doesn't matter, I told myself. *It's their loss.* But a little voice inside my head said, *Except Claire. That's your loss*.

A wave of angst washed over me, followed by anger. The party had hurt me. I looked at the faces in the window and started singing "Like a Rolling Stone" with the full strength of my lungs.

Someone came out of the house toward me and rushed to where I'd fallen on the sidewalk. "Please," Duncan said, "stop yelling."

He didn't appreciate all I'd done for everyone. I'd put so much of myself into the song, the party, the night. I'd poured almost my whole self out onto the sidewalk. "You're stepping in me," I told him. Or maybe I yelled it.

As I looked up at him, my anger was like a wave that had already peaked. It was crashing and fading back into the night. I could see he was afraid. He was like a child who has suddenly found himself at the edge of a cliff he can't back away from.

I felt for him because he was alone, like I was. I missed being part of the MFA clique. I missed Claire. *But here's someone else.*

"I can't walk," I said.

He stared down at me like we were all out of options.

"Help me," I said.

He did. He knelt and put my arm around his shoulders. I was shocked by their smallness. I thought I would remember the feel of his smallness forever. The bones beneath my bare arm were the only physical things I had truly felt all night. I didn't feel the sidewalk or the night air I wasn't properly dressed for. It felt so good to be touching someone.

Duncan no longer had his tweed sport coat on. He was wearing a wrinkled dress shirt with yellow underarm stains. He must not have had anyone to look after him. He was like a cat you find on the street: mangy, with a dirty, frayed collar and a rusty bell sadly announcing its arrival.

Someone once loved him. Otherwise he would not have been so heartbroken, so stooped, even before he had to bend to take some of my weight, as much as I thought he could bear. Too much, perhaps; we still hadn't risen from the sidewalk. Which was fine with me. I enjoyed studying him, imagining what his life was like. The longer I was near him, the clearer it became: he hadn't figured out how to be in the world. Maybe his wife had just left him or he was living with his mother and she'd died without leaving him any instructions on how to take care of himself. He'd eaten all the meals she'd cooked and frozen for him before she died, and he was as alone in the world as I was. More. There wasn't even any cat or dog fur on his shirt. The only thing attached to him was a stale smell. He'd started drinking before the party too. He was one of those unlucky people who got weirder and more uptight when they drank.

"I'll take you home," he said. We stumbled to his Subaru and I directed him to my apartment, watching his face light up and then darken as we passed between streetlights. He was at least fifty, maybe older. The lines in his face weren't from smiling. Maybe they were from bracing himself for whatever the world threw at him.

"It's that old brick one on the right," I told him.

He pulled over. Without asking if I needed help, he leaned over to unlatch my seatbelt. I wondered if he was going to kiss me, but instead he pulled back and said, "I'll walk you up."

He followed me into my apartment and kissed me awkwardly. I liked the warmth of his body pressed against mine and the taste of red wine on his lips, so I let him continue kissing me. When he started to pull at my clothes, I said, "Can we just kiss?" He yanked on my zipper.

"Duncan, *stop*." But he didn't. Not until a couple minutes later when I punched him in the balls so hard that his hand released my hair. He doubled over.

I stumbled away. "Get out."

"I will," he gasped, nearly breathless from the pain. "Don't become hysterical."

Hysterical?

I'd thought he was shy, and that's why he was so strained. But actually he was a heartless asshole. Once he'd dressed, he grabbed his phone off the end table and walked out without looking at me.

I stood there, paralyzed for a moment, before rushing to lock the door—the deadbolt and the chain. I took deep breaths, trying to calm myself. But my emotion wouldn't subside. Maybe I didn't want it to. My fear was turning to anger. I didn't feel afraid anymore.

It feels so good to be unafraid.

It was *him* who should be afraid. I ran to the window and screamed, "This isn't over."

He jumped a little. He was worried someone had heard.

Motherfucker, I thought as I watched him drive away, *you have no idea how dangerous I can be.*

CHAPTER

35

Then

IN WORKSHOP JUSTINE smirked at me and Claire's eyes were filled with even more pity than the week before. My only solace was writing. I'd lost track of how many notebooks I'd filled. Sometimes, when I ran out of paper, I wrote on my hands and arms. Writing was the only way I could express myself. My peers might not have to listen to me when I spoke, but they'd have to read my story.

When I looked up from my notebook, everyone was gone, even the professor.

Over the course of the next week, I devised a plan to take revenge on Duncan. I would pull a move I called "The Justine." I was sure it was her who had switched her name and Claire's in my contacts. She'd done it while I was distracted tying the cherry knot. I would do something even worse with Duncan's phone. I hoped it hurt him as much as what Justine had done with my phone. My relationship with Claire felt irreparable. I tried not to think of a text I'd gotten from her Sunday: I heard you had a breakdown last night. Have you talked to your doctor yet?

Her message had deflated me as completely as if I were a balloon popped by a wrecking ball. How had anyone mistaken my singing for a breakdown?

CHAPTER 36

Then

THE SATURDAY AFTER the assault, I was ready to take back the power Duncan had stolen from me. As soon as I arrived at the party, he saw me across the room of buzzing alumni and students. He tensed, the little points of his face pulling tighter. Getting what I wanted would be harder with him on his guard, but I was planning to get it anyway.

When Duncan went to the bar, I went too. The smell of red wine nearly made me gag, reminding me of tasting it on Duncan's lips. If he had permanently ruined red wine for me, even the punishment I had in store for him wouldn't be enough.

Duncan turned to walk away from the bar, but he was too slow. I blocked his path. "I'm sorry about what happened," I said. "I'd like to make it up to you."

He tried to go around me, first one way and then the other, but I shifted from side to side to keep him in front of me. He started to panic. I knocked against his arm, sending wine splashing onto his shirt.

"Damn it," he said. He put his glass down and took his iPhone out of the front pocket of his shirt to make sure it wasn't wet. He set it on the table and took a napkin someone offered him. I picked up his phone and clicked the button on the side to wake it up. Then I turned it to his face so the face recognition would unlock it. I hastily dropped it in my purse and walked away.

The voices of the host and other people attending to the director faded as I made my way down the hall into the farthest bedroom. I locked the door behind me.

They say iPhones take the best pictures, and as I took off my clothes and lay on the bed, I had to agree. I'd practiced keeping my camera-holding arm out of the frame when I took selfies. I got some shots of my face and body. I closed my eyes and let my mouth go slack so I looked like I'd passed out. I took about a dozen photos that way. Then I took some in which my eyes were half open. I held a hand in front of the camera and turned my head away as though I didn't want to be photographed.

For those few moments while I believed I was in control, all was right with the world.

I put my clothes on, and started texting the pictures from Duncan's iPhone to mine.

With the first one, I texted the beginning of a sentence: Only a drunken whore doesn't wake up.

On the second one, I texted the rest: no matter what you do to her.

Some of the pictures I sent without a message. But with the last one, I texted: I fucked you hard, because otherwise you probably won't know anything happened.

Then, I couldn't resist, I went online to search dick pics. I sent this last picture with the text: C U Next Tuesday.

I unlocked the door, went back out to the bar, and put the phone down next to a bottle of stinky wine. I filled a glass with vodka. I'd achieved what I had set out to do, and it was time to celebrate.

* * *

I woke up the next morning with a pounding headache and a great sense of satisfaction. Time to make sure he saw the picture texts sent from his phone to mine.

I decided to simply text him a sad face: ☹

Then I waited.

A couple of hours later, he texted back: Who is this?

I responded: *Who is this?!?!* Seriously. How many women did you assault last night?

I waited. Waiting sucks. I wished I hadn't responded so quickly. I wished that it was him and not me waiting. But it turned out to be worth the wait.

My phone made the special sound that I'd programmed for his texts: a pig oinking. The phone was closer than I'd like to admit—it was in my hand. I took a deep breath and looked at the screen: Let's talk.

CHAPTER

37

Then

I READ DUNCAN'S TEXT several times.

It was satisfying to know he was quaking in his boots.

I replied: What is it you need to say?

He texted: I'd like to speak with you face to face.

It sounded kind of ominous. Except that I wasn't afraid. And even if I were, there were two things I needed:

1. To make sure Duncan regretted what happened.
2. To see Justine's winning story.

I texted back: Okay. Where?

The phone rang. I picked it up and swiped right.

"We can't meet in public," he said before I'd even said hello.

"We can't meet in private," I replied.

He sighed. He was the weariest person I'd ever met. I'd thought he was weary because he carried the weight of the world on his shoulders. But no, he was weary from straining to hold back his strange, unexplained rage.

"The Arch," I said.

When he didn't immediately agree, I added, "No one who lives in St. Louis goes there. It's just tourists." At least, that's what I assumed. "Tomorrow at noon. And don't get any ideas. I've set it up so if I don't log into my computer within the next forty-eight hours, the screenshots of your texts to me will be automatically emailed to the dean," I lied.

Usually his voice was clipped, tight. Now it was loose, uneven. It increased in pitch over the course of four little words. "Are you busy *now*? " The desperation in his voice both satisfied and scared me.

"Yes," I said, and hung up.

Let the bastard wait.

CHAPTER 38

Then

THE NEXT DAY, just to make him nervous, I wore a skirt that didn't go all the way to my knees and a tank top that had shrunk in the dryer. For a moment, the world felt lush and green and fresh. The future looked bright. Maybe too bright. As I approached The Arch, the reflection of the sunshine in the stainless steel was like a blade entering my brain, reminding me that I drank too much the night before. I pulled my shades down over my eyes.

During one of the many scenarios I'd played out in my head in the wee hours of the morning, Duncan stabbed me and then pushed me into the Mississippi. I was happy to see that The Arch wasn't close enough to the river for him to pull that off. Still, when I saw an artificial pond, I steered clear of it. I walked out among the tourists to stand directly beneath the huge arch. I didn't look up at it. I wouldn't let him catch me by surprise.

He wasn't hard to spot. The tourists were wearing shorts and T-shirts. He was standing at the base of The Arch in a black turtleneck, tweed sport coat, and nice jeans.

He scanned the crowd. He was the type whose nervousness made other people nervous. In groups of people, he was always either furtively looking around or bracing himself as though he'd just felt the first rumblings of an earthquake. When he saw me, it was the latter.

"Duncan," I said as I approached.

He frowned. Meeting with me in public while 70 percent of my body was visible was making him even more nervous than usual. He took a shaky breath. "Shall we?" he asked, gesturing toward the entrance to The Arch.

Neither of us wanted to go first and be the one who walked in front. But I was too impatient to just stand in place. I turned and walked toward The Arch. We were going to go up to the top together.

I got in line and turned my body so that I could keep an eye on him. His face was pinched and he smelled like whiskey.

The pods each held five seats. There were three freshman-aged girls behind us in line. One of them was wearing a red, oversized Washington University in St. Louis T-shirt, and the other two were wearing baggy T-shirts. Good girls didn't wear tight shirts during the day. I mean, it was Monday, after all.

I wondered if people thought I was a hooker.

I hoped so. Or I would have hoped so if Duncan didn't already look like he might be on the verge of becoming the sort of man who goes on a murderous rampage and then calmly makes sweater vests from the hair of his victims. Beads of sweat had started to collect on his brow. I had already pushed him further than I intended to, and I hadn't even made my demand yet.

The girls were watching us. They looked up from their iPhones for whole seconds at a time, and there was even eye contact between them. They were probably texting each other: WTF is with the silent weirdo and his silent hooker? Don't they speak the same language?

Yeah, what Eastern Bloc country did he order her from?

LOL

The pods each held five seats. They formed an incomplete circle. I sat as close as I could to the door. As it slid shut, the smell of whiskey seeping from Duncan's pores grew stronger.

"I don't care for heights," he told me.

It was humiliating that this queasy coward had been able to overpower me for a couple moments. "It's only six hundred and thirty feet," I said. I was happy when he winced.

The pod rose with what would be a peaceful rocking motion if I weren't disgusted by the thought of my knee accidentally touching Duncan's. My whole body was in an isometric hold.

We rose past a series of spiral staircases, a bunch of metal boxes with screws, and an unsettling number of fire extinguishers.

The girls were taking selfies, or I guess, "usies."

"I can take one for you," I told them.

I took several. Then I gave the iPhone back and asked, "Will you take one of us?"

I handed my phone to one of the girls and slid onto Duncan's lap before he could protest.

Click.

I hopped off his lap like it was going up in flames. When I got home, I was going to take the hottest shower possible and scrub as long and hard as I could without bleeding.

At the top of The Arch, the pod door slid open. As we disembarked, a woman's voice blared from the loudspeaker: "Welcome to the top of the Gateway Arch. Please exit out of your tram car to the left. No photographs, please."

Too late.

"Hannah," Duncan said, using my name for the first time that day, "I know you're upset about various things. I'm sure you don't like that you don't have any sort of university support."

Various things? I was about to tell him off for dismissing the assault, but he quickly continued, "I can see what I can do about getting you some funding for next year."

That would be nice, but I doubted I'd survive the MFA program for another year unless I exposed Justine as a fraud before she completely ruined me. "I need a copy of Justine's story," I said.

He looked at me blankly. Was I moving too fast for him, a man who thought that trying to force a woman's head to his crotch within two minutes of arriving at her apartment was acceptable?

"I-I don't have it," he stuttered. "The file is missing."

"Find it. If I don't have it in twenty-four hours, the pictures will be in the dean's inbox marked 'urgent'."

As I turned away from his panic-stricken face, I felt a wild, powerful high. He protested, but he didn't follow me. He was no match for me. I was making things happen.

I stopped to peer out a window. The view from the top was spectacular; I could see for miles. Little dots, which must have been people, were swimming in a rooftop pool. Busch Stadium was empty, the red seats making me imagine some sort of violent abandonment. An old cathedral, an old courthouse, and some corporate buildings seemed to be standing at attention, paying their respects to me and the other people who'd made the slow, claustrophobic journey all the way to the top of The Arch. It was all rather lovely, actually. I wished I had someone to explore the city with me. It hurt to think of how I'd hoped Claire, Justine, and I would be friends. We could have gone into all the places I was looking at now. Looking at by myself, from the top of my world.

The sadness creeping in was taking away my high. I turned away from the window, but not before I saw something out of the corner of my eye.

A streak of girl, skinny with long brown hair flying straight up from her head as she fell.

Justine?

I got as close to the window as possible, trying to see the ground.

"Did you see someone falling?" I asked a man next to me.

"Falling?"

He hadn't seen her. I looked around at the other people milling about. They were in little groups, staring out the windows in blissful awe, not terrified awe like me.

When I was back in a pod, slowly being lowered to the ground, I pinched my neck so I had something to focus on besides my anxiety. I felt trapped. I felt like screaming. I tried a trick my therapist had taught me. I counted down from three hundred by threes. I was at forty-five when my pod reached the ground.

I ran to the spot where the girl would have fallen, but there was no one there. Had someone taken the body?

I noticed people were starting to look at me.

"Are you okay, miss?" a man asked.

"Yes," I lied.

When I got home, I had a drink to settle my nerves. One didn't do it, so I had another. I couldn't get the vision of the falling girl out of my head, and I couldn't stop wondering: *Was it Justine?*

CHAPTER

39

Then

I PARKED A BLOCK away from her building. I'd dressed in unremarkable clothes, and I had binoculars tucked under the top of my shirt. As I made my way toward her apartment, I repressed the urge to run around an old couple walking slowly on the sidewalk in front of me. Until you're teetering on the edge of mania, you never really know how unbearably slow everyone else is.

From the sidewalk, I studied the brownstone, looking for some clue as to which apartment was hers. There was a corner garden-level window with a box unit poking out. I planted myself beside a tree and checked to make sure no one was around before peeking into the window.

The living room was dominated by a huge leather couch that definitely wasn't from IKEA, and a glass coffee table that was probably worth more than the contents of my entire apartment. Several large art books were piled on top of it. I didn't need to see Justine in the apartment to know it was hers.

In she walked, very much alive. I could tell it was her by her huge sunglasses and elegant but understated dress.

I was relieved, but also disappointed. If she'd disappeared, would all the things she'd said about me have disappeared with her? Would I have been able to start again?

She threw what looked like a $3,000 Bottega Veneta tote bag on the large leather couch and locked the door. She looked agitated. She paced, holding her iPhone so tightly it was like she was trying to squeeze something out of it.

She seemed to be someone else entirely.

I lowered the binoculars and walked around the corner to get a better view of the rest of the apartment. The bedroom had one box unit, but luckily there were two windows. Through the empty one, I was able to see a king-sized bed. Justine could probably fit in a child's bed with room to spare, yet her bed was threesome-sized. She didn't plan on being lonely.

Did she sense me watching her? She closed the blinds. At least I could still see her silhouette. Curtains lurked at the edges of the windows, but she didn't bother with them.

She finished her conversation, set her phone down, and unlocked the front door. I noticed she didn't open it. She walked calmly across her living room, disappeared into the hallway, and reappeared in the bathroom. I saw her silhouette through the shade. She put her finger down her throat and doubled over the toilet.

Was this the reason she hated me and had made me an outcast? Because I knew she did this? I hadn't seen her eat anything. Was she just throwing up milk and coffee?

Perhaps I should've had compassion for a woman who felt the need to throw up after drinking a latte. But I couldn't repress the thought that followed: *she goes to great lengths not to look like me.*

It would've been easier to like her if bulimia or her thinness was ruining her looks. Though Justine was thinner than most women—thinner than me by at least the weight of a small kindergartener, so thin that she'd probably have to gain a few pounds before she would be legal to model in France—she didn't look old or sick the way some of the cardio queens at the health club did.

Justine employed the midsession "courtesy flush" that reduces the odor. Was she expecting company?

Through the living room window, I saw a man enter the apartment. He was about four inches taller than Justine, who was about five inches taller than me. Maybe five eleven. I hadn't seen anyone pull up, so he must have parked in back. He started closing the drapes, one set of windows after the next—the first living room window, the second, the kitchen—then he entered the bathroom and reached around Justine to yank the curtain closed.

I brought the binoculars up to my eyes and looked through a gap in the drapes, confirming my fear: it was the stranger.

Suddenly, the curtain was yanked open and huge, enraged blue eyes stared out at me. I lowered the binoculars. Justine turned from looking out at me to grab something from her purse. I was certain it was her phone. I sprinted away before she could snap an identifiable picture of me.

When I got home, I had another drink to calm my nerves. Lucy looked at me with the usual judgment in her eyes. "In my situation, you'd need a drink too," I told her.

C H A P T E R

40

Then

AT THE END of the twenty-four hours, my phone rang.

As soon as I answered, Duncan said, "Please. I've looked everywhere. It's not here."

What did Justine have over Duncan? Why was he risking my wrath? There was no way he didn't have her story somewhere.

I really didn't want to send the pictures to the dean of the English department as I'd threatened to, though. The dean might look for a way to blame me and squeeze me out of the program. And regardless of what happened, I'd be on the radar.

"Contact the fucking *Atlantic*," I said.

"I did. I emailed them that we had a server crash and we lost a lot of our files. I asked them to email it." He took a deep breath and continued, "They responded that they can't give it to me."

I'd thought the pictures were an easy way to get what I needed. But it turned out, all they were offering me was a hard choice. Duncan was calling my bluff. He knew the pictures could take me down too.

"This still isn't over," I told Duncan. "But I'm not going to send the pictures. Not yet."

CHAPTER

41

Then

I WAS AGITATED, PERHAPS paranoid, and the only way to end the agitation was to sleep. But I couldn't sleep without drinking.

When I woke up alone, I should have been relieved, but instead I was afraid. Anything could happen to me in my apartment and no one would know.

The next two days passed in a blur. On Monday I took my notebook and a flask of vodka to campus, intending to write. The lawn was crowded, but I found a place to sit in the shade of a tree outside the English department. When I woke up, the sun had moved; it was blinding. I closed my eyes again and touched my face. I knew by the heat and swelling of my skin that I was sunburned. Dammit. I probably looked like one of the street people who got drunk and fell asleep in the sun.

Tuesday my head pounded too hard to write, so all the dark thoughts remained trapped in my brain. Had I gone crazy? Was there any value to my life? Would it really matter to anyone if I disappeared? I took my medicine and did a yoga routine I found on YouTube, but the thoughts wouldn't stop. I drank until, mercifully, I passed out.

Wednesday, as soon as I walked into workshop, I knew I'd entered enemy territory. I was five minutes early. Why was I the last to arrive? Were they hanging out before workshop? Justine must have told everyone how I spied on her; everyone was looking at me in the worst sort of way, out the sides of their eyes. They wanted to watch me without having to interact with me. What did they see? I felt my scar start to throb beneath the thick layer of cover-up I'd carefully applied before leaving my apartment.

For the first time, I realized how cruel it was to hold the workshop in a lounge with easy chairs and overstuffed couches. The preposterousness of anyone being able to relax while their soul was being dissected mocked us. Workshop should take place in a windowless, underground room lit by only a few candles, with everyone standing around the rack where the workshopee will be pulled apart. A torture chamber.

I sat in the only place left, on the couch beside Andrew. He nodded slightly at me, enough to acknowledge my presence but not enough to invite further interaction.

I pulled out my notebook, desperate to escape the shame and disappointment I felt sitting alone in that group I'd so badly wanted to be a part of. I opened it and gasped. Staring up at me were three words:

Die bitch, die

My heart started to pound. Did someone want me dead? Were the words a threat? They were shaky, slanted backward.

Were they mine?

I suddenly remembered there were people on either side of me who could easily see what was written in my notebook. I slammed it shut.

"Excuse me," I said, stumbling over Andrew's legs as I hurried from the room.

As soon as I was in my car with the doors locked, I opened the notebook and looked at the words: *Die bitch, die.* They hit me again as hard as they had a few moments before when I first saw them.

Or maybe that wasn't the first time I'd seen them. Maybe it was the second. Did I write *Die bitch, die* in my own notebook and then forget?

I didn't know which was worse: someone else writing it, or me writing it and not remembering. I ripped the page from my notebook and tore it into tiny pieces. There was only one place to turn, besides the bottle, and it was the same place that was causing me pain: my notebook. Writing was the only way I could make sense of my feelings and avoid acting them out in real life.

CHAPTER 42

Then

THE NEXT MONDAY, I had my first formal talk with Duncan.

Perhaps because I hadn't closed the door behind me and people were passing by in the hall, he said, "Hello, Ms. Silver." He shook my hand as gingerly as if he was picking up a dirty syringe from the floor. He sat down and then gestured to the chair in front of his strangely uncluttered desk.

I didn't accept his invitation to sit down. I needed to be sure I could get away quickly if I had to. As I looked at the pristine, paperless surface of Duncan's desk, I managed to keep from saying, "Do you work here?" Instead, I asked, "Did you find Justine's story?"

He ignored my question. "I hope you have a good experience here," he said. "I hope you grow as a writer, explore new ideas, make valuable connections, and publish in a wide array of literary journals."

"Are you reading from a brochure?"

"No, these are my sincere hopes for you."

"Did you find Justine's story?" I repeated.

"No," he said. "I called you in because I need to speak with you about another matter."

"I hope you're kidding."

"Please have a seat."

"Is there something you can't say while I'm standing?"

"We've received a complaint," he said.

I was pretty sure I knew who had complained. I was surprised Justine had waited this long to report seeing me outside her apartment. I couldn't tell Duncan that I thought I had seen her falling from The Arch and had gone to her apartment to check if she was still alive.

"Is the complaint you've received as awful as what you did to me?" I asked.

He jumped up and hurried around me to close the door. He sat back in his chair and said, "Please have a seat. I called you in here for your own protection. Justine says you're stalking her. She has a photo of you running away."

"Maybe I was just out for a jog."

He looked at my body pointedly, and continued, "In addition to stalking her, Justine said that early in your obsession with her, you lured her to your apartment and showed her the urn you stole. She said it's not missing—it's at your apartment."

"You were in my apartment," I said coolly. "Did you see it?"

His face flushed. "I'm doing you a favor by telling you about this, and by advising you to write Justine an apology for stalking her. Maybe that will appease her and keep her from bringing her complaints directly to the dean."

Write an apology? That would be a confession. "Do you think I'm stupid?" I asked. My voice was louder than I intended.

There was a knock on the door. Before Duncan had a chance to answer, Professor M peeked in at us. "Is everything okay in here?" he asked. He looked at me with concern.

"Hannah's just a little emotional about a personal issue," Duncan said.

Professor M ignored him. "Are you okay?" he asked me.

I am now, I thought as I looked at him. I would much rather have been flirting with him over a couple glasses of wine than stuck in an office that was so neat and clean it looked like an operating room.

I nodded. "Yes, I'm fine."

"Okay," Professor M replied. Before he walked off down the hall, he opened Duncan's door all the way and, with his eyes still on me, said, "Let me know if you need anything."

Duncan sat glaring at the open doorway. "Take my advice, Hannah," he said quietly. "Don't ruffle any more feathers."

"Goodbye, Duncan," I said as I stood up. "Don't call me in here again."

CHAPTER

43

Then

I SWISHED INTO THE next party like it was my sweet sixteen. I wasn't going to let Duncan think he could intimidate me. I wore my best dress and a pair of heels that could puncture a man's heart. When I approached the other fiction MFAs, Amelia handed me a glass of red wine. "They were out of white," she said. I was so grateful for her kindness that I sipped the red wine, even though I nearly choked from the memory of red wine on Duncan's lips.

I bided my time mostly at the edge of the group, making a game of trying to stay in the circle while it morphed and tightened and migrated, trying to exclude me. When the game began to feel ridiculous, I turned to see if there was anyone else to talk to.

Professor Barkley Newhouse called out to me, "Young woman, spare a moment for your favorite professor, or has all courtesy gone out the window with the advent of MyFace?"

"What would you like, Professor?"

He didn't lower his voice or look sheepish as he replied, "What you're having, unless there's something stronger."

"I'm surprised you don't have a flask."

He laughed. "I'm an old man. I forget things. Such as, why aren't you taking my class?"

I trusted him enough to be honest. "I'm afraid that soon I'll be kicked out of this university and won't be taking anybody's class."

He raised an eyebrow. Before he could ask any questions, I continued, "I wanted to talk to you about what you mentioned before, about Justine's work feeling 'familiar.' Then I'll get you something from the bar." I took another drink from my wine glass.

"Oh dear," he said playfully, and motioned with his gaze to something on my right. Justine was approaching.

"What happened to your entourage?" I asked her.

"Poor Hannah," she said. "It's sad when someone has so few friends that they think five people enjoying each other's company is an entourage."

"You're right," I said, "wrong word choice. Entourages are for stars. You're more of a cult leader."

Professor Newhouse took my wineglass out of my hand and downed all that remained. "Ladies," he said, and promptly started to cough. He set the wineglass down on the mantel and raised his hands over his head. I hit him on the back and he started to choke.

"You're getting it in his lungs," Justine said calmly. She didn't try to help.

Newhouse's face was swollen, his eyes bulging out of his head.

Maybe I *had* gotten it in his lungs.

I got behind him again and gave him what I hoped was the Heimlich maneuver. Something flew out of his mouth; it looked like a cherry pit. Justine hurried to swoop it up.

"What was in that drink?" Professor Newhouse asked me.

"I don't know," I told him. "But I think I know who does."

As Justine walked away, I yelled, "Come back. Show me what's in your hand."

She didn't stop.

I ran after her. "If you don't show me, I'll tell everyone about your story, and how it's not really yours. I'll get you eighty-sixed from the program."

"You couldn't even get me kicked out of a Hobby Lobby, much less this program."

"Is that a dare?" I asked, but already I was starting to sway on my feet. *What's wrong with me?* Had someone slipped something in my drink besides whatever Professor Newhouse choked on? Justine? I needed to get out of there before anyone noticed I was losing my balance.

"Goodbye," I said to Professor Newhouse, trying to speak clearly and make confident but not unduly lingering eye contact.

He was also woozy. He was having trouble keeping his eyes open. "Be good," he said.

"Always," I replied, and then we both started laughing. It was as close as I'd come to bonding with anyone in a while.

I closed the front door securely behind me. I barely made it to the bushes before I fell to my knees. The world went black.

CHAPTER

44

Then

WHOOPS.

I was in my car, on a huge expanse of green grass, in front of the first buildings on the campus quad.

Please be dreaming, please be dreaming, please be dreaming.

My head was pounding so violently, I could hardly see. I pulled some sunglasses out of the console in a feeble attempt to disguise myself. I needed to get the hell out of there before someone from the department saw me. Where had I put the keys? I looked on the passenger seat, where I usually set things, but they weren't there. I didn't want to be even more conspicuous by getting out to search under the seats. I vowed to purchase one of those magnetized key boxes as soon as I got the chance and put a car key and my apartment key in it. *This can never happen again. In fact, it can't even happen now. Yet here I am.*

How long had it been since I'd taken my mood stabilizer? Did I have any with me?

When I put my hand down between the seat and the door, I noticed my purse beside my lap, my license sitting on top like it was on display. I quickly rifled through it, taking inventory. My iPhone was still intact, the screen locked as it always was when I hadn't used it within five minutes. There were no pills and no cash. I always carried at least a few bills in my wallet, so either I'd lost them or someone had taken them.

Suddenly, I noticed lights flashing in my rearview mirror. *Oh, for fuck's sake.*

The officer stopped behind me, as though we were on the road, and that gave me some sense of relief, as if everything was normal. He got out of his cruiser.

I fastened my seatbelt and got my insurance and registration information out of the glove compartment, noticing for the first time that my arms and chest were sore. I rolled down my window. "I'm so sorry," I said, handing my license and registration through the window. "I don't know what happened."

He leaned down to study me. He didn't look like the sort of cop who would write you a speeding ticket for any fewer MPH than he clocked you at. The sun hadn't been up for more than a few minutes and already he was wearing sunglasses, aggressively shiny ones that made it hard to look at him. He had a "high and tight" haircut and his forearms were as big as my thighs.

"So you probably didn't notice that No Parking sign down there."

I looked to where he had nodded and saw the sign. It was at an odd angle, as though it had been hit by a car.

"Please take off your sunglasses and step out of the vehicle."

I was confident I could walk a straight line and sing the ABCs backward. The Breathalyzer would trounce me, though.

"Turn and face the vehicle. Put your hands behind your back." He touched one of my wrists. I had a raw, sore feeling where he pressed on my skin. "Looks like you had a wild time last night," he said. "Unless these welts are from something else."

Without waiting for an answer, he started putting the cuffs on.

"Can you at least cuff me in front?"

He hesitated, then told me to turn around.

I obeyed, looking at my wrist as the cold metal settled against my skin. The raised flesh was red and angry.

I glanced around, seeing if there were witnesses to my humiliation. A few undergrads pretended to play Frisbee higher up on the hill, but they were mostly watching the officer and me. Grad students and faculty walked past. Some had stopped in their tracks to stare. A small crowd was gathering at the bottom of the hill.

I didn't want Duncan and my fellow MFAers to find out about this. I searched for a way out. "You can't prove it was me who hit the No Parking sign."

"I don't think the case against you is going to hinge on the sign, but you might want to take a look at the side of your car before you argue about it."

A very long, very incriminating scrape decorated the driver's side of my car. Tire tracks led all the way from the sign to my rear tires.

I was relieved when he finally put me in the back of the cruiser. I slouched low in the seat while he ran my license.

Perhaps the welts on my arm and wrist should have scared me, but I was too full of shame to feel anything else. I was so drunk that someone had hurt me and I didn't even remember who.

What the hell is wrong with me?

As the officer gave me a Breathalyzer, I could hardly close my mouth around it because my nose was running and I felt like I was hyperventilating. I knew the officer wouldn't let me get away with not sealing my mouth around the straw because I'd watched my mother attempt to outsmart a Breathalyzer after crashing into the neighbor's truck when I was ten. The police know that "trick" and I didn't have a better one, so I blew the way I was supposed to and what I blew was a .29.

The officer got on his radio and summoned a tow truck.

"What will happen to my purse and car?" I asked.

"You can take your purse. As for your car, the nice folks at the impound lot will be happy to look after it for you."

CHAPTER

45

Then

I EXPECTED TO BE taken to detox, but instead the cop brought me directly to jail.

The orange jumpsuit wasn't just something people wore on TV. I was thrown into a cell with another woman in the same attire. She was sitting on the bottom bunk, and she gave me a once-over and promptly lost interest.

"Looks like we both got the memo," I said, gesturing at our jumpsuits. She had about a hundred pounds on me and didn't think my quip was cute. I tried something more straightforward. "What are you in for?"

"Jaywalking," she said, barely looking at me. She had a weave, lots of makeup, including glitter over her eyes, and long acrylic nails. You'd think her scowl wouldn't fit in with the look, but it did. She didn't ask me what I was in for.

"I—"

"You're drunk, and you should shut your mouth before something foolish comes out."

I felt like I was drunk *and* had a hangover at the same time. "I don't know what I am," I said.

She slowly stood up, and I saw that she had *more* than a hundred pounds on me.

I held out my hand as though she had risen to her feet in order to properly introduce herself. "Hannah," I said.

She looked at my hand like it was giving off an odor. "They cuff you that hard, you must have fucked up good."

"My car ended up on the lawn of the university I attend."

Maybe I shouldn't have mentioned that I attended a university. That probably wasn't the sort of thing that wins friends and influences people in jail. But all she said was, "Huh. Maybe it's not too late for me to go."

She was at least fifty, so I guessed I wasn't looking very youthful at the moment. "I'm going to graduate school," I said. Because I was an idiot.

She scowled harder and came toward me. There was nowhere to run, so I just waited for whatever was going to happen.

She grabbed my face in her hand. The corners of her acrylic nails were sharp. One dug into my scar. She studied my face, turned my head, and looked into my nose as if searching for something.

When she let go of me, I stumbled back against the bars and watched with relief as she made her way back to the bed.

From all the television I'd watched, I knew she'd gone relatively easy on me. I needed to clean up my act before I ended up in prison, where I'd be eaten alive.

I closed my eyes against tears. When I opened them, I saw that my cellmate had thrown a tissue on the floor. I almost had too much pride to take it, but using the back of my hand wasn't working very well. I picked up the tissue and blew, slowly at first so it wasn't too loud, then, fuck it, I blew it all out, breaking the tissue and giving myself a bloody nose. My cellmate fished another one out of her bra and threw it toward me.

"You're a damn mess," she said. "Who's beating on you?"

"Just me," I said. "I don't know how I got these marks."

"Don't you know what they are?"

I shook my head.

"The marks of a man who don't love you."

I couldn't stop the pitiful thought that followed: that's the only kind of man there is in the world. My psychiatrist pretended to care about me, but I knew how much he made per hour. Anybody can pretend to care for that much money. I'd skipped the video call we were supposed to have that month.

She continued, "You better run as far as you can before he does that to your face."

CHAPTER

46

Then

THE UPSIDE OF not having many friends was that when I got my one phone call, I didn't have to deliberate about who to call. I hadn't texted Luke in weeks, and besides, I didn't want him to know what a mess I'd made of myself. Only one man could help me, and I had the leverage to motivate him. Plus the boldness from not taking my pill for . . . I didn't know how long.

"Yes?" he answered.

"Good morning, Duncan," I said. "It's Hannah."

This announcement was met with a brief silence. Then he said, "Yes, Hannah?"

"I'm in jail."

He sighed. I probably should have been insulted that he wasn't surprised. I wished he would at least say *something*. But it looked like if anyone was going to move the conversation forward, it was going to be me.

"This won't look good for you."

"Why is that?" he asked.

I decided to hold off on mentioning the pictures for now. I needed to provide him with an argument he could bring to the university. "The department must have gotten me pretty drunk last night."

Silence.

I continued, "And then allowed me to stumble out to my car and allegedly drive so drunk I ended up on the campus lawn after possibly taking out a No Parking sign." I didn't mention that there were marks on my wrists even before the police officer cuffed me. I didn't know how it all fit together.

Another sigh.

"I'm going to need an attorney. And bail."

"I'm sure you have student loans that you can use."

I ignored him and continued, "The university can provide me with a lawyer who can get these charges dropped. Nothing like this has ever happened to me before. My driving record is spotless. I blew a .29, but I don't believe I was driving. The keys were gone." As I spoke, I realized it sounded like I was claiming I was set up, and that suddenly seemed like the most likely possibility. Whoever did this to me took my keys so I'd be stuck there for the cops.

I wasn't sure what else the person had done to me, but in addition to my sore wrists, my chest was sore and my head was throbbing.

"The university doesn't provide lawyers," Duncan said.

"Just copious amounts of alcohol? The alumni who provided me with it and then let me stumble out to my car are liable for any damages."

Again he was silent. I'd had enough.

"There's also the issue of the naked pictures texted from your phone to mine. My hearing is tomorrow. Have a lawyer here before then," I said, and hung up.

CHAPTER

47

Then

THE LAWYER WAS the happiest person I'd seen in forty-eight hours. His gaze only lingered on my scar for a couple seconds.

"You've come to the right place!" he said as we shook hands.

I assumed he was being sarcastic, but then he explained that Missouri was the leading alcohol-producing state in America, and that Anheuser-Busch was looking out for people like me. "They've got your back," he said, "and, they hope, your wallet." He looked through some files on his laptop. "Seeing as this is your first offense, if you're willing to agree to one condition we have here," he pulled out a piece of paper, "I have no doubt you're going home today."

"About that," I said. "'Going home' needs to involve a few other things: I need a lift to the tow yard, someone to pay for the tow and whatever they're going to charge me for having it there for two days, and the five hundred dollar fine for the DUI—unless you can get that charge dropped, which I highly recommend you do, for the university's sake."

"All that can be yours. Just sign this."

He handed me the piece of paper. It said I had to go to treatment in order to maintain my enrollment in the Washington University

MFA program. The university would pay for it. At the bottom was a place for me to sign.

"I can't miss school," I told him.

"You can go to an expedited, one-week program. I'm sure someone at Wash U will take notes for you while you're gone."

"I'm getting a master's in creative writing and my story is due the Wednesday after next. I won't have time to finish it if I'm in treatment."

He winked and said, "You'd be surprised at all the things you can do in treatment."

"Can I drink?"

"That's the only thing you can't do."

I couldn't imagine not drinking, but I also couldn't imagine continuing as I was. I didn't want to be vulnerable enough to wake up with strange marks—or worse—ever again.

"Dammit," I said, taking the pen from his hand. Of all that had happened recently, nothing seemed as surreal as the thought that in two days I'd be in treatment.

* * *

First thing I did when I got back to my apartment was pour myself a drink. I took a swig before going to the mirror. The concealer had worn off my scar. My mugshot was probably wretched. I had another swig before taking off my tank top, another before taking off my bra, and another before kicking off my shorts.

Suddenly I was looking at a well-proportioned girl who could use a little more exercise and a lot less drunken human contact. My chest felt sore, but not so sore I was prepared for the purple, handprint-sized bruise above my breasts. Had someone pushed me away or held me down? There was an ache in my head that wasn't just from vodka. I'd had it since coming-to in the driver's seat of my car on the campus lawn.

I reached up and touched the back of my scalp. It was tender. Had I hit my head?

If I hadn't wanted to go to treatment just to sober up, I had another reason to go: whoever did this to me was still out there.

CHAPTER 48

Then

I DECIDED TO USE the two days before I went to treatment to get a gun and learn to use it. I immediately found something online that I liked—a .22 that was so simple, so classic, it almost looked like a toy. I went onto my cleaning job app and signed up for every cash shift available. On the second day, I put cover-up not only on my cheek, but over the bruise on my chest as well.

It was no time to have to wear a turtleneck. My cleavage could come in handy.

I only had two shots of vodka before I went, and I left the bottle at home, even though it was hard to drive away without it. These were the sort of accomplishments that made me think I wasn't an alcoholic. The world was just too averse to people who didn't want to remain conscious of it every moment of the day. Reality was a spoiled brat who craved constant attention.

When I entered the liquor store where the seller worked, the bells on the door chimed. He looked like a former defensive tackle who had just recently gone on a diet and was feeling a little vain. He was wearing a T-shirt so white it must have been new. It strained across his chest in a way that reminded me I once dreamed of dating a quarterback.

I figured he was the owner of the brand-new GMC Sierra in the parking lot. Either the store was very profitable, or he sold more than liquor.

I got a bottle of Absolut vodka and brought it to the register. He was standing behind it, looking me over. When I set the bottle on the counter, I leaned over farther than I needed to.

"Will this be all for you?" he asked, eyes tumbling down the front of my shirt and then back up to meet mine. His pupils had dilated. I imagined he'd like to look back down my shirt but was afraid of what he might miss in my eyes.

"No," I said. I thought I could hear his heart pounding, or maybe it was my own. "I saw your ad."

"Which one?"

"For the .22. I have the cash," I said.

He dug around beneath the counter and then set the gun in front of me. I reached out to touch it. It was cool beneath my fingertips. Would it stay that cool when I held it in my hands?

I looked up and saw that he was staring at the bruises on my wrist. I took my hand back and pulled my sleeve down. I stuck out my chest a little more and looked at him expectantly.

"Don't you want to know why the hell it's so cheap?" he asked.

"I thought maybe you needed cash." *But from the new truck, I'm guessing I was wrong.*

"The serial number has been filed off."

Oh, for fuck's sake. "For any particular reason?"

"Not that I know of."

"I hope there's not a bullet from this gun in an evidence room somewhere," I said.

That had the desired effect of reminding him he wanted to get rid of it. "You want it or not?" he asked.

I dropped the cash onto the counter. Who knew committing a felony could be so easy?

As I walked away, he called after me, "I get off at six."

"Poor thing," I replied. "I get off whenever I feel like it."

CHAPTER 49

Then

But at six I was leaning against his pickup, back seductively arched to emphasize my assets, eyes on the liquor store door. When the clerk/firearm salesman opened the door and saw me, he smiled.

"Take me somewhere." I put my hand on my skirt, over the new holster underneath. "Show me how to use this."

"Bad idea," he said. "Really bad idea." But his eyes didn't move from my body as he let the store door slam shut. "Ranges close soon anyway. Let's go get a drink."

"I wasn't talking about the range. We still have a couple hours of daylight."

"I'm guessing you don't have ear protection."

Jeez. Aren't boobs and ammo enough? I'd only had a gun for three hours and already it felt complicated.

When I didn't answer, he asked, "How the hell did you know this was my pickup?"

"It was here earlier and it's here now. Unlock the passenger door and take me to the range."

He considered for a moment before saying, "Oh hell, all right." He opened the door for me and offered me his hand to help me up into the passenger seat.

His skin was rough, but I still liked his hands on me.

He closed my door, then walked around the front of the truck and got in.

I looked over at him, and he looked back and winked. I could feel my face break into a smile. He was the closest thing I'd had to a boyfriend since moving to St. Louis. When he turned the key, the engine roared to life. The seat vibrated beneath me like one of those vintage hotel beds you put a quarter in. I wondered if he was thinking the same thing. I could feel myself blush when Heart's "Crazy on You" came on.

We headed west, taking Interstate 44 to US Highway 50, while listening to classic rock. I was relieved we weren't going to East St. Louis. We were probably going somewhere you could set an empty beer can on a stump and shoot it without waking the neighbors.

After a while, we pulled onto a dirt road; the shadows of the few trees we passed were long enough to reach all the way from one side to the other. He pulled up behind three men firing at a row of targets. They were wearing headphones, but they still sensed us and turned to look at us.

I wished I saw even just one woman among them. "Friends of yours?" I asked.

"Close enough," he said.

I didn't want to get out. "So it appears we don't have to check in anywhere?" I asked for lack of any other way to delay.

"You're with me. You're checked in."

"Robert," I said, reaching across the seat to grab his arm. It was reassuringly large. "I'm nervous about these guys."

He put his calloused hand on mine, completely covering it. "They're not as bad as they look. And they'll fade back into their little worlds after they get the chance to look us over."

"I'm glad you're bigger than them."

I was relieved he didn't respond, "Me too." But then I remembered that size didn't matter here. Guns were the great equalizer. That was, in fact, why I needed to learn to use one—so the size of the person who'd bruised my wrists and chest and left me drunk in my car didn't matter.

We let go of each other, and Robert came around to open my door. The silence outside swelled into the truck. I didn't move. I didn't put my hand in Robert's awaiting palm.

I jumped when a shot broke the silence. It was followed by several more shots.

Robert was looking at me. "How many shots was that?"

"I don't know."

"Eight. From now on, count when you hear shots fired."

Our lesson had begun. I took Robert's hand and hopped down from the truck. He handed me a pair of earplugs and put another pair in his own ears.

As we walked toward the firing range, one of the guys nodded at Robert and vacated the nearest lane for us. Robert thanked him. I looked at the target he had given us—a simple bullseye with a lot of ventilation from whatever the guy was firing.

I pulled the gun and ammo from my purse. Robert studied the ammo, checking to make sure I got it right.

"I read good," I said loudly enough for him to hear through his earplugs.

"Just making sure."

Before he took the magazine out and showed me how to load it, he said/yelled, "Always keep it pointed downrange." We turned toward the target, and he handed me the gun.

As I held it loaded in my hands for the first time, I started to shake. It was heavier with the ten bullets inside. I couldn't even imagine firing one.

He saw me shaking and came to stand behind me. He extended his arms out and placed his hands over mine, one holding the gun, the other cupping the bottom of the grip to steady it. "Take a deep breath," he said. "Relax." His lips were close to my ear. His nose, too.

He sniffed. "Do I smell vodka?"

I considered pretending I didn't hear him through my earplugs, but then he might repeat his question loudly enough for the three other guys to hear. "Vodka is odorless," I said. "You can't smell it."

"How much did you have, and how long ago?"

He was still behind me, holding my hands steady so the gun didn't shake.

"I haven't had a drink since this morning," I said.

"This morning?" I felt him take a breath, and not one of relief. I should have said someone spilled vodka on my clothing or something.

"And anyway," I continued, "that's not why I'm shaking."

"Set the gun down on the ground and step away," he said.

I thought of the bruises on my wrists. "No. I can't," I said. But I did as he asked.

He picked the gun up and ejected the magazine, slipping both into his waistband. He reached for where I'd let one of my hands fall to my side and pulled up my sleeve. "Who gave you these?" he asked, running his fingertips over the bruises on my wrist.

"I don't know."

"I shouldn't have sold you a gun."

"But you did. Now help me."

"I'm going to give you your money back."

"I'm not returning it."

"And I'll buy the ammo from you."

Wow. He really didn't want me to have the gun. Which just made me hold onto it harder. "I'm not selling."

The guy who made space for us was packing up. "First time?" he asked as he walked past.

"Not yet," I replied.

He laughed, and told Robert, "Go easy on her." Then he looked at me and said, "My hands shook the first time I held a loaded piece too."

After he walked away, Robert looked me hard in the eye. "You really want to do this?" he asked.

I nodded.

"Don't just nod. Tell me if this is something you want to do, because I think, if you really wanted to do this, you wouldn't smell like vodka."

"You sell people liquor all day. Is there a correct and incorrect time to drink it?"

"Hell yes."

"Okay. Give me a sobriety test."

He smiled in a way that made me think he was going to insult me or ask me to do something dirty, but instead, he said, "Sing the alphabet backward while walking a straight line."

Perfect. That was easier than tying a cherry stem with my tongue, and I could do that even when I was almost in a blackout. As I sang, I blushed again. My voice was so terribly awkward, neither smooth nor intentionally husky. When I got all the way to *A*, he smiled and said, "Good, but don't quit your day job." I was reminded that I hadn't told him anything about myself. He didn't even know I was a student. I was glad. I wasn't giving him any information about me. I was like the gun with the serial number filed off.

He came to stand behind me. When I started to turn around to face him, he said, "Nope." I faced forward again, listening to the gun click as he loaded it. I wanted to lean back into him. I wanted to have a normal sexual experience with someone who wanted me, but I stayed still as he pressed against me to place the gun in my hands again. Then he covered my hands with his. *This is what he gets out of it, the chance to press against me. He doesn't know that I'd touch him for nothing.* I had to keep my willingness a secret; my power came from him thinking he had to work to get me in bed. My mother once told me: "You don't know if he'll stick around, so you have to get something up front."

"Line up the sights," he said.

The target was fifteen yards away, and my hands shook only slightly. Maybe I could hit it.

"Take a deep breath."

As my lungs filled with air, my back pressed against him. The target slipped from my sights.

"Re-aim."

"I've got it," I said.

He eased his grip but didn't let go completely.

I stepped forward—away from him—and squeezed the trigger.

I didn't hear the shot, but I heard the shell casing hit another one on the ground, followed by another round sliding into the chamber. The gun had shifted in my hands. I knew I hadn't hit the target—or anywhere near it.

"Don't worry," he said. "It gets better the more you do it."

My heart pounded and I didn't think I could steady myself until it slowed. I lowered the gun.

"Take a deep breath," he said. "Try again."

I raised the gun and emptied the magazine, relieved when there were no bullets left. I wanted to drop it and walk away. I had thought I'd feel powerful, in charge of my destiny. But using a gun wasn't like it looked on television or in the movies. Instead of feeling strong, I felt like a child playing grown-up.

None of the ten shots hit the target.

"I don't like how this feels," I told him.

"The only way to change that is by practicing."

"My hands aren't steady."

"Maybe we went too fast. Pick it up. Try again."

I was relieved by how light the gun felt unloaded.

Hold the gun at arm's length with both hands. Look through the sights at the bullseye. Take a breath and hold it. Then take the slack out of the trigger. Slowly start to exhale. When you've exhaled fully and the sight is on the bullseye, pull the trigger.

I dry fired. Once, then again. Soon, I lost count.

"Okay," Robert said, "that's enough. You don't want to do that too often; it can damage your firearm. You can get snap caps if you need more practice."

"I don't have time for snap caps," I said, ejecting the magazine and reloading.

My hands were steady now. I felt comfortable with the grip. Robert adjusted my stance.

"I've got it," I told him.

"Hell yeah, you do," he said.

I hit the target with my first round. I kept going, working my way through the ammo I bought, until I got my first bull's-eye. I wanted to jump up and down and scream, but that didn't seem like proper range etiquette. I turned to Robert.

"Thank you," I said, and kissed him before he could finish saying, "No problem."

In that moment, I was in love. Not with Robert, and not with the gun, but with the bull's-eye. I felt powerful in a new way, one that didn't involve male attention. I'd set out to do something, and I'd done it. I finally understood why people liked to shoot. I wasn't sure which felt better: training a loaded gun on the target, or the release after firing.

"Hey," I said to Robert, who was smiling at me with genuine happiness, "let's see what you've got."

I only had three rounds left in the magazine because, well, three strikes and you're out.

He took the gun and fired two near bull's-eyes and one bull's-eye.

I wished it didn't make him so attractive to me.

I noticed we were alone on the range. The other two guys and their pickups were gone.

"Go ahead," Robert said, "now that you've seen how it's done."

There were only eight bullets left in the box, and I wasn't parting with them. "No, let's pack it in. We're done here."

His smile vanished. "We're not done," he said. "Time for a sponge bath."

For a few awkward, exhilarating seconds, I didn't realize he was talking about the gun. He started walking back to the truck with my gun, and I followed.

I fell in love with his hands while watching him clean the gun with a silicone cloth. The small, precise movements, the calm concentration—was he the man I'd been searching for?

He handed me the gun and the magazine, wrapped in a cloth. So much for the sexual tension. I guess it was a little less creepy than putting on gloves, but not by much.

"Looks like I don't get to keep your prints," I said, slipping the gun into my purse. I wasn't comfortable with the holster yet.

"I can still leave you with some prints," he said.

He touched my cheek. It was almost supernatural how good it felt to be touched. In a dating app survey I'd taken once, the first question was: "Are you more lonely or horny?" I'd answered "horny" because it sounded less pathetic. But right then, as I guided Robert's hands to the buttons on my shirt, I wasn't sure what I was. *I just want more of whatever this is.*

CHAPTER

50

Then

WHEN WE WERE done, we drove back to Blue Spirits and idled in his truck. I thanked him for the lesson.

"You didn't leave me much choice. It was hard to say no." I was glad he was looking at my face instead of my boobs as he said it. And he was smiling; he didn't regret anything.

I wasn't sure when I'd have an opportunity to touch someone again; I knew people could get kicked out of treatment for sleeping together. So I reached for my gun specialist one more time.

Afterward, we caught our breath with the air conditioner blasting over our sweaty bodies. My muscles were cramping from trying to move around in such a small space and I didn't have much to say, but I didn't want our time together to end. After a moment, he said, "You'll need to get a safe or a gun lock."

I nodded.

"I hope you take care of whatever you need to," he said.

I realized I was delaying getting out because I didn't want to do what came next: give up vodka and go to treatment. If I smelled like vodka, they'd watch me more closely, so I was going to try to go in sober. A knot was already forming in my stomach.

"Okay," I said again.

"You know where to find me."

I couldn't stand the seriousness. I wanted to lighten the mood. I thought of saying something like, "And you obviously know where to find my boobs" because of how he'd stared earlier. But I liked him, so I searched for something else to say and couldn't find anything. I gave him a quick hug. If I let myself linger, I wouldn't want to let go.

"Hey," he called as I walked away. "I'd love to try this in a bed sometime."

I blew him a kiss and got into my car.

CHAPTER 51

Then

I DIDN'T WANT TO risk anyone from Wash U seeing me in treatment, so I went to the Twin Cities. Minnesota, the land of ten thousand lakes and ten thousand treatment centers. Unfortunately, Wash U wouldn't pay for Hazelden; I wasn't going to get cleaned up like a celebrity. Instead, I was going to St. Vic's in St. Paul, where I only had to go for a week as long as I passed all their tests.

My first question: "What do I have to do to get out of here?"

"You need to pass all the piss tests and do a fourth and fifth step," my treatment counselor answered.

We were sitting in his office, a far cry from Duncan's at Wash U. The chair I was sitting in was wobbly; one of the legs was shorter than the others. It was hard not to rock back and forth, feeling a bit mentally ill. I was getting nauseous. The office smelled like coffee and old fabric. Perhaps the brown, gold, yellow, and burnt-orange colors of the couch, carpet, and walls were meant to be cheerful, but they just reminded me of the shows I'd seen about the seventies, which are probably the last place someone trying to stay sober should go.

"It sounds like I'll also have to figure out what a fourth and fifth step are."

My treatment counselor's chair creaked as he leaned toward me. When he took a deep breath, I realized he was about to give me a long-winded explanation, and I added, "Just the short version, please."

The chair creaked again as he leaned back and put his hands behind his head. He was probably relieved that this would be quick. "You have to confess your sins to a priest, rabbi, or sponsor."

"I don't know what a sponsor is, but he sounds like the best option."

My counselor sighed, filling the air with the smell of coffee breath. He took his hands from behind his head and placed them on the desk, which, unlike Duncan's, was cluttered with papers, wrappers, and what appeared to be his children's art projects: macaroni creations, a crayon drawing, and either a piece of origami or a crumpled ball of paper that didn't make it to the trash. He explained that a sponsor was another recovering alcoholic or addict. "Someone who has what you want."

"I want to get out of here."

"Something besides that."

That evening, a group of "working women" was brought in from detox. I immediately saw that *Pretty Woman* had given me the wrong idea of what a prostitute looks like. One woman, Lynette, was particularly jumpy and agitated. She was missing a conspicuous amount of body fat and several teeth. Unlike a couple of the other women, she didn't seem to worry about her appearance: no red or pink lipstick, no fake lashes, no LBD and heels, no fuck-me boots.

I stood in the doorway of the common area and stared as she was led to her room. She dragged her feet along the floor and swore at no one in particular. I liked that she was wearing tennis shoes, not cheap boots like a few of the other women.

Suddenly, her head whipped around on her neck and she spit at me. It hit my arm. Maybe this should have upset me, but I'd been so suffocated by insincerity and anonymous aggressiveness that it was refreshing, or it would have been if she wasn't an intravenous drug user who probably gave fifteen-dollar blowjobs. I used a towel to gently wipe off the spit. The skin underneath was intact, so I probably wouldn't contract whatever she might have.

I didn't know where my pills were, but it didn't matter. I was given a new prescription. That night a nurse dispensed my mood stabilizer in a little clear cup and watched to make sure I swallowed it.

CHAPTER

52

Then

THE NEXT DAY, I saw Lynette in the common room, talking to The Body, a huge, tattooed man who was rumored to have a meth and heroin connection. His hand was on her leg under the table, squeezing. When the only staff member watching over us went in search of coffee, Lynette got up and led The Body from the room. They ducked into a closet.

After a couple of minutes, I heard commotion, things falling, a thud, and then screaming. There were no locks on the doors, except the one between us and the rest of the hospital. I ran to throw open the closet door, afraid I would find her bleeding, broken, and/or dead.

"You stupid motherfucker," she was screaming. Her hair was in disarray. "I said a *hand* job!"

Her foot was on The Body's throat. He was on the floor, his nose bleeding. She spit on him.

"I'm sorry," he said, trying unsuccessfully to duck. I imagined that he was Duncan. It was a beautiful moment.

Lynette took her foot off his throat and looked at me. "You got something to say?"

"No. I mean, yes. Will you be my sponsor?"

My treatment counselor called me into his office to ask if I'd filled out the "Fourth Step Searching and Fearless Moral Inventory" worksheet.

"Yes," I lied.

"Good. Have you decided who you'll do your fifth step with?"

"My sponsor."

"You found a sponsor?"

"Lynette."

His eyes widened.

Is he surprised that I asked her, or that she said yes?

She didn't seem like the type to be careful about what she got into. She wasn't only an alcoholic, but a meth addict, still twitchy. She claimed she'd only snorted it, but her veins were flattened, used up. Her gaze, too, looked a little used up.

The counselor must've been surprised that I'd asked her.

After a moment, he said, "Good choice."

Later that day, Lynette and I sat together in art therapy, making collages to communicate our feelings without using words. We'd been given a stack of ancient *People* magazines.

I assumed she was on the first of the twelve steps, admitting she had a problem. When I started to explain the fifth step to her, she interrupted. "I've done more fifth steps than I can count."

A woman in SpongeBob SquarePants pajamas said, "More than you can count on your teeth?" Apparently the woman didn't know what had happened to The Body. He'd told the staff he fell.

I waited for Lynette to clock the woman, or at least tell her off. "Thank you for the opportunity to be Christlike," she said to the woman.

I stared at Lynette incredulously.

She turned to me and explained, "I have to be a good role model for you." She smiled, revealing the few teeth the woman had referred to. "So, thank you, too."

She was really taking the sponsor thing seriously. I hadn't seen anyone so happy since I'd arrived.

"Can we do my fifth step after art therapy?" I asked. I was in a hurry to get it done so I could get out of there within a week. I didn't want to miss more than one workshop.

"Let me check my calendar," she said.

We continued to paste pictures on our papers for a couple of minutes before I realized her reply was a "yes."

"Should we use your room or mine?" I asked. I was confident Lynette could convince either of our roommates to find somewhere else to be.

"St. Vic's will allow us a private space for this."

Considering that there weren't even doors on the bathroom stalls, I doubted they'd leave us alone together.

I was wrong. The counselor agreed to let us use the group therapy room, and even allowed us to close the door most of the way. "Leave it open enough for one eye to peer in," was all he said, which creeped me out but was also a relief. I was only 50 percent sure Lynette wouldn't end up clocking me after I told her all my problems.

The group therapy room had no windows and was at the edge of the ward. We turned two of the orange chairs to face each other. Once we settled in, she studied me. Her eyes only lingered for an instant on the faded scar on my cheek. "What does a swanky piece of ass like you have to confess?" she asked.

I was relieved that despite the harshness of her words, she was looking at me with something veering on affection.

"I drink too much and mess everything up," I replied. "When I try to have anything good in my life—graduate school, friends—my life just turns to shit." I told her about Justine, how she'd caught me peeking into her apartment window, and how I suspected she'd spiked my wine at the department party and had Amelia wait for me to come in so she could hand it to me. I told Lynette I ended up coming-to on the campus lawn.

She snorted and shook her head. "I know girls like you, Hannah. You have it all and it could be perfect, but you won't let it. You'll scream and kick and fuck it all up for no reason. I used to think I wanted stability. But I'd rather give a stranger a hand job than be someone's wife. Unless I had a husband I fought with most of the time, and then maybe one man could hold my attention. I don't know."

Was she right? Since the day of the scar, I'd told myself I just wanted to be safe, but I no longer felt I fit into a safe world. And my behavior didn't make any sense if what I truly wanted was stability. Had some part of me always seen the little white pills I was supposed to take as the enemy?

"You and I don't have much in common," she continued, "except that we both hate to be bored. Lucky for you, it takes a lot less danger for you to feel entertained than it does for me. Watching some princess through her bedroom window wouldn't keep my attention. Maybe I have ADHD; it would take some really good shit to get me to stay in one place, staring at one girl." She studied me for a moment. "Are you a sapphist?"

It took me a few seconds to figure out what she was asking me. "Well, in college—"

"I've never been to college, and even I know that doesn't count. So what is it about this girl?"

"If she didn't exist, I would be able to feel successful."

"Is that why you drink?"

"One of the reasons."

"I drink because my father left when I was two, I was molested by my stepfather, my older brother killed himself because he didn't stop it, and now, because I have Hep C."

I didn't know if I should comfort her, or if she would find that insulting. "I'm sor—"

"Save it. That was all bullshit. I mean, all that happened, but I don't know why I drink. I suppose because I don't think I have a reason to stop. But you? You've got lots of reasons to get your shit together. The door to the world is wide open for you. There's not a mark on you."

Maybe my scar had faded more than I thought, and I only saw it because my brain hadn't registered its absence. Or maybe comparing me to what she herself saw in the mirror had left me looking pretty spotless. I wanted to say something comforting, but it would have been condescending to tell her she wasn't marked. She was, heavily. Her cheeks were sunken in from all the teeth she'd lost, and her skin looked like an old, ill-fitting tarp. She was the first woman I'd liked in a long time. I told her so.

"That's because I'm safe. Not competition."

"I guess learning to take a compliment isn't in any of the early steps."

"Be quiet for a minute. I have to fill out this sheet. 'Identify behavior patterns in individual's past that may have contributed to his/her alcohol and/or substance abuse.'"

I saw her write, "Drinks too much." After a moment of consideration, she added, "Complains."

"I'd like you if you had more teeth too," I said.

"What if I looked like this Justine you hatefuck-yourself-to-sleep about every night?"

"I'd like you a little less."

"And if I'd won the friction award."

"As long as you still called it the friction award."

"This isn't rocket science. You're jealous. What if you pictured her trapped in a little box with a colony of zombies and a teenager who just got a drum set?"

"That helps," I said, wondering if she meant a colony of lepers.

* * *

But when I returned to St. Louis, I still hated Justine. Was it the chicken or the egg? Was my hatred keeping me awake, or was it because I was awake that I hated her?

Sometimes I wanted to drink, but I didn't. Instead, I took my pill every night

CHAPTER

53

Then

FOR WORKSHOP, I turned in a story about a graduate student whose pills were stolen by a fellow student. Out of curiosity, the thief tries the pills. After the thief is medicated, the original woman no longer has any need for medication. It was the thief who was causing her angst, and with the thief medicated, she feels just fine.

The night before the workshop discussion was to take place, I was filled with anxiety, but also, elation. Writing had given me an uninterrupted space to speak.

I took extra time getting ready. I put cover-up on my scar, then wiped it off, then reapplied it.

As I entered the workshop lounge, I didn't focus on the eyes of my peers. I looked at Professor M, who smiled at me and started off the discussion by asking me to read the first page aloud. I read in a shaky voice that got stronger with each line. But as soon as I was done, before Professor M even had a chance to open the discussion, Amelia spoke up, "How can we trust a narrator who's on psych meds?"

I pushed down the shame that started to bubble up in my chest and lifted my gaze to meet hers. She wasn't looking at me; she was looking at Justine like a puppy who wanted to be praised for doing what it's told.

"If someone's on a mood stabilizer, does that mean nothing they say matters?" Claire asked.

Andrew jumped in, "The problem is we don't *know* if it means anything."

"So, because we don't know, we dismiss everything she has to say?" Claire said. "Someone can steal from her, and it's okay?"

"The thief takes pills too," Phong said, "and the pills make *her* better. The story is about the absurdity of calling one person ill when we're all ill and we're all making each other sick."

"I don't think the story is true," Ben said. "And I don't think it's a delusion caused by mental illness. It's a *fantasy*. It's like *Annie Hall*. At the end, you realize the narrator's told the story the way he *wishes* it had gone, instead of how it actually happened. The narrator here is imagining she isn't mentally ill by putting the blame for her mental illness on someone else."

"Stop dismissing what the narrator is saying," Claire said. "Does this narrator's claim that her pills were stolen not matter because she was taking pills? Does she have no protections under the law?"

"People are innocent until proven guilty," Ben said.

"Are you talking about the thief or the woman who takes medications?" Claire pressed.

"We're craftsmen," Professor M said. "Right away, the narrator tells you she takes medication. It's the reader's cue that she's unreliable."

"We're *all* unreliable narrators," Claire said. "Everything that's written is just someone's perspective. Even the news stories we read. And writing about ourselves changes us. We're distorted by observation. Separating imagination from observation isn't possible. We filter everything through our own biases. Haven't you heard of 'observer bias'? Even how we treat each other *outside* of workshop can shape what we bring into it and how we approach it."

"Claire," Justine said, clearly agitated. "You're censoring the workshop. You're trying to stop us from workshopping Hannah's story."

"Claire isn't allowed to dismiss our dismissal?" Ben teased, looking at Justine.

Professor M tried to steer us back to the story. "Would this material be better suited to a novel than a short story?"

"No," Andrew said. "The story serves the author's purpose. She wants to see if we'll believe a narrator who takes psychotropic medication. Otherwise, why would she mention it?"

I cringed at the first mention of "the author."

Professor M stepped in. "Remember, we're workshopping the story, not the author."

Claire said, "How could she—whether we're talking about the author or the narrator—tell this story *without* mentioning she was on psychiatric medication?"

"And *why* did the narrator choose to tell this story?" Professor M interjected. "That's a question we should always ask. What motivates this character, and what is she really trying to say?"

"Should the reader have to wonder if the story is true?" Justine asked.

"Isn't this a *fiction* workshop?" Professor M said, his green eyes sparkling playfully. "Am I in the right room?" He looked around, feigning confusion. "There are many great books with unreliable narrators, such as Jaimy Gordon's *Bogeywoman* and Dostoevsky's *Notes from Underground*."

"We're *all* unreliable narrators," Claire said. "Anyone relating something they've observed introduces observer bias. Even observing yourself changes you."

"Are you talking about the author observing herself or the narrator observing herself?" Andrew asked.

"Is there a difference?" Phong asked. "All stories are memoir, if we're being honest. And memoir is really the greatest fiction, because if observing something changes it, then writing memoir changes you from the person you were writing about into a new person. As you're writing a sentence about yourself, it's already not true."

"You're basically saying no one can truly see anything," Justine said. "Then what's to talk about? We're all in our own worlds, and that's where we'll stay?"

Professor M chimed in, "Fiction, and some 'memoir,' isn't concerned with what really did or didn't happen. It's about getting to a *larger truth* than the facts: the emotional truth, or some truth about human nature or the universe."

The writer isn't supposed to speak in workshop, but I did anyway: "I wrote this story because I think whoever made me drive my car onto the lawn or drove it onto the lawn themselves needs medication even more than I do."

For a moment, there was a shocked silence. People were embarrassed and uncomfortable, and no one knew where to look. Then Amelia started laughing and Justine joined in.

"We can come back to Hannah's story," Professor M said. "Let's turn to Justine's work now. What did people like about the story?"

"It's very dramatic," Ben said. "The author really went for it."

"What is 'it'?" Professor M asked.

"Action."

"Did the action feel natural, satisfying?" Professor M prodded.

"Everything worked really well together," Amelia said. People nodded, except for Claire. Amelia continued, "The story was seamless."

"Is this workshop one of those social experiments where people mindlessly conform?" Claire asked. "Like when someone walks into an elevator, if everybody is facing the back, they face the back too?"

"What do you mean?" Professor M asked.

"The story feels like one of those driverless cars. There isn't a human being at the wheel."

Wow. Claire was fearless. Her comment gave me the courage to say what I was sure we were all thinking: "The story feels like *Single White Female* rewritten by AI."

A couple of people gasped. Professor M rushed to say, "Let's not go making any allegations. I think we all had big expectations of the story going in. If we hadn't had those expectations, I'm sure we would be having a different discussion. As for the story itself, we all go through periods where we're not writing our best. Often after a big success." He looked at Justine, who had grown pale. Her lips were pressed so tightly together that they were trembling.

I didn't feel bad for her. The villain in the story was me. She was described as: "Unremarkable, except for a scar on her cheek that hints at a violent past." Justine was ruthless in her quest to ruin me; unlike in *Single White Female*, her story ended with the unremarkable girl killing the protagonist.

The story wouldn't have gotten Justine funding. It wouldn't have even gotten her into graduate school.

"I do think there are a lot of personal dynamics at play here," Andrew said.

"Everyone is jealous of Justine," Amelia said. She looked at me. "One of us didn't get funding, so naturally she's looking for a reason to tear apart Justine's story."

Andrew nodded, and Ben said, "I really liked the story."

I thought of the piece of notebook paper Justine had left in my car. I knew the pain she must have felt as she'd tried to write something flawless. I'd also put plenty of slash marks through my own writing, just not literally. The writing process is hard, even more so for writers because we want to get it right. But instead of continuing to fight to get the words right, Justine had given up. She'd taken the funding that should have been mine. In return, the university was getting writing generated by ChatGPT in the graduate workshop.

I wasn't going to let Justine get away with it, not just because of how she treated me, but on behalf of all writers still slugging it out in the trenches instead of surrendering the written word over to AI. "The story uses repetitive phrases," I said, "and I see a lot of the words AI overuses, such as 'resonate'—"

Justine cut me off. "Hannah has been stalking me. I'm not comfortable with her being here."

I wanted to defend myself, but how could I explain that when I went to her apartment I'd just been checking to see if she was still alive after I thought I saw her falling from The Arch?

Professor M raised his hands up to signal a time-out. "It sounds like there are too many outside factors at play here. We're going to end the workshop early today."

I needed to leave before I said something I regretted. Everybody was still sitting down, taking notes or shutting down their laptops. I stood up and stumbled over people's feet as I ran for the door.

CHAPTER 54

Then

EVERY TUESDAY, I had to go to a local treatment aftercare program. "I feel like appearing more badass than I actually am," I'd told the local counselor last week. "I'm tired of being messed with. I need to be my own Mafia family—a wolf pack of one."

"You have to learn to be vulnerable," he'd replied, causing the fading bruise on my wrist to throb. He looked nothing like the counselor at St. Vic's. His biceps seemed on the verge of exploding, and though he was sitting, it was clear he was tall. As he'd gazed down at me across the tiny table that served as his desk, he looked like an adult sitting at a Fisher Price play set. "In group," he continued, "with the other women, don't close yourself off. Don't believe you're different. You're not the only one who thinks she has a good excuse to drink."

"It's easy for you to say I should make myself vulnerable. Have you ever imagined what it's like to be a woman?" I'd considered carrying that day since I was wearing a jacket to protect against the late October chill, but at the last second I decided to bring pepper spray instead of my gun.

"I meant that you can be emotionally vulnerable here, in group," he'd said. "That's very different from the way you make yourself vulnerable physically. I was going to say something to you last week about your outfit. You don't need to be overly provocative here or elsewhere. A tight shirt and short skirt send the wrong message."

"Yes," I'd replied, "they do send the wrong message: the message that I'm not carrying."

That had startled him. "Guns aren't permitted here."

"I know. I saw the sign and I read good."

"Well!" he'd said, to end our meeting.

When I'd stood up and smoothed my jeans down, he'd looked me over carefully. Not to imagine me naked, but to see if I was dangerous. It felt good. Before walking out, I'd said, "I bet you'd rather have me in a tight shirt and short skirt now."

CHAPTER

55

Then

October 2024, graduate school, St. Louis

LATER THAT WEEK, when I called Lynette, she answered the phone, "You really need a hobby."

Was I leaning too heavily on her? I decided to go to another party. When I told Lynette, I added, "What do I have to lose?"

"You know exactly what you have to lose," Lynette said. "Your sobriety."

"What good is my sobriety if I can't even take it anywhere?"

"It's still young. Would you take a two-week-old to a flea market?" she asked. I heard an inhalation, an exhalation. I thought I might be the only nonsmoker in the world who'd gone to treatment. "Go ahead, though, if that's what you want," she said. "Go do a little research. I'll be here when you get back."

"You're on probation. You have to be."

"Selling meth is against the law, and it didn't stop me."

I didn't say what I was thinking: *You didn't only sell meth. You sold your body.*

"A probation officer isn't what keeps me here," she said. "I'm trying this *life on life's terms* thing, and I suggest you do the same."

"I don't plan to drink."

"If you want to make God laugh, tell him your plans," she replied.

"You're not supposed to belittle me. You're supposed to make suggestions."

"I suggest you do whatever it is you usually do when you're not at one of those things where everyone just stands around doing nothing." She didn't understand how a gathering without drugs and sex could be called a party. "Write. Stalk that silly girl—and all the other people you're jealous of—on the internet." I liked that Lynette had never bothered to remember Justine's name. "Pray. Fuss around in fancy panties. Stay inside your damn apartment until Sunday," she said, and hung up before I could protest.

* * *

The next day, before the party, I slid my gun into my new thigh holster. Whoever had bruised my wrists was still out there.

I arrived earlier than usual. I saw my fellow MFAers, Andrew, Amelia, Justine and company, the department professors, a few alumni, and Duncan. Then there were the spouses. I could tell they were spouses because they looked slightly uncomfortable. *Will they find a way to fit in, or is fitting in here impossible for the less lettered?* The poets' lovers made a better showing. They hadn't failed to be interesting. One woman's bangs formed a sharp square over the center of her forehead, and another had a haircut that looked like it was modeled after a staircase. I imagined the poets falling quickly into tangled love affairs, then ending them for months—as tortuously as possible—writing one poem after another, hoping to produce enough for a collection.

I stood on the edge of a circle of my fellow MFAers. They barely acknowledged me. One day I wanted to throw a party, just so I could not invite them.

They were talking about a piece in *The Atlantic*. The author argued that stories should be less descriptive and more plot-based. That was a reversal of the previous widely held MFA workshop stance that plot was a cheap device needed only by authors whose prose lacked truth, beauty, and intellectual depth. I wanted to tell my fellow MFAers, "Just write whatever the hell you want," but then I'd need to find another circle to stand on the edge of.

"People here have taken William Gass's emphasis on the sentence—on simile, metaphor, and experimentation—and brutally misconstrued them in order to feel superior to ordinary 'middle brow' readers who want a story arc and some semblance of a plot," Phong said. "Stories have been plot-based for thousands of years. Have you ever considered that people have an innate, *natural* need for structure?"

"I understand what you're saying," Andrew said, "but this is a writing program. Why would we simply want to tell stories the way they've been told for thousands of years? If we wanted to churn out mindless imitations, we wouldn't need to be here."

At the words "mindless imitations" I looked at Justine. She was still in the circle, but she was leaning back.

"You can't say that stories have always been the same," Phong said. "Literature is always changing. Important writers do things differently from the writers who came before them. Obviously you know literature has different periods," he added, as though Andrew probably didn't know. "Are you against the stream of consciousness writing of Virginia Woolf?"

I hadn't noticed Claire standing beside me, but suddenly I heard her voice. "Personally, I'm not 'against' any writing. I'm against deciding which stories are worthy of being told."

I felt a hand brush against my arm. By the horrified expression on Justine's face, I knew who it was. I turned around, and the stranger smiled at me, holding out a beer.

"I don't drink," I said.

He set it down on a coffee table and turned his gaze back to me. His eyes weren't merely looking at me, they were going as deep as they could.

"I've been practicing going slowly," he said. "It's why I was late."

Only trouble is interesting, Professor M had told us in workshop. *Hell is very story-friendly.*

I didn't care if the stranger was only hitting on me to make Justine jealous. He was beautiful, and I was lonely. "Do you want to get out of here?" he asked.

I glanced back and saw Justine glaring at me as the stranger took my hand and led me out of the party.

His building was newer than mine, sleek. The floor didn't creak. A large black leather couch drew me deeper inside.

"Do you like Father John Misty?" he asked.

I was so nervous I didn't trust my voice. I nodded.

The opening notes of "Real Love Baby" flowed from the speakers as the stranger sat beside me on the couch. "I never introduced myself," he said. "I'm Eli."

"Hannah."

"Nice to meet you, Hannah," he said, sliding closer. My leg flinched away from his. I needed to take off my thigh holster and hide it somewhere. I asked him where the bathroom was, and he pointed down the hall.

I locked the bathroom door behind me. I took the thigh holster with the .22 in it and slid it into the cabinet beneath the sink.

When I returned to the living room, he wasn't there. I went back down the hallway toward an open doorway, lit only by the faintest glow from within. He was lying on his bed, fully clothed, with his hands behind his head. The candles he'd lit all around the room were the only hint of seduction.

"Hey," he said.

"Hey."

"Come here."

I got closer, but I didn't get on the bed. As I leaned down to kiss him, I kept my weight balanced on my feet so I could run away if I changed my mind. He pulled his hand out from behind his head and touched my face. He was so gentle that I didn't feel afraid. I didn't want to run. I wanted to stay there, going slowly, for as long as we could stand it.

* * *

We lay in bed afterward, cooling off as the air from the ceiling fan whisked over our bodies. Only one candle had managed to stay lit. I studied Eli in its soft glow. I didn't feel I knew him any better than I had a couple of hours before; he was still a mystery. My hand roved over his body, searching for an answer. I ran my fingertips down his taut stomach, his hip flexors, his thighs. Even the spongy flesh behind his cock.

Suddenly he grabbed my wrist so hard I gasped. "Not there," he said.

For an instant I was too shocked to speak, but then I said, "Let go of me, motherfucker." He released me. I rolled to the edge of the bed and put my feet on the floor.

"Hey," he said, "I'm sorry. Don't go yet."

"What's wrong with you?"

"I don't like to be touched there."

"Why?"

He rubbed my back, making it so I didn't want to stand up and move out of his reach. No one had ever touched me so deftly, as if my skin was braille and he was memorizing every word. "I don't want to talk about it now," he said. "Please don't go."

Has he been abused? Did someone hurt him?

I lay down again, turned to him. *Okay*, my body told his, *I won't leave.*

Sometime in the night, I woke up and thought of my cat and how horrible I look in the morning. Then I thought of my gun and how I didn't want to have to sneak it out of his bathroom or explain it to him. I decided to leave.

I used the light from my cellphone to look for my clothes.

I heard him shift in bed. "Really?" he said, sitting up.

"If I'm gone too long, my cat will pee in the corners."

"You rent. Why do you care where she pees? Come back to bed."

"You seemed classier last night," I said. Then I remembered him with a cheap beer in his hand. "Classy" wasn't what brought me to his apartment.

He turned on a lamp and squinted at my clothes in my left hand, and my cellphone in my right. The evidence that I was going to sneak away. "You too," he said.

"I wasn't going to ghost you."

"It's okay, you can ghost me. But first, come here one more time."

I did, and then I went to the bathroom to get dressed—dressed *all the way*, which now included my gun. "Say hi to your cat," he said at the door.

"Come over sometime and say hi to her yourself."

"I will," he said. He kissed me so sweetly I had no doubt that I'd be alone with him again.

As I left his building, I had a terrible thought: *Justine has been in the bed I just slept in*. Would she to try to make her way back there? I was going to do whatever I had to do to stop her.

CHAPTER 56

Then

October and November, 2024

THE NEXT TIME we went to his apartment, we were kissing even before he opened the door. Even with me nibbling on his neck, he was able to slide the key into the lock and turn the knob. He pushed open the door and said, "I got something for you."

A stuffed cat lay on one side of the leather couch in the living room, staring at us with big blue eyes. It looked so odd in the otherwise masculine apartment that I burst out laughing.

"I know you miss your cat when you're away too long," he said. "I thought this might keep you here longer this time. Hopefully, all night. I make a brilliant breakfast soufflé."

It *was* brilliant. Fluffy and light with just the right amount of garlic salt and cheese.

After that, he always had something for me. A toiletry kit with a toothbrush, a boar bristle hairbrush, an awaiting bubble bath, a silk bathrobe, an espresso machine. *I'm the queen of this castle,* I thought as I stood in the kitchen one morning in my new robe, making espresso. I left everything he gave me at his apartment, and I always found it exactly where I left it. That's why I assumed I was the only woman who came over.

One night when we were in bed, our limbs tangled and warm, catching our breath, I realized I didn't think about Justine anymore. I used to try to anticipate her next move because I didn't feel safe. Now I had Eli. I felt safe with him, but not so safe I was bored. He was so thorough with me I felt like he was writing the manual for my body.

"You push me to the edge of my range," I told him one morning. "The edge of my control."

I knew I wasn't explaining it right. My feelings for him were like a limb that had been stretched beyond its natural range of motion, beyond where my muscles had control of it. It was like I'd gone into the splits; I couldn't lift myself up the same way I'd come down. I was in a fragile position, but I didn't want to move because everything was perfect if it stayed exactly as it was.

"I push you to the edge of your control?" he asked. "I'll take that as a compliment. But are you sure we've reached the edge yet?" He held my wrists in his hands, pressed them over my head.

"Do you remember that interview we heard, with the singer who goes to the end of her range, and it's raw and awkward and sweet, and it makes everyone shift uncomfortably in their seats? And that's when she knows she's most real. She can't put on any airs. She can't do anything but let it come out as messy and strange and beautiful as it is."

He was kissing my neck. "Hmmm," he said.

"That's how I feel with you."

I hadn't spoken like that before. I needed him to look at me. I needed to see his reaction. I pulled one of my hands from his grasp and tried to lift his face up so his eyes were looking into mine. He resisted. I'd said too much. I'd taken things too far.

And that wasn't even what I really wanted to tell him. It was just the lead-up.

"I have to pee," I said. I disentangled myself and went into the bathroom to get dressed and retrieve my gun. I felt stronger with it. I shouldn't have let my guard down. I needed to be more careful.

I stepped out of the bathroom, fully dressed.

"Come back," he said.

"I've got things to do."

"Hey," he said. Now he did look me in the eye. His gaze was unwavering. "I'm in deep with you, too."

In order to gather my thoughts, I would have needed to look away, and I couldn't. He was too beautiful not to believe. I wanted to come back to bed, but my gun was strapped to my thigh.

"My cat—"

"There's always some sort of urgency about you when you leave, Hannah. I think one day you'll leave me and you won't come back."

"I'll always come back."

"Good. Otherwise, I'll have to kidnap you." He winked.

"Promise?" I asked.

He half smiled. "I'll see you tomorrow." The next day was Saturday, the only evening of the week we never spent apart. "Go."

I did. The secret I wanted to tell him about was my gun, and something told me to leave it under my skirt for the time being.

As I walked home, I wondered: *If it comes down to him or my gun, which will I choose?*

CHAPTER

57

Now

I CAN HARDLY BREATHE after Eli says, "You're the only woman for me, Hannah. I can't live without you. And you can't live without me." I have to get away from him.

I send him out for supplies, and when he returns, I seduce him but refuse to go all the way until he drinks. An hour later, I watch him pass out from the rum I made him drink.

As soon as he starts to snore, I slip out.

Outside, the cold hits me, and I run as though he might be chasing me. I try to think only of putting one foot in front of the other, following the trail of footprints to his truck and my freedom.

But soon, his footprints become fainter. I stop.

I've only made it a hundred yards from the cabin. I could turn back. If he's woken up, I could say I just went outside to go to the bathroom. Otherwise, if I keep going toward the truck, it won't be safe to return to the cabin.

I take a swig from the vodka I brought. I also brought a candle, but it went out almost as soon as I stepped out the door, leaving only moonlight to guide me.

I squint down at the snow. His footprints are a couple of hours old, but just as deep as mine. They're a reminder that he's heavier, denser than I am. I don't want to go back.

Keep going, I tell myself. *Hurry.*

The snow seeps through my boots, the wind sneaks under my coat, and my fingers start to freeze. I'm not sure I can pry the magnetic key from under the truck, if it's even there.

And then, I see the truck. The dark red F-150 that always looks purple in the moonlight. Its wheels are angled to the side, giving off attitude. I'm hoping there's cash hidden in the truck—Eli has money somewhere. Maybe I'll find enough to make it home.

I crouch beside the truck and peer underneath. It's too dark to see anything. I put the candle and vodka in the snow and slide under. My fingers find the magnetic key box. It's attached to the frame. He must think I'm really stupid. He didn't even consider that I might try to take the truck.

I retrieve the candle and vodka, open the door, and climb into the cab. I plunge the key into the ignition, eager to crank the heat. The engine turns over, but doesn't start.

Shit.

I try not to panic. He just came back with groceries a couple of hours ago. The truck must be working. Is it out of gas?

I get out and unscrew the gas cap. The smell of gasoline is overpowering. I have the thought that I could huff this until I'm not afraid anymore. I could huff it until I pass out.

I know this is a bad thought—one I can't afford. If I mess up now, I might not survive. I screw the gas cap back on.

I pop the hood and search for the problem. After a moment, I realize that the distributor cap is gone.

Dammit.

I need my gun now, more than ever. If I can't start the truck, I'll have to go back to the cabin. Eli will know I wanted to leave. That I planned to abandon him. He must have known, already, and taken the distributor cap to prevent it. So maybe he doesn't think I'm an idiot after all.

Without the gun, there's little chance of getting the distributor cap back.

I climb back into the cab. My fingers are freezing, but I shove them into every possible place the gun could be. It's not in the glove compartment, the console, or under the seat. It's not in the door shelves. I turn the cab inside out looking for it.

It's not here.

Now my only hope is that he hasn't woken up, and that it'll start snowing again, covering my tracks.

I'm panicking so badly that I almost forget to put the magnetic key back in place. As soon as it's fastened, I run. My feet are half-numb, and I fall twice. But each time, I pick myself up and keep going.

When I get back to the cabin, I open the door and hurry inside before the rush of cold air can wake him. Not that the cabin isn't cold. The fire in the stove is no longer burning. The shades are drawn against the moonlight; the room is completely dark.

I know he's on the bed by his snoring. I strip off my wet pants and socks. I'll tell him I went out to go to the bathroom and fell in the snow. Or perhaps the clothes won't freeze, and I'll just say that the reason I'm not wearing pants is because I fell asleep immediately after sex, like a man.

I slide under the covers, not touching my feet or hands to his skin, but seeking his warmth. He startles a little when my cold cheek brushes against his chest.

It's okay, I tell myself. It will be as if this never happened. As if I never tried to leave him.

But then, I think that maybe what I need is a drink, and it hits me: I forgot the vodka in the truck.

CHAPTER

58

Then

November 2024, graduate school, St. Louis

SOMETIMES ELI AND I didn't go to the graduate school parties together. Instead, we met there and pretended to be strangers picking each other up for the first time. Our game made me feel high, like a manic episode. Especially if I didn't take my pill.

One night, I let him go to the party first. I wanted to walk in knowing he was watching me. I was wearing a new shirt and a skirt that was almost too short to carry in. I had boots on so he would hear me coming.

But when I walked in, he didn't look at me. He was talking to Justine. They were standing by themselves near an old bay window with a bench on one side of the living room. I had the terrible thought that if they were completely alone, they would lay down in it. No one had dared to breach their space. I saw a hint of a smile on the side of Eli's face that was visible to me. I saw the way Justine leaned toward him. I saw her hand reach out and touch his arm. He leaned even closer.

It wasn't just that they wanted to rip each other's clothes off. There was too much familiarity; it didn't surprise him that she was touching his arm. They'd slept together recently, and they wanted to do it again.

My hands started shaking. I didn't even think I'd be able to hold my gun steady on a target. Or in this case, two.

A sharp, searing pain entered my head right behind my eyes.

I didn't know what else to do; I looked for the old professor. It wasn't hard to find him. I followed the smell of a pipe. He'd need a ride home later, and who better to give him one than me? I wanted Eli to see us leave together.

The professor was standing near the bar. A few graduate students were gathered around him. "If you need to hide something, you may as well put it in your memoir," he said, waving his pipe around. "Everyone believes people lie about themselves in memoir and hide the truth in fiction. But really, the god-awful truth is that no one reads carefully anymore. People want to read enough to say they've read something. They'd rather talk about it than read it. No one really gives a sturdy turd about anything anymore." He stopped to suck from his pipe. When he was done coughing, he said, "Are you writing this down?"

No one was holding a pen or typing into their smartphone.

I was going to ask Professor Newhouse something that would probably shock the other students. They enjoyed him at parties, in a group, but they wouldn't want to spend time with him alone. I didn't care what they thought of me, though. I only cared about the hurt I hoped to see in my lover's eyes as I left with the professor.

"Professor Newhouse," I said, "I can give you a ride home when you're ready." I didn't mention that I'd have to walk back to my apartment to get my car.

The other graduate students snickered; I could only imagine the cruel things they'd say later. But the professor no longer cared about them. He waved them off. He looked at me. I thought I looked pretty good when I checked the mirror before leaving my apartment, and seeing his expression, I knew I was right.

"Hannah!" he said. "Pour me another glass, will you?"

As I did, I looked back to where my lover was talking with Justine. She stood alone now. "Pour yourself one, too," the professor said. "You'll never be able to stand all these people sober, and you don't want to be a dropout, do you?"

"They didn't tenure you for nothing," I said, considering the options. I needed something clean and hard. I needed vodka.

"Don't be hard to please," he said. "Graduate students can't afford to have good taste. If it's free, you like it."

However free the wine was, it wasn't relapse-worthy. I needed to go home and drink what I wanted. I wished I hadn't offered Professor Newhouse a ride in front of everybody. I wished I had just turned around and left when I saw my lover with Justine. I felt sick.

"Excuse me," I said to Professor Newhouse. "I actually need to leave."

CHAPTER

59

Then

"HANNAH!" PROFESSOR NEWHOUSE called after me. I kept walking. I hated crying, but at least if no one *saw* me, I could pretend it didn't happen. On my way to the door, I saw that my (former?) lover and Justine were talking again. The sexual tension between them was so intense they didn't even notice me.

It usually felt good to open the door, step outside, and enter a space that wasn't the party. But not that night. I needed one last look at them.

I went around the house to peek in the window. Unfortunately, my boots were made to look good, not to do anything that boots for men do, such as make it easier to walk. I stumbled up against the window. Before I could duck, everyone inside turned to look at me.

Justine tried to mask her satisfaction with a concerned-looking frown, but the corners of her mouth trembled. She was fighting a smile.

How transparent.

"Amateur," I yelled at her. Her eyes widened, but I knew she wasn't really surprised. She just wanted to direct everyone's attention to my bad behavior. I stumbled away from the window and fell to the ground.

Wow. I'm not even drunk. Maybe if I were drinking, I wouldn't have stumbled. Maybe being sober all the time was making me moody and klutzy. I'd had no relief from myself except sometimes with my lover, who didn't appear to be mine any longer.

If this is sobriety, I don't want it. Fuck treatment and cognitive behavioral therapy and everything else I've done to try to get better. I'm too messed up to be fixed.

One advantage St. Louis has over Minneapolis is that you can get liquor until 1:30 AM instead of only 10 PM. Before I went to treatment, I would make sure to go to different stores so no one thought I drank too much. I even told a couple of clerks I was the social planner for a twenties dating site that had actual get-togethers with mixed drinks. It turned out one of them was younger than he looked and wanted to know the name of the site so he could sign up. "Plenty O' Twenties," I said, and never went back there again.

But that store was the closest one to the party, and I couldn't bear to be sober one more second than I had to.

I started to stand up, but then I saw his shoes. Neatly polished black dress shoes.

"Hey, are you okay? What happened?" Eli crouched and looked around. "What did you trip over?"

I was afraid he'd see my gun. I rose to my knees. "It's hard to explain," I said. I was dizzy, and my fingers were tingling. Side effects of stopping Lamictal too suddenly. I hadn't taken it last Saturday because I was at his apartment, and I hadn't taken it this week because I'd been futilely hoping he'd invite me over. I didn't want to dull the high that being with him gave me. But he wasn't worth it. "And besides," I said, "I don't have to explain myself to you."

He stood and offered me a hand. "Yes, you're clearly not in a position to explain anything."

When had he become so condescending? I lurched to my feet, refusing his help. "It's hard to enunciate as well as Justine."

"Who's Justin?"

Even in the moonlight he was beautiful. Why was life so cruel?

"The girl you were standing close enough to fuck a few minutes ago."

"I'm standing near the only girl I want right now."

"You know I'm an English major. Do you really think I don't see both meanings of what you're saying? Right now you only want to sleep with me, but two minutes ago you wanted to sleep with her?"

"You know that's not how I meant it."

"I don't know anything anymore."

He shook his head. "Is this the romantic moment where I'm supposed to declare myself a serial monogamist?"

He was trying to be playful, but other than dumping me on the spot, it was the worst thing he could say. "Serial monogamist? What does that even mean? If you sleep with one person at two AM, another at three, and another at four, can you say you're a serial monogamist because you only slept with one at a time?"

"Oh, sorry, I misspoke." He smiled. "Now that I think about it, I'd prefer to be in a threesome."

I couldn't help picturing him, Justine, and me. That was one too many people. Or perhaps two.

"How could you say something so stupid?" I asked. "What the hell are you thinking?" I started walking in the direction of the liquor store.

He hurried to block my path. "Hannah, listen. I'm taking you home so you don't embarrass yourself anymore tonight."

"Fuck you," I said.

"Famous last words."

I wished my anger at him tempered my attraction. He was almost as appealing as a drink, except that a drink never talks to another girl.

I pushed past him. I couldn't wait to be buzzing. I stopped to try to take off my boots. They were slowing me down.

"Really?" he said, coming up beside me. "You're going to walk home barefoot?"

"No, I'm not going to walk home barefoot. I'm going to walk to the liquor store barefoot." I put a hand on his arm for balance while I yanked the boots off.

"You shouldn't be drinking, but if you're going to do it anyway, do it where I can keep you from doing anything crazy. Come over. I'll make you a drink that will curl your toes."

"Isn't Justine available?"

"Who the hell is Justin? I talked to a couple of people."

I was certain that by "people" he meant women. Without knowing who the other women were, I could say with confidence, "Justine was the hot one."

He grabbed me by the shoulders. Without my boots on, he was a head taller than me again. "I can't let you go anywhere like this. We're going to my apartment or yours."

"There's nothing to drink at mine."

So we went to his.

I was going to drink all I could and then leave. I'd go straight home and take my pill.

We bellied up to the bar, and I stopped him from mixing me a drink. "Just vodka," I said.

He raised an eyebrow, then poured a little into a glass and handed it to me.

It traveled quickly down my throat, into my stomach. The burn was so, so good. I knew it took twenty minutes to start really feeling the effects, but the vodka's incredible warmth, its wonderful fire, held me. I felt safe.

Suddenly he was behind me, and the feel of him pressed against me, combined with the warmth in my belly, was so nice that I almost didn't care about him finding my gun. *Hide it*, one part of my brain yelled at the other. *Oh, for fuck's sake*, the other part responded.

I poured myself more vodka and moved away from him. "I have to pee." I hurried to the bathroom with my drink. Now that I had it, I didn't want to let go of it. I closed the door and slammed the vodka. *How have I deprived myself of this for so long?*

I took off my holster and looked at my gun. I was blessed. I had vodka, a gun, and the man of my dirtiest dreams. I had everything.

I wasn't going to let Justine fuck it all up.

CHAPTER

60

Then

IN THE MORNING, I woke up with my head pounding and bruises on my wrists. I didn't remember what happened. Worst of all, I'd lost my sobriety. I hadn't thought I'd miss it, but I did. Especially the remembering things part.

I couldn't think of why Eli would have held my wrists that hard, except he didn't like for my hands, my mouth, or even my gaze to go beyond his cock.

He was on his back beside me, snoring softly, innocently. I shook him. "What the hell?"

He opened his eyes and looked from my face to the bruises on my wrists, which I was holding out to him.

"You attacked me," he said. "You said you were going to kill me for talking to Justine at the party."

For a moment I was too shocked to speak. Then I asked how I attacked him.

He tilted his head to show me the marks on his neck. "I was afraid you were going to kill me."

I stopped myself from saying, "If I'd wanted to kill you, I would have shot you." I still didn't want him to know I had a gun. "No," I said, trying to keep my voice steady so he couldn't hear how close I was to crying. "I'd never hurt you."

He turned back to me. "Do you know how hard it would be to choke yourself? I would have passed out before bruising myself this badly."

"How do you know how bad it looks?" I asked. "Did you look into the mirror while you were doing it?"

"Because it hurts. It hurts even to talk." He closed his eyes. Was he done with the conversation? Was he done with me?

"You're not dumping me, are you?" I asked.

"No. There's nothing you could do to make me fall out of love with you."

Love? Did he actually mean it? I wanted to believe he loved me, but did that mean I had to believe I tried to strangle him?

He opened his eyes and turned to me. "I know it was just the vodka," he said. "I forgive you."

This doesn't feel right. I didn't remember ever being violent, sober or drunk. I grabbed my clothes off the floor and hurried to the bathroom. My .22 was still where I hid it. I had thought it would protect me from waking up with bruises, but I'd been wrong. I felt a little heartbroken as I secured the thigh holster and placed my gun inside it. Was this the end of my romance with the .22?

I put my clothes back on and assessed my appearance in the mirror. *Could be worse*, I thought, taking in the mascara smudged around my eyes and the sallowness of my skin, *but not much.* The concealer had worn off the scar. Had seeing it made him think he could do whatever he wanted to me? Had he decided that I was damaged goods?

I ran cold water over my wrists, though I couldn't tell if they hurt. My head pounded too hard to feel anything else. When the pounding subsided, I was pretty sure I was going to hate myself for giving up my sobriety and for doing whatever it was I did last night.

When I came out of the bathroom, he was sitting on the couch, waiting for me. "I forgive you, Hannah."

I ignored him and pulled on my boots. He stood up and approached me.

"You don't understand," I told him, holding out my hand to stop him from coming closer. "If I'd wanted to hurt you, I could have."

He raised an eyebrow. "Okay."

He didn't believe me. I needed to prove it, even though it meant giving up my secret. "Sit back on the couch," I said. I slipped off my boots. "There's something I've been hiding."

I started by taking off my shirt and bra. I don't know why. I waited for him to say something smartass, maybe, "Nothing I haven't seen before." He was silent. I reached behind me to unzip my skirt. I worked it down my hips.

His eyes were already in the right place, even before I carefully pulled the skirt down past my thighs.

"Your panties too," he said.

I'd never tried to take my underwear off with the thigh holster on. I hesitated.

He stood up and came so close we could kiss. Instead, he pulled something from his pocket. There was a click and a flash of movement. I looked down and saw the switchblade. He gripped my panties with one hand and cut them off me with the other.

Then he backed away and looked at me standing naked with my gun strapped to my thigh, my torn underwear on the floor beside me.

Now he knew that I didn't really want to hurt him. My gun was proof that I could have.

"Beautiful," he said. "Perfect."

He came and put his forehead against mine. His lashes brushed my skin as he closed his eyes and said, "I love you, Hannah Silver. You, and only you. There's no one else."

CHAPTER

61

Now

As soon as it hits me that I forgot the vodka in the cab, I get out of bed. My pants and socks are too wet to put back on, so I go over to where his jeans lie near the woodstove. I start pulling them up over my long underwear.

"What are you doing?" he asks.

"I have to pee," I say.

"Isn't that what you were just doing?"

"I have to go again."

A pause. Not good. The last thing I need him to do is think. If he gets out of bed and finds my pants and socks frozen on the floor, he'll know I didn't just step out of the cabin to pee. I wandered through the cold snow until I was soaked.

"Light a candle and come closer," he says.

I let his jeans slip from my hands and fall down my legs. I go back to bed without the candle, heart racing, and crawl under the covers. "I'm sick. I woke up feeling like I was on fire, so I went outside to cool off. I don't know what happened after that. I must have fallen down. I woke up shivering in the snow. I came in and took off my wet clothes, and now I can't warm up."

"Who did you catch the flu from?" His sarcasm comes out in a breath of rancid rum.

Should I say I wandered out with the bottle of vodka and dropped it somewhere in a blackout? "I don't remember anything clearly."

"Clearly."

He hasn't touched me. Hasn't felt my forehead, hasn't reached out to comfort or harm me.

"I thought you had to pee."

"It's too cold to go out."

Faster than a drunk man could, he grabs my wrist and squeezes it so tightly I cry out. "Next time you're gone for more than a few minutes, I'll lock the door."

"Let go of me!"

He releases my wrist and moves back to his side of the bed, leaving me shivering in the dark. I'm angry and cold, in that order.

For hours, I lie awake. My anger turns to fear, and my resentment is replaced by my need for his body heat. I roll across the middle of the bed, the chill deepening as I cross over Justine's ghost, until I reach Eli's warmth. His arm falls over me. He's been expecting me.

"I'm sorry," he says, his voice softer. "You know I would never leave you stranded outside."

"I don't know anything right now," I say, cutting him off before he can press me to find out why I was gone so long. "I'm too exhausted."

* * *

The next morning, I'm awakened by the pounding of a hammer. I'm warm even though he's not in bed anymore. I reach out for Eli, but instead I touch a heated rock. There's one near my feet and another one by my side. The cabin smells good, homey, like wood and cinnamon.

Eli is hammering some boards together. When he notices I'm awake, he smiles. "Today is your spa day, starting with breakfast in bed. I'm almost finished making your tray table."

When he's done nailing the three boards together, he tells me to sit up. He puts a pillow behind me and then brings me a plate of pancakes with butter and syrup. "You can get syrup on yourself, but don't let it get on the bed. I won't lick it off the bed." His smile is teasing, but it doesn't reach his eyes. I try to hide my anxiety and act normal. He kisses me, but I can feel something is off between us. He says, "Oh, I almost forgot something." He goes back and gets me some bacon.

Despite my anxiety, I'm ravenous. "Aren't you going to have anything?" I ask him between bites.

"Yes, as soon as you're finished."

After breakfast, he tells me to turn over, and I do as he asks. He gives me a massage, which I try to enjoy. "You're so tense," he says. I'm relieved when he takes his hands from my back. "I'm going to read to you."

"From what?"

"My memory."

He tells me the story of *White Fang*. I know he's making things up as he goes along, but as a fiction writer, who am I to be critical of that?

Sometime in the middle of the night, I wake up to Eli mumbling in his sleep. "Justine," he says. "Justine."

I start to shake. I roll away from him, my fists clenched so tightly that my nails dig into my palms. I speak to him in the darkness. "You slept with Justine. Worse, you lied to me about it." He doesn't wake up, so I press my toe against his leg. When he stirs, I say it again.

"What?" he says groggily.

"You heard me."

"Hannah, I didn't—"

I don't give him a chance to speak. I fly across the bed and my hands are on his face before I even know what I'm doing. I grip his cheeks like I can squeeze the truth out of him. "Don't you *dare* deny it again," I tell him.

He slaps my hands off his face. "Okay. I *did* sleep with her. But who wouldn't?"

"*Who wouldn't?* A man in a relationship with a woman he loves!"

"You're overcomplicating things, Hannah. It was just lust."

"Well, it seems like you're still in lust with her since you're still saying her name."

"I'm not the only one who says her name at night."

"I don't believe you," I say. I shift back to my side of the bed. "I'm breaking up with you."

He snorts, then takes a breath like he's going to say something. But he must not know what to say. I feel his shock in how the air suddenly goes still. Finally, he says, "No. You're not."

"At soon as the sun comes up, you're taking me to the road. From there I'll hitchhike."

"Where will you go?"

"Away from you."

"Good plan," he says, his voice steady but with an undercurrent of rage. "Except there's one problem." Even in the dark he's able to grab my wrists, roll me onto my back, and pin my hands over my head. He's done this playfully dozens of times, but now it's not playful. "I'm not letting you go."

"Let go of me," I say, trying to twist my arms free.

But he's too strong, I can't release his grasp on me. His knuckles are pressing so hard into my skin that I know I'll have bruises. He leans so close I can feel his breath on my face. "I'm not ever letting you go. You wanted us to be together, and now we are. For forever, or until I can't take it anymore."

C H A P T E R

62

Now

It's dark here, a dark no one who lives in the city knows about: utter blackness. And yet, I'm too afraid to shut my eyes.

I pretend that I only said I wanted to break up because I was caught up in the heat of the moment. I pretend I still want to be with him more than anything else in the world. But he doesn't believe me. His body is a blockade now. When I try to move, he's there—standing between me and the door, taking up all the space. He questions why I want to go out, then watches through the cabin window to make sure I really am squatting in the snow. I can feel the weight of his gaze on me, heavy and unyielding. Afterward, he comes out to check that the snow is yellow.

* * *

The worst thing about realizing that Eli kidnapped me and I'm a prisoner here is that it doesn't keep me from seeking the warmth of his body at night. I wish it were Luke's warmth I could burrow into. Imagining being in his arms, feeling the comfort of someone who truly cares about me, gets me through the humiliation of needing Eli. Here, my pride battles with the cold, and loses every time. Even with the hot rocks we warm on the stove, it's too cold to sleep without pressing against Eli.

Somehow, even in the cold, he retains his heat.

He could survive out here alone. I can't. If I go running toward the road in the hopes of someone coming along, I'll freeze to death.

I have to wait for a warm day to get the hell out of here. Or die trying.

CHAPTER

63

Now

WE'VE BEEN HERE three weeks and already I've lost so much weight that I can feel it. My clothes hang more loosely on me. I have no protection from the weight of Eli's body pressing against mine or the intensity of his unrelenting gaze.

Another side effect of not eating much is that I haven't gotten my period this month. It's one more thing to add to the list of things I've lost here. It disappeared with the last bit of extra flesh. I'd be worried I was pregnant if I didn't have an IUD.

One day, as he's tending the woodstove, Eli startles me by calling out to where I'm shivering under the covers. "Do you think your mother is starting to worry about you?" His voice is casual, but there's something under it, a quiet challenge.

The last time my mother contacted me was on my eighteenth birthday. She'd reached her monthly limit of Sudafed and the pharmacy wouldn't sell her any more. She wanted me to get her two packages, the maximum allowed in one day. "Then we'll celebrate your birthday however you want," she'd said.

I'd said no. A few months later, she moved without giving me her new address. I'd lost her, though not as much as I wanted to. I wanted to lose even the memory of her. I was angry that she could have found me if she'd wanted to and yet she hadn't. When I'd first made an account on Facebook, I checked to see how many Hannah Silvers there were. There were dozens, but not hundreds. She could easily have contacted me if she wanted to. Wasn't she even curious about me? Luke is the only person I've ever spoken honestly to about my mother.

"Yes," I tell Eli. "We're really close. If anyone ever hurt me, she wouldn't rest until she got justice."

"Where is she now?" he says. I realize he knows she's not worrying about me. He just wanted to point out that no one really cares about me. I'm completely alone.

I have to do something. He'll either catch me in my lie or be more careful about how he talks to me. "I have the gun," I lie.

"But you don't have it on you now," he says. And that's how I know he doesn't have it.

Where the hell is it? I wonder. He must think I hid it somewhere. *Did I? If so, where? My apartment? My car?* I have no memory of our last night in St. Louis, but I think I'd have some recollection of the gun if I ended up with it. I don't think either of us has it, in which case, *who does?*

Eli starts coming closer. I don't want to be a sitting duck here in bed. I hop up and shove him aside as I run toward the stove. Where's the ax? It's usually by the stove or door, but I don't see it.

I look back just in time to see Eli trip, his body slamming into the floor with a sickening thud. A bottle rolls away from where he tripped over it.

Suddenly, I don't care that I hate him. I don't care about the things he's done to me. I care about him. I set the candle on the floor and drop down beside him. "Oh god, are you okay?"

He moans, swears.

A glint of white on the floor catches the light. I pick it up. It's smooth on both sides, sharp at one end. My chest floods with relief. It wasn't his skull I heard hitting the floor—it was just a tooth. I need to take advantage of his position to get the distributor cap back.

"You need to go to the hospital," I tell him.

"No, I don't. But even if I did—" He clears his throat, struggling to get the words out. "You couldn't go." I see what's stopping him from speaking clearly. I see it on his lip and on the floor. Blood. "Not after what you've done."

"What have I done?"

I help him roll onto his side so he doesn't choke. I see the chipped tooth in his mouth. "What have I done?" I repeat.

"As long as I don't tell you, I might be safe."

"Don't be ridiculous," I say.

"You were going for the ax."

I squeeze my eyes shut. I *was* going for the ax. I'm not sure what I intended to do with it. But what choice did I have? I don't know what he's capable of. I don't even know what I'm capable of.

"I thought you were going to kill me," he says.

"I'm not a murderer," I reply. But my voice isn't as sure as I'd like it to be.

"You killed Justine."

"I don't believe you."

"Help me to bed, and then I'll show you something."

When he's settled in bed, he tells me to reach under the mattress.

I feel the spiral first, and then the thin cardboard cover. My long lost friend. I didn't realize how much I missed my notebook, but now, as I pull it out, my hands tremble. I want to kiss it. Instead, I hold it to my chest and start to cry. I hope this notebook will help me remember who I was before everything got muddled in my head. It's the only tangible link I have to the woman I used to be.

I open it. Every page is full.

"Read the last chapter," he says.

"You read my notebook?"

Instead of answering, he says, "Read it."

I grip it more tightly. "You've kept this from me all this time?"

He looks away. I want to scream at him, but not as badly as I want to know what's in my notebook.

I see the date on the last entry. November 30, 2024. My heart slips down my chest. November 30 is the last night we were in St. Louis. It's the night Justine went missing.

The words in my notebook pick me up and drop me back in.

November 30, 2024 Journal Entry

Or is it December 1 now?

I'm in the hallway of the alumni's house. Naked. Justine is here too. She's just torn my dress off and now she holds it in her hands like a cheap tent she's uprooted from the ground. What's going on? I don't understand what's happening. The air is vibrating as though a bomb has just gone off. I'm afraid of Justine. I'm afraid of what she's already done to me, how she's framed me for stealing the urn, and what she'll do next. And I'm angry. *Where is my gun?* The gun holster isn't strapped to my thigh as it usually is. Someone must have taken it.

I look around and see that Duncan is down on all fours, trying to grasp a pearl necklace that's rolling away from him.

Eli gave me a few bumps of cocaine earlier, but my high is over. I felt invincible for a little while, but now I'm crashing hard. Things have gone out of focus.

People from the living room are gasping, their voices sharp as they take in the scene in the hallway. They stare at me, shocked, eyes wide as they absorb the full sight of my naked body. "Give me back my dress," I tell Justine. I can see by the hatred in her eyes and how she tightens her grip on the dress that she's not going to let me have it.

I lunge for her, eliciting more gasps from the crowd that has gathered to gawk at us. I take hold of the dress and pull until I hear a rip. Justine's face contorts in rage. She releases the dress, spins on her heel, and runs. I yank my tattered dress back over my body and go after her.

I feel the steady pounding of my heart, the life force surging through my body, and I know: I'm on the hunt.

I also know both Justine and Eli are out here. I know they have some connection.

Where are you, Justine? You don't get to just disappear. Not now, when I need to look you in the eye, and turn the anger there to fear.

I feel a hand grip my shoulder. I recognize the grip. Eli always holds me too tightly or not at all.

"Come on," he says.

"I need to find Justine."

"No, you definitely don't need to find Justine. I'm bringing you home."

It's the first time he's said her name. It rolls off his tongue too easily and fits itself into the night as surely as the street, the houses, the stars.

I feel my gun against my thigh, reach down, and it isn't there. It's like the aching of a phantom limb, a reminder that something is missing.

But is the missing gun my true handicap, or is my handicap Eli's hand on my shoulder? His direction, subtle and not so subtle, charting the course of my life? "Hannah," he says. He spins me to face him and starts to shake me.

This is too familiar. He's hurt me before.

I hold his hand in place on my shoulder. With my other hand, I twist his elbow up, inward, and down. When he doubles over, I knee him in the face and start running.

The street seems to stretch on forever. Where is Justine? It's as though she's vanished from the real world, and slipped back into her usual place: my mind. What's real? Is she actually out here in the night, or am I just chasing shadows inside my own head?

I run until I spot her a few houses ahead, Amelia at her heels.

I would never have dared yell her name before tonight. But now it feels natural, primal, like howling at the moon or sounding a ram's horn before battle. *"Justiiiiiiiiiiiiine."*

She whips around. I feel her gaze lock onto mine. She starts walking toward me.

Amelia reaches out for her, but Justine doesn't stop walking. "Fuck off," Justine tells her.

"Don't worry about Hannah," Amelia says. "She's not worth your time. Just ignore her."

Not breaking eye contact with me, Justine repeats herself. "Fuck. Off."

Amelia lowers her arm, glances briefly in my direction, and then does what she always does: obeys. She stumbles off like a kicked dog.

I'm the last person Amelia sees with Justine.

But Justine and I aren't alone. A hand grips my upper arm so tightly that I feel myself shrinking, getting smaller in its grasp. Eli is like the villain in a horror movie, the one the naive hero should have dealt a harder, more final blow. I can't escape his grasp. Not without risking my shoulder. Even now, I'm thinking of the things I'll write. Of greatness. I need my shoulder for writing. And if writing doesn't work, I'll need it to carry heavy trays for the rest of my life.

Though I can't move much, I can still speak. "Everyone already suspects you're a fake," I tell Justine, "and I'm going to show them they're right."

She turns to Eli as though this is all his fault. "You know what you have to do."

"I tried, Jus," Eli says, his voice catching. "But I–I can't do that to Hannah. I'm sorry."

"Do *what?*" I ask.

But Justine is talking over me. *"Sorry?"* she mocks Eli, stepping closer. "How the hell does that help me? You've turned on me, haven't you?" She drives a finger into his chest and he releases my arm. I stumble back, away from whatever is about to happen. "If you don't pin it on Hannah," she says, "one of us will have to take the fall. And it's not going to be me."

Justine lunges for his waistband. Before she can grab the gun, the gun which must be *my* gun, he shoves her away. Then he pulls it out.

I think of her life line. How short it was.

Justine screams at Eli: "Now I see: you were never going to follow through."

"I was," he says. "But come on, Jus. I'm not a fucking monster." He lowers the gun but doesn't tuck it back in his waistband. "We'll figure this out later."

"Eli," I say, my voice tight. I want him to give me my gun.

Justine looks at me and laughs. "You bloated cow. He feels too sorry for you to do what he promised me he'd do. You, whose life is such a pathetic mess. What do you even have to live for?"

Finally, she's saying all the things about me I'd suspected she was thinking. I tried to tell myself it was just me projecting my feelings of self-hatred onto her. But I don't completely hate myself. "At least I believe in myself enough to write my own stories," I say.

Her laughter falters. For a couple of seconds it sounds like she's choking, then she says, "How's that going? Any publications yet?"

I tell her what I sometimes tell myself: "Life is a marathon, not a sprint."

"Oh, Hannah." Her eyes narrow with contempt. "You'll never figure it out, so I'll make it simple for you. You *reek* of desperation and failure. People can't get away fast enough. You'll never write anything worth publishing, and you'll die all alone. Your cat will end up eating your face, and no one will find you until the stench is strong enough to seep under the door of your crappy, low-rent apartment."

I grab the gun from Eli's hand. I think of what Robert said to me during target practice: *control your breathing.* I focus on lengthening my inhale.

Before I can exhale, Eli turns to me. "Hannah, give me the gun."

I ignore his outstretched hand and point my gun at Justine. I want her to see that I'm the one in control. I want her to beg me for mercy.

She starts running.

"Justine!" I cry. But she keeps getting farther away. "*Justine,*" I scream again.

I chase her through the night, past stately homes and flowering dogwood trees and the squares of light emanating from the windows of the houses we pass. She's nearing an intersection. The lights there are too bright. Someone will see us.

If I don't catch her before the intersection, I'll lose her.

There's a sharp pain behind my eyes. It feels like I'm being stabbed in the head with a knife. But there is no knife. I need more or less vodka. I should go home.

My hand is on the trigger, trembling.

Suddenly Eli is beside me. He tries to yank the gun from my hand and a shot rings out—then another and another.

Justine jerks as if struck by lightning, then collapses, her body going limp.

The air, my ears, the whole night shudders with the echo of the shot. And then there is complete, perfect stillness.

Eli curses so quietly I hardly hear it. I turn to him and see that what I feared is true: I shot Justine. I can see it in the tears in his eyes.

I start to run toward her, but Eli grabs my arm, his grip unyielding. "No," he says, "don't."

I look back at him, at my gun in his hands. "What were you going to do to me? What was Justine talking about?"

He wipes a tear from his cheek with the back of his hand. "I was never going to do anything, Hannah. I just let Justine think I was so she wouldn't do anything to you herself."

His face is unusually raw, stripped of its usual guardedness; I believe him. It was only Justine who plotted against me. But still, I didn't mean to shoot her.

I start to run toward her, but Eli cries, "Don't. There are cameras in the intersection."

"But Justine . . ."

He deliberates for what feels like a long time but is probably only a few seconds. "It's already too late for her. We can only look out for each other now."

For a moment, I can't move. I find it impossible that the world could exist without Justine. But then something inside me shifts, the world recalibrates.

Justine has fallen. Eli and I have survived.

"Come on," he says, and then tells me what I've been longing to hear. "It's just you and me against the world."

I let him take my hand and pull me along behind him so quickly that I'm stumbling. We are confused, horrified, euphoric. The future is ours.

CHAPTER

64

Now

I LOOK UP FROM the notebook. "It's fiction," I tell Eli.

"No. It's you, Hannah. It says 'Journal' on it, for fuck's sake."

"But that's part of the story. The title 'Journal' is fiction."

"Do you even know the difference between fiction and truth anymore?"

Do I?

"Don't try to gaslight me," I say. "It'll just make me hate you."

"Hannah, why would I lie? I wouldn't have let you read all the shit you wrote about me if I didn't have to."

I stand and look down at where he's lying in bed. "Then what is it you were going to do to me?"

"What didn't happen doesn't matter now," he says. His voice falters. Is he afraid of me? Suddenly, I feel like Kathy Bates in *Misery*. I sit back down in the chair.

He points to the notebook in my hands. "*That's* what matters. It's your writing, Hannah. You know it is. It's like the other confessional thing you wrote."

"What other thing?"

"About wandering frat row before you were legal."

"That was fiction too!"

"Justine told me you passed it off as fiction to get into graduate school."

Shame and anger swell up inside me. "Justine is a liar."

"*Was* a liar," he says.

Why do I keep forgetting she's dead?

Eli continues, "But she didn't lie about everything. When I read your story, I knew it was true. Justine got Duncan to show it to her, then used it to manipulate him, threatening to turn him in for violating your privacy if he ever crossed her. She told me it wasn't fiction."

"It's hard to say what's fiction and what isn't."

"In terms of what you've written or what you've said?"

"Maybe both."

"Hannah," he says softly, "it's okay. It doesn't matter to me. I mean, if I love you even though you killed Justine, do you think I care what you did in high school?"

"*We*," I correct him. "If the chapter you had me read is true, *we* killed Justine."

He starts to cough and blood flies from his mouth. I look at his beautiful, contorted face.

"Can you get me some snow for my mouth?" he asks.

I grab a bowl and rush out into the cold. My hand stings from the bite of it as I pack the snow into the bowl, desperate to gather enough so I don't have to come back for more. I know it can't be good to be this cold.

When I try to reenter the cabin, the door won't budge. I push my shoulder against it, but it's solid, unyielding. I set the bowl down and knock on the door with my other hand—the one I didn't use to pack the snow—but my knuckles feel raw against the wood. No answer. I begin pounding. "Eli!"

The door doesn't lock automatically. He would've had to get out of bed to latch it. Why would he go through that effort? Am I truly dangerous? Is that why he's afraid, or is he just punishing me?

"Eli!"

The wind whips my hair across my face, stinging my eyes and filling my mouth as I scream for him to open the door. My fists are numb. My words are choked by the cold.

The realization guts me: he's not letting me in.

I know I can't stand still—not if I want to live. I force myself to move, even though I'm not sure where I'm going or what I'm doing.

I wander until I come across a huge rock. I have the urge to pick it up. I wrap my arms around it, but I can't lift it. Is it heavy, or am I weak? I start pushing. My boots slip out from under me, and I crash to the ground. I wonder if the impact and the cold are the last things I'll ever feel. No more self-doubt, no more chasing things that always seem just out of reach: answers, happiness, friendship, oblivion. I'll never have to stand outside a circle of people, wondering why I can't fit in.

Everything goes black.

CHAPTER

65

Now

I WAKE UP IN bed with my hands and ankles bound. The ropes are rough and my skin is raw. He's ripped one of our blankets into three pieces and put them over the windows. The piece over our eastern-facing window is lit up with sunlight. A lit candle is flickering in a draft coming from the western-facing window. He's wrapped around me, skin to skin, rubbing my limbs to bring the circulation back.

This can't be happening. "What the hell?" I say.

"I don't want to die," he calmly explains, "and I don't want you to die. So this is the best we can do for now."

He gets up. He's completely naked and his body is the most familiar sight in the world to me. But what about the rest of him?

He's always kept his cards close to his vest, but what I can know of him, I know by heart: the efficiency of his movements, the decisiveness, the finality—as though he's already mapped out every step he's about to take. I suppose, all along, this was part of his appeal. He doesn't hesitate. When he does something, he does it with the certainty of someone who's made up their mind.

If he plans to kill me, I don't have much time.

The empty rum bottle is nearby, but not close enough for me to grab it with my feet and break it to cut through the rope around my wrists.

I can't escape with my body. I'll have to do it with my mind.

* * *

When I wake up the next day, the light slanting through the window tells me it's already afternoon. How did I sleep so long?

He gently pushes my hair back from my face and unties my ankles.

He pulls out several packages. I read the label and wonder if I'm dreaming.

"Halcion?" I ask.

Is that why I slept so long? Did he give me Halcion last night?

When I was little, I found some Halcion in my mother's medicine cabinet. I Googled it and found that during H. W. Bush's presidency, he threw up on the Japanese prime minister after taking it. And now Eli is saying, "Yes, these will help keep you calm," as he places some of the little blue pills into my hand. I stare at them as he brings me a cup of melted snow. I can't think of any innocent reason he'd want me to take these. I need to say whatever it takes to stay alive.

"Eli," I say, "I have to tell you something."

He tilts his head, studies me coldly. "So do it."

I take a deep breath and look him in the eye. "I'm pregnant."

CHAPTER

66

Then

November 23, 2024, graduate school, St. Louis

AT THE DEPARTMENT party, Professor Newhouse called to me, "Hannah! There's no place to sit near the bar. Bring something over here."

Something. I knew exactly what he meant—something strong, with just enough mixer to hide that he had his mouth on the tailpipe of his alcoholism. It scared me that I knew what he wanted, because it was also what I wanted. We were connected by our desire.

It was always me he asked to make his drinks.

At the last party, I'd seen him stumble to the bar, lift a bottle of scotch to his lips, and—noticing me watching—simply wink and keep drinking. If someone else had noticed him, shame might have lowered the bottle.

I poured three parts rum to one part Coke into a glass and held it out to him. He took it with shaking hands. None of the students gathered around him anymore. The other professors, the alumni, even the spouses who were usually desperate for anyone to talk to, kept their distance.

"Sit down," he said. But I was getting a bad feeling. Eli had disappeared the moment we'd arrived, and I still hadn't seen him.

I tossed back a couple of shots to steady myself. "I was just leaving," I told the professor. I pushed through the people milling in groups, talking and laughing. It sounded like they were speaking a foreign language.

Where the hell is Eli?

The doors of the bedrooms and studies were shut, but I could still see inside a couple of them: book-lined walls, heavy desks, plush comforters. Elegant headboards, mirrors stretching the rooms into infinity, lamps that gave off the gentlest light. A life I could never have.

Which of these rooms was Eli in? And more importantly, *why?* Suddenly I pictured him with Justine.

No. *No no no no no no no.*

If I find them together, which of them will I kill first?

I tried one door and then another. Beds, books, computers. No Eli. Not until the very last door on the left. He was alone, looking down at something in his hands.

"What are you doing?"

He quickly straightened up. "Waiting for you." He smiled. "I knew you'd come looking."

Does he want to make love to me here, in the bed of the alumnus?

I heard voices in the hallway growing closer. Eli must have heard them too. He slid one hand in his pocket and took me by the elbow with the other. He guided me silently out of the room, past Duncan and a group of alumni. "She's just had a little too much to drink," Eli said smoothly as we pushed past them.

All I could think was: *What the hell is going on?*

CHAPTER

67

Then

November 25, 2024

I WAS CALLED INTO Duncan's office on the following Monday.

"Hannah," he said, and then hesitated, as though he regretted what he had to say next. "Your . . . behavior at the department parties has become a concern among some of the alumni. Men and women who give a great deal of money to the department. Money that pays students' stipends."

The word *stipends* stung. Was he mentioning them because I was the only one who didn't receive one? Was he trying to keep me in my place?

"Some things . . ." Duncan cleared his throat, as though the words he was going to speak would somehow make this conversation harder than it already was. "Some things . . . have gone missing."

"What things?"

"Some jewelry, cash, a watch."

I stood up, the chair scraping loudly against the floor. My skin crawled as Duncan's eyes went up and down my body. I was wearing a skirt just long enough to cover my piece, and a shirt that I'd worn for the last week. "Just because I'm not getting a stipend doesn't mean I need to steal. Don't try to pin a bunch of senior moments on me."

"We're not talking about 'a bunch of senior moments.' As you may have heard, one of the alumni's houses was broken into a few days after he hosted a party. The thief—or thieves—knew exactly where to go and what to take."

I hadn't heard. I was out of the loop, but I wasn't going to admit it. "It was probably just a coincidence." I paused, then added pointedly, "But you're welcome to search my apartment. You know the way."

A shadow passed over his face. "This is a warning," he said. "If you drink next Saturday, don't come to the department party."

Without being excused, I turned toward the door.

"And please know that student health services are always available to you," he called after me. "If you have to miss any class time or request an extension on your workshop story to get whatever help you need, I'd be happy to figure out a way to accommodate you, just like we did when you went to treatment."

I turned back. "We both know I'll do whatever I want, and you're not going to stop me. I still have the pictures and texts."

His lips pursed as though he'd just tasted something sour. He opened them just enough to say, "Your behavior undercuts any accusations you might make. I didn't do anything wrong. When I tell people how you set me up, who will believe you instead of me?"

"We can check, if you'd like."

His eyes crawled up my body and locked on my face. Was he staring at the scar? "Look at yourself. No one will believe you."

I calmly met his gaze. "People don't have to believe me," I said. "They'll believe the photos."

This time, he didn't call after me as I left.

CHAPTER

68

Then

Early evening, November 30, 2024

"No," I immediately said when I opened the door to Eli's knock. He was dressed for the department party in a neatly pressed dress shirt, jeans, and Italian shoes. I rarely saw him in Nikes and old jeans anymore because he only wanted to hang out with me on Saturdays. I hadn't seen him at all since the previous Saturday.

"I'm taking you to dinner, then the party."

"Incorrect," I said, my voice firm. "Duncan called me into his office and—" I stopped. Duncan's warning not to go to the party didn't really concern me. The real reason I didn't want to go was simpler: I was tired of being on the defensive around the other MFAers. "I'm staying in tonight."

"What did Duncan want to talk to you about?" Eli forced a casual tone, but there was an edge to it.

"It was nothing important," I lied, shrugging it off. "Some clerical error with my registration." I didn't want to tell Eli anything about my interactions with Duncan because then I might also have to tell him about the pictures I took. *It's better if he doesn't know what I'm capable of.*

"Then why are you worried about it?" Eli asked, irritation creeping into his voice. "Let's go to the party. You can't go out on a performance like last week. You were so drunk even I was surprised."

"You'll get over it."

"I have something for you," he said. He turned to the counter and shook out a couple of lines from a little vial.

It looked so pure, so fresh and innocent. Maybe it was just what I needed. Would it bring me clarity? Focus? There was only one way to find out. I stepped up to the counter and thought, *Here we go.*

CHAPTER

69

Now

THE WORDS HANG in the air between us: "I'm pregnant." Other than how his eyes widen, he hasn't moved.

Finally, he takes a deep breath. Without a word, he collects the pills, opens the cabin door, and throws them out into the snow. Then he comes back to where I'm lying in bed and unties the ropes around my wrists.

I say I have to pee. I go outside, gather up every last pill, dry them on my shirt, and hide them in my bra. Then I yank out my IUD just in case he thinks to check for the string. I break it into three pieces and hurl them in different directions.

CHAPTER

70

Now

December 25, 2024, northern Minnesota

THOUGH I'M THE one who's bipolar, Eli is all over the place mentally too. For Christmas, he builds me a snow family—a snowman, a snowwoman, and a baby bulging from her belly. When he leads me out to see it, he must think the tears in my eyes are tears of joy. He puts his arms around me and looks at me the way men look at their wives in Viagra commercials—like he's full of a sweet, tender lust for me. As though what we do when we put our bodies together is make love.

If he figures out I'm not pregnant, how will he look at me then?

CHAPTER

71

Now

January 1, 2025

He always wants to make love, and he never wants me to get up afterward. He keeps me on my back so he can continue touching me or sleep with his head on my chest. Is he turned on by the pregnancy?

"I was told it would be hard for me to have kids," he says.

I try to keep my face still. I try not to panic.

He takes one of my hands, guides it down his body. I know where we're going, even before he puts it on his scrotum. He's kept my hand from this place so many times before that I knew something was wrong.

"Do you feel that?" he asks, pressing my fingers against his skin. "The left one is just a little egg-shaped piece of plastic. I had testicular cancer when I was twenty-two. They froze some of my sperm, but due to . . . what happened on our last night in St. Louis, I'm not planning to ever go back to get it."

I need to get out of here before my flat stomach gives me away and/or I gain enough weight to menstruate. I need to get out of here before my head and heart explode from being jerked around by my emotions. My feelings for him are bouncing around inside me like a super ball. One moment I loathe him, and the next, he does something kind. I briefly feel cared for, wanted. Relieved.

The only definition of pleasure I've ever understood: the buildup and release of pressure. I tell myself that life is pain, and life without pain wouldn't be pleasurable at all because there would be no release.

But I wonder if what's really happening is that I'm rapid-cycling. Going from mania to depression and back again. I've never cycled this fast before. My thoughts race through my head until I feel like I've hit a wall. Then, mercilessly, they start up again.

CHAPTER 72

Now

January 15, 2025, northern Minnesota

I SHOULDN'T HAVE EATEN so much pudding. Eli opened the industrial-sized can and handed it to me, along with a spoon. I held it, my whole arm wrapped around it, and something came over me. All my dread about eating and gaining enough weight to get my period vanished. For a moment, I was possessed. I've made it all disappear in just the last few minutes. It's on my mouth and chin. A few dollops are quivering on my arm. At least that's a couple of ounces that I didn't eat.

I feel sick with fear, and also—quite literally—sick.

I stumble outside. I feel so nauseous I think I might just throw up naturally, but no. I have to use my fingers.

Later, in bed, Eli takes my hand. We've blown out the candles. It's too dark to make out much in the moonlight edging in around the blanket pieces draped over the windows. "I know what these marks are," he says. Of course he does. He was with Justine.

As he runs his fingertips over the teeth marks on the back of my hand, it starts to shake. He doesn't let go.

I try to yank my hand away, but his grip is too tight.

"I was afraid I was gaining weight," I say. It's best to tell the truth when I can.

"You need to gain weight. Twenty-eight to forty pounds."

We don't have a scale, but I was 125 pounds before my mania for him and vodka started to ruin my appetite and stop my periods altogether. I probably weigh 100 pounds now.

He squeezes my hand tighter. "You're done sticking your fingers down your throat."

"Stop! You're going to break my hand!"

"Only if I have to," he says before releasing it.

CHAPTER 73

Now

February 2025, northern Minnesota

I'm on my way to 125 pounds, the weight at which I'm certain I'll menstruate. My pants no longer flirt with my hipbones, no longer threaten to slip down to the floor. My breasts are getting bigger. When I raise my arms above my head, I can no longer glance down and count my ribs.

I can't keep gaining weight. But I also can't have teeth marks on the backs of my hands.

I try everything. Hiding food in my clothes and burying it in the snow. Just eating the food he gives me, then going outside to swish mouthfuls of snow until I've drunk enough water to easily throw up without using my hands. Pushing a spoon down my throat so I won't have teeth marks on my hands. But he keeps catching me.

I watch with trepidation as he roots through our supplies. He turns to me with a package in his hand.

I've been dreading this moment since telling him I was pregnant.

He hands me the pregnancy test. "Go pee on this."

I've prepared as well as I can. I've coated a can of Dr. Pepper with mud to disguise it and left it in the sun so it won't freeze. I wait for Eli to tend the fire, then I slip on my boots without lacing them up and go outside. I open the can and stick the strip in.

Another server at the restaurant I worked at told me this is how she checked to see if her boyfriend was in it for the long haul. She handed him the stick with the double line, and the next day he was gone.

"Did you ever tell him you weren't really pregnant?" I'd asked.

"No. Fuck him. He came up on Tinder a couple weeks later and I swiped left."

I don't know if Dr. Pepper will work for me like it did for her, but what do I have to lose?

"Turn around," Eli calls out to me.

Shit. He's seen me. At least his voice isn't right behind me. I set the Dr. Pepper down and turn around slowly, making sure to keep it hidden from his view. He's standing in the doorway of the cabin. He starts to take a step toward me, but I yell, "You know I have a shy bladder. I can't pee if you're too close." He stops, about ten feet from me.

I hope he can't smell the Dr. Pepper. I pee the smallest amount I can get away with on the strip and hold it out to him. He yanks it from my hand, takes it inside, and slams the door shut behind him. My heart is hammering in my chest as I crush the can beneath my boot and hurl it into the trees. If the test is negative, will he leave me out here?

A few moments later, he throws open the door and tells me to come in. I don't see the test. I futilely search his face, looking for some sign of the result. He makes chicken wild rice soup without a word to me. My throat is tight from fear, making it hard to swallow. But he's watching me, so I do.

* * *

The next day, I tell him I have intense and very specific cravings. I ask for Jell-O, pickles, saltines, and most importantly, strawberry pudding. These are foods that some people think of as high calorie. I hope Eli is one of those people. He doesn't take long to assess our supplies and leave with a list. It's unsettling how much power the imaginary child has over him.

The strawberry pudding will be his downfall.

CHAPTER

74

Then

Early evening, November 30, 2024, continued, graduate school, St. Louis

As soon as I snorted the first line of cocaine Eli laid out on my counter, my nerve endings felt exposed. My eyes strained wider. I was ready for anything. I even wanted to see what Eli was like coked-up, pushed to his edge.

I did another line, then said, "Now you."

"I'm won't be able to sleep with you for a while if I do this," he warned.

"You won't be able to sleep with me *forever* if you don't."

He shook out a couple more lines. I took a slug from one of the bottles on the counter, my eyes glued to him as he hoovered up a line and threw his head back. Watching him felt like some kind of deeper relapse.

How did I get here? How did I fall in love with this strange, elusive, beautiful man? Are we a hot mess or just an above-average train wreck?

After a moment, he looked at me and smiled like he wanted to be up to no good.

I was hoping we weren't really going to the party, but he said, "Get dressed." He pulled something from my closet. "Wear this."

A dress that was both too big and too flimsy, yet I hadn't given it away because it was really fucking expensive and maybe someday I'd take it to a tailor.

"No way. I'll look pregnant. Besides, it's so big it'll fall right off me."

He didn't seem to hear me. He dug around and pulled a coat from the back of the closet. He handed it to me along with the dress.

"I need a bump," I told him.

"As soon as you get dressed," he said.

I've never dressed so quickly.

He pulled out a switchblade and gave me a bump off the end. My heart thumped wildly in my chest. I went to the bedside table in my bedroom and slid my gun into my thigh holster.

"Let's go already," I told Eli as I walked back down the hall, through the living room, to the door. "I want to get this party over with."

CHAPTER

75

Then

When we arrived at the party, I avoided the bar. I had a flask in my purse, so I could drink discreetly. The cocaine would stop me from getting sloppy.

I was clear-headed. Invincible.

Justine must not have known how powerful I was. When I pushed past the spouses and minor alumni to make my way deeper into the room, she didn't try to block me from joining her circle of MFAers. Instead, she stepped back to let me in.

"Are you okay?" she asked loudly. "Why do you keep touching your nose? Do you have a cold?"

Ben's gaze flicked back and forth between Justine and me. Amelia looked at me with big eyes. She and Justine were both wearing little black dresses. I noticed Amelia had lost even more weight. That's why her eyes looked bigger. Justine's LBD flowed down her body with only the elegant interruptions of her breasts and slight hips, while Amelia's looked like it was hanging from a cliff with only a couple jagged rocks sticking out—her hipbones.

"No," I told Justine. "I don't have a cold. I feel like a fucking rock star."

"She looks like a hobo," I heard Amelia say as I pushed through the circle, moving deeper into the house. I wandered through the kitchen and down the hall, remembering the Saturday before. The bedrooms, the studies, the lives lived inside them, lives that I thought were so unlike my own. Perhaps they weren't so different. Surely everyone had moments when they wanted to float up over their mundane worries, and really see around them. They just didn't know how, or they were afraid. I could show them.

That's what I would dedicate my life to—helping people be truly free. *I will own one of these homes, make love in these beds, write critical essays at heavy desks surrounded by bookshelves. Children will run through these halls, screaming and laughing, making a mess. I'll welcome it all. No mess is too much for me. There is nothing I can't handle.*

I slipped into one of the bedrooms, pulled out my flask, and let the warmth flood my body. I needed to try the room on. I took off my coat, lay down on the bed, and closed my eyes. I thought happily of Eli waiting for me in one of the bedrooms at the party last Saturday.

As though I'd summoned him with my thoughts, the mattress shifted beneath me and I felt a hand on mine. Eli was lying beside me. He started moving his hand over my body under my dress. He touched my thigh.

"I thought you couldn't have sex if you did coke," I said.

"I just want to touch you however I can."

Sometimes I wasn't sure how he felt about me, but as his hands moved across my skin, I felt loved.

"This is nice," he said, taking his hand off me and standing up. "But we need to get out of here before someone comes looking for us."

I still loved it whenever he used the word "us."

"Let's stay here just a little bit longer," I said, "This is heaven."

"*Now.* I hear people coming down the hall."

"I don't care about them," I said, reaching for him.

Before I could touch him, he grabbed my wrist. "Get the fuck up," he said, yanking me out of bed.

"What the *hell?*" I yelled at him, my happiness quickly turning to anger. "What's *wrong* with you?" With my free hand, I smacked him hard across the face.

When he turned his head back to me, his eyes blazed with such fury that a strange sound escaped me. His anger was even more violent than mine. I recoiled. He pressed a hand over my mouth. "Shut up, or I swear, I'll hurt you."

I believed him. I'd wanted to push him to his edge, but now I saw that his edge was farther than I wanted to go with him. I could have pulled the gun, but I didn't. He was too close.

He made me walk in front of him, his grip tight on my arm. "Keep going, out to the truck," he said. I complied, and he let go of my arm.

Duncan saw me stumbling down the hall and frowned as his eyes moved over my face and body. I turned quickly, searching the hallway behind me for Eli. But he was gone. *Where did he go?* Should I go out as he had instructed, or cry for help, or run?

Justine appeared behind Duncan, her eyes hungrily raking over me. "Duncan, Hannah is hiding something beneath her dress. I told you how she conned people out of their money at Minneapolis gyms. She's a thief. She must be the one stealing from the alumni." Justine was speaking too loudly, as though she wasn't just speaking to us.

My thigh holster with the .22 was all that was beneath my dress. I wasn't even wearing a bra or underwear. "You're twisting what I told you, Justine," I said. "I sold people overpriced energy drinks. I'm not a thief."

Guests from the living room started to crowd the hall, peering at us with curiosity.

"Prove it," Justine said.

Did she really want me to take off my dress? "Go to hell," I told her.

"See?" Justine said to Duncan. "I *told* you she was hiding something. I'm not going to let her get away with it anymore."

She lunged at me. Her hands scratched my shoulders, and I heard my dress tear as she yanked at the fabric. I grabbed it, trying to keep it from coming off completely, but then I saw: there was nothing beneath it. Nothing at all. The thigh holster with the gun was gone. Was it in the jacket I'd forgotten in the bedroom?

I let Justine pull my dress all the way to the floor.

She stepped back, her gaze sweeping over my naked body and then up to my face, her eyes locking onto mine with a look of betrayal. *I* hadn't betrayed her. But someone had.

"What the hell is going on here?" the host called, rushing toward us, his face contorted in disbelief. I recognized him—he was an important alumnus who had been featured in the department newsletter. He was staring at my naked body in shock.

"This junkie stole from you and then handed it off to a man who fled," Justine said, stumbling back away from me. She'd lost her composure. She hardly resembled the refined, confident woman she'd pretended to be. And why had she called me a junkie? All she knew was that I drank.

Without taking my eyes off her, I pulled my dress back up.

"I'm calling the police," the host said.

"Please," Duncan said, "let's make sure there's a reason to call them first. You know the department doesn't need more attention right now. And besides, you'd need to tell the police what was missing if you were reporting a burglary. What exactly are you going to tell them?"

The crowd in the hallway pressed closer while the host searched the bedroom to see if anything was missing. Justine's eyes were still wide, big enough to hold both rage and surprise.

The host emerged a moment later, holding my coat. "The window screen is lying on the ground below the window, and I found this." He handed the coat to Duncan. "Turn it upside down," he said. When Duncan hesitated, he said, "Do it."

I was afraid I might have put my gun in a pocket. "No," I cried as Duncan flipped it over. I was about to say, "There's a gun in there," but I bit my lip when only a pearl necklace and earrings fell out. The crowd gasped and started murmuring. Duncan dropped the coat and frantically gathered the jewelry up. "Don't bother," the alumnus said. "The real jewelry is already gone. This is counterfeit—planted here after the real jewelry disappeared last time we hosted."

"This won't happen again," Duncan said. "I'll make sure of it."

The alumnus shook his head. "My wife and I aren't hosting again. There's something wrong in your department, Duncan. You need to deal with the responsible parties," his eyes flicked toward me. "Before the department's reputation gets dragged through the mud."

"Don't let her get away with anything," Justine cried, her voice a mix of fury and frustration. "She's not just a thief—she has a gun."

How did Justine know I had a gun?

Justine fell upon the coat and ripped the lining. She swore when she didn't find anything. She stood up and flung the coat against the wall.

The alumnus stumbled back. "Somebody call the police," he yelled.

Justine dashed down the hall, parting the crowd like Moses parting the Red Sea. Soon I heard the heavy front door creak open. I hurried to the living room, ignoring someone calling after me, "Young lady, this will be much worse for you if you flee the scene of a crime."

Justine hadn't bothered to close the door behind her, and Amelia rushed after her.

I didn't hesitate. The energy had spilled out into the night, and it carried me along with it. I needed to see her.

I started running.

CHAPTER

76

Now

April 30, 2025, northern Minnesota

I'M AWAKE WHEN the sun starts to peek over the horizon. For over two months, I've been waiting for it to warm up enough to make my escape. I have a good feeling about today.

I crawl out of bed and step outside. It's cold, but neither my breath nor my pee steams. The sky is blue, the sun bright enough that I cast a shadow. The world is finally warm enough to flee into.

When I reenter the cabin, Eli is sitting up in bed, staring at me. His brows are drawn so close together that there's hardly any space between them.

"Give me your clothes," he says.

I just stare at him, waiting for him to take back his words. But he doesn't. He waits.

"Why?" I ask.

"To keep you from getting any ideas about running away."

How does he know that's exactly what I'm thinking of? He stands up and starts walking toward me.

"Okay," I say. I slowly unbutton the flannel, to give him time to change his mind. But I don't take off my long underwear top slowly; I rip it off, so there's only an instant when I can't see him.

When I've stripped down, he looks at me—at my stomach, mostly. Then he grabs my clothes and throws them into the woodstove. I lunge forward, trying to take them out, but Eli grabs me and holds me tight. I watch the clothes burn to ash, the smoke curling up into the air.

I hate him. I want to be as far from him as possible. Clothes or not, I have to leave today. It's time for him to eat the Halcion I've saved for him.

He hasn't complained about any of the food combos I've given him: pudding with dried fruit, cream of mushroom soup with parmesan and croutons, and peanut butter and jelly sandwiches with fruit rollups instead of jelly.

So I'm confident he's going to eat a bowl of strawberry pudding with granola. But when I hold it out to him, he just looks at it.

"I'm not sure I'm secure enough in my masculinity to eat something this purple. What is it?"

There's a spoon in the bowl, which he nudges to one side and then the other, studying the pudding. I'm shivering so hard that the spoon clanks against the side of the bowl.

"Pudding with granola," I tell him, and then point to my own bowl. It's sitting on the bed, empty but for a few smears of purple. "It's like strawberry shortcake, but with more texture."

"Texture? That's how you sold me on the crunchy peanut butter with pickles, relish, and mayo."

"And you liked it."

"'Liked' is a strong word. But close enough." When he smiles at me, little lights flicker in his eyes. He's relieved. He thinks I've forgiven him for burning my clothes, even as I stand here naked and shivering in front of him. I hand him the bowl.

This time he takes it. He puts a spoonful in his mouth. "Not bad," he says, "though I'm afraid eating this is going to turn me into a little girl."

I briefly picture him as a little girl. He's just as terrifying in that form as he is now. There's something besides just his wiry strength that makes him intimidating.

He doesn't eat all of it, but he eats enough. We never waste food, so I take the bowl and set it on the closest thing we have to a table now that we've used the actual table for firewood, one of the large boxes he uses to transport food from the truck to the cabin.

He needs to be distracted while the Halcion kicks in so he doesn't make himself throw up in time. I lie on the bed. "I forgive you for burning my clothes," I lie. "Come hold me."

When he comes to me, I close my eyes and turn my head away so he doesn't kiss me. I don't want to be drugged by whatever Halcion might be on his lips. I touch his hair, his ear, his cheek, the perfect bone pressing up out of his skin into my palm. This is the last time we'll hold each other.

I hold him until he starts to grow heavy. Then I push his body off mine and move a safe distance away.

"Where are you going?" he asks. His words are slow and they stick together.

"Wherever I please."

He stares me, confused.

"I'm leaving," I say. It feels strange to say when I'm naked.

"You can't."

"Yes, I can. It's you who isn't going anywhere. I've given you the Halcion you were going to give me before I told you I was pregnant."

It's like I'm watching him over a bad internet connection; he shakes his head in stops and starts as though he's in a movie that isn't loading properly. "I picked the wrong one of you," he says.

"Who are you talking about?" I ask, even though I know: Justine.

He doesn't answer.

"I need to get our baby to safety." I use the word 'her' because he wants a girl: "I need to give birth to her in a hospital. I need the distributor cap."

He laughs, then coughs, a dry, hacking fit that shakes him. It won't be long until he has cotton mouth and can hardly speak or swallow.

When his coughing subsides, I step closer. "Tell me where the distributor cap is. If you don't, I'll take your clothes and leave you here for the cops. Which option do you choose?"

"Those weren't all the options." He says it so clearly I'm afraid the Halcion won't knock him out. He stands.

I back all the way across the room, until I feel the door behind me.

"I could kill you," he says, "or I could kill myself, or I could kill both of us. All our problems solved."

"What about our baby?"

"I'll cut her out."

He suddenly crumples to the floor. His left leg is spasming. I hurry to the bed to grab a blanket to wrap around myself. I tie it over my left shoulder so I'm not naked anymore. Then, I go to stand over him, one foot beside his hip and the other pressing against his trembling thigh.

"Where's the money?" I ask.

"The floorboard," he says, pointing to one next to him. But none of the floorboards around him looks loose. If there's money here, it's somewhere else.

I go back to his side of the bed and drop to my hands and knees. As I test the floorboards beneath the bed, he grabs my foot.

I kick him off and slide under the bed, pulling the backpack in after me. He's too disoriented to follow. I scrape my knee on something—the corner of a floorboard sticking up. I grab the fork from my backpack and wedge it under the protruding board. Below, I find a bag with $79 and my purse. Is this all the money he has?

I pull myself along the floor and out from under the other side of the bed.

I open my purse. No phone. Dammit. My purse is empty, except for my license and my pills. My pills! Did Eli steal them so I couldn't take them? Why did he keep them?

I can't believe how many months I've gone without medication. How long I've gone without knowing what my next thought would be. Tears sting my eyes. I break one of the pills in half and swallow it dry.

I pull my license out. The numbers are familiar: Height 5-2, Weight 125. DONOR. My signature is familiar, too. But the woman in the photo is someone else entirely. All this time without a mirror, I'd forgotten what I really looked like. I'd had a picture of myself in my head: an okay-looking girl with good cheekbones. My license photo always embarrassed me. I'd hated handing it to bouncers and servers.

But if I still look like the woman in the photo, I'll consider myself lucky. Round cheeks, straight white teeth, a healthy flush. Not the face of a killer. Not even the face of a woman who would tell a guy she was pregnant and then leave him delirious on the floor.

I know I don't look like her anymore, though. I don't have any cover-up for the scar on my cheek. Now I really feel naked. But my true vulnerability is the notebook. I look under the mattress for it, but it's not there.

"Where is my notebook?" I ask Eli.

He's still on the floor, his leg shaking violently. "Your journal?" he asks. Though his body is faltering, his voice is steady. "I don't remember."

I'm not going to waste time arguing with him again about whether it's a journal or a notebook.

"I know your name isn't Eli," I say. "Because you don't answer to it at night."

"It's Alex," he says. "Alex Bazin."

"Was it you who drove my car onto the campus lawn?"

"No.

"Who was it?"

"I don't know."

"But you did other things to me before bringing me here."

"I did them for Justine. She wanted to get you kicked out of Wash U. She told me you were bipolar. Said we could push you over the edge, get you to crack. But even after we did, Duncan didn't get rid of you."

I was right not to show the pictures I took with Duncan's phone to the dean. I'd gotten a lot of leverage out of those pictures.

"Was it your idea or Justine's to steal from the alumni and blame it on me?"

"Hers. She didn't care about the stuff, she just wanted to ruin you. She sent in an anonymous tip, saying you were stealing. But Duncan didn't kick you out of the program, so she decided you needed to be caught. With a gun. I was supposed to plant something from the alumnus's house in your pockets. I did, but I also took the gun off you." He reaches for me, and I see that he's crying. "Please, Hannah, don't leave. I love you."

His declaration of love disgusts me after all he's done to me. I ignore his outstretched hand.

"Later that night, she wanted me to kill you," he says. "That's the final thing she wanted me to do to you."

"Maybe you weren't willing to kill me then, but you were going to kill me here in this cabin if I didn't do whatever you wanted."

"After you told me you were pregnant, I was happier than I've ever been in my whole my life. But then I found your IUD in bloody pieces in the snow." His voice fills with rage. "I couldn't believe you'd think I was such an idiot or that you'd be such a selfish bitch. But I didn't give up. I gave you the pregnancy test, let you think you'd passed, and kept trying."

He struggles for breath. His eyes are losing focus. The intensity with which he always looked at me, like he might ravage me and/or look away and never look back, had held me captive. But now, he's not looking at me anymore. And even if he were, I wouldn't let his eyes keep me here. I'm free.

I'd planned to take his clothes and leave him as naked as he'd made me. But trying to get his clothes off him is too dangerous. Instead, I grab his flannel jacket off the door handle and pull it on.

"Goodbye, Alex," I say. Then I leave him there.

CHAPTER 77

Now

I EXIT THE CABIN and enter the world with nothing but a backpack. No, I take that back. I can't afford to be negative. I do the cognitive behavioral therapy exercise my therapist taught me: I reframe the situation. I'm out in the world with a backpack and all I have to offer.

Unfortunately, I can't think of anything I have to offer except my body. I hope someone doesn't take advantage of me. It's hard not to look desperate when you're wearing a blanket as a dress, but hopefully, I don't look quite as desperate as I actually am. My Active Bitch Face and the fork I took are my only defenses.

It's hard to believe I haven't checked Facebook, Instagram, or TikTok in four and a half months. No calls, no texts, no cyberstalking. In some ways, I'm freer than I've been in a very long time. Free of possessions, free of contacts. No one but Alex knows anything about me right now.

Who do I want to be?

I have plenty of time to figure it out before I reach the road. I'm making my way through pine trees, their branches reaching out for me as I pass. At first, I don't notice the moisture they leave behind. But soon it builds up, and Alex's flannel becomes wet and heavy.

Before long, I'm only dry where the backpack covers me. I'm exerting myself enough to stay warm, but I know that once I reach the road, I'll start to feel the cold. I'm afraid the wet flannel will make me look tossed-away, discarded. I don't want anyone to think they can do whatever they want with me.

I have to pretend I'm someone else, project an attitude that says: *I could be wearing Dolce and Gabbana, but instead, I turned a blanket into a dress because I wanted to be earthier. I'm taking the Bigfoot out of my carbon footprint.*

I always rolled my eyes at the upper-middle-class kids who hid their nice clothes beneath flannel jackets and begged because it was cool. But now, it's better to look like them than what I am: a woman very much alone in the world.

Finally, Alex's truck comes into view. The magnetized key box isn't underneath, and the doors are locked.

Goodbye, truck. You've disappointed me for the last time.

I walk past it, grateful for the dirt road. It's wide enough that I can avoid the wet pine limbs. The sun is still high in the sky. I continue my cognitive behavioral approach by telling myself nature has rolled out the red carpet for me. The future beckons: *come this way. Good things lie ahead.*

I stay positive for a good mile or so. That's when I hear an engine in the distance, speeding past on a paved road up ahead.

My heart starts banging hard in my chest. I haven't seen a human being besides Alex in four and a half months. I can't remember what to say. It's hard to think of anything over the merciless thumping of my heart.

My backpack slips down my spine and spanks me with each step. I tighten the straps, but they keep coming loose.

I reach the road just as clouds start passing beneath the sun. They're moving in from the northwest. I wish the wind blew from the south instead, sending up warm air. At least the wind is mostly at my back as I walk along the road.

But where are the cars?

Finally, as the daylight fades, I see headlights. I stick out my thumb.

CHAPTER

78

Now

I VOW THAT I won't get into the vehicle if the driver is drunk, high, or if his gaze drops beneath my chin when I ask for a ride to the Twin Cities.

I'm so blinded by the truck's headlights that I can't see inside the cab. I have no idea if the driver has seen me. But then the brakes screech.

I see it's a truck hauling lumber. I run to where he's stopped and hoist myself onto the metal step. I look into the window he's just rolled down. I like that there are two seats, not just one long bench seat. I like that there's a thermos in the cup holder and it smells like coffee, not Rock Star or some other barely legal stimulant. What I don't like is the classical music coming from the speakers. More than a few fictional psychopaths have been portrayed as fans of classical music. I think of Hannibal Lecter chewing a prison guard's face off to one of Bach's arias. But the trucker doesn't look like a psychopath. He looks like a weathered Santa Claus.

I hope he doesn't recognize me from the news story about how I'm "missing." I wonder if there's been another report about me being a suspect in Justine's murder. But the trucker doesn't show any signs that he recognizes me. I'm breathing heavily, but I try to hide it as I say, "I'm trying to get to the Twin Cities."

He nods and says, "Hop in."

I jump back off the step to open the door. I heave the backpack in and then step up into the cab.

"Ron," the man says.

I pull a name out of nowhere. "Gina," I reply. Immediately, I remember a coworker telling me that 'Gina' is short for 'Vagina' and regret my choice. At least I won't forget it.

"I've gotta get this load of lumber to The Cities by midnight," he says, "and I've got a few stops to make along the way."

I guesstimate it's about 6:00 PM. In seven hours, I'll know if I'm going to be able to blend back into the real world. I need to look on the internet to see if I'm wanted for murder. I haven't decided whether I'll go on the run or turn myself in.

It's been a long time since I traveled on anything except my feet, and as the truck picks up speed, I have to sit on my hands to keep from reaching for the "oh shit" handle to steady myself.

I assume Ron is lonely, and that's why he picked me up, so I wait for him to start a conversation. It's only a couple miles before he asks, "What were you doing up here, alone in the cold?"

I think about how I must look: dirty hair, grimy face, and chipped fingernails, wearing a blanket dress and a man's flannel jacket. "I thought it would be fun to hitchhike around for a while," I say, "try to make it on my own, without a bunch of modern conveniences."

He asks me how long I've been trying to make it on my own.

"A while." To end the conversation, I add, "I'm going to meditate now."

I keep an eye out for Alex's truck. After a few minutes, a vehicle approaches from behind. Ron keeps an eye on it in the rearview mirror, but then it slips into our rear blind spot. I have to resist the urge to peek to see if it's Alex; if it's him, I need to stay hidden. It's irrational to think that, after everything, he somehow made it to his truck and is now driving soberly within the lines, following us. But after spending four and a half months unable to escape him, it seems impossible that I'm free.

The car's engine is loud enough to hear over the noise of the semi. When the car gets into the oncoming traffic lane and passes us, Ron breathes a sigh of relief. "Not the 5-0," he says, "just some dumb kid."

As we approach I-35, other vehicles come into view. A strange feeling washes over me. After a moment, I realize it's shyness. This is the first time in months I've been around so many people.

Traffic increases by about 5000 percent when we hit Duluth, and the speed limit drops to 45 mph. Ron grabs the CB radio and complains about the "Turtle Race." It's mostly college students in a mix of cars from beaters to SUVs, but there are also other semis on the road. I wish Ron weren't on the CB with other truckers. They're talking about cops and bear bait (an erratic driver in the middle of a very important text), but at any second, he could mention me. Someone might recognize me from the news, and that would be the end of my new freedom.

CHAPTER

79

Now

"WE'RE GOING TO stop ahead," Ron says. It's my favorite rest area in Duluth, high enough to overlook the bridge to Superior, Wisconsin. On a cloudless day, you can see the curvature of the earth. But it's an odd place for a truck with a load; we'll have to climb at least fifty feet to reach the top. I was hoping we'd stop at a gas station instead, so I could grab some 3.2 beer. I'd have to show my license, but I could put my thumb over the name since the clerk probably wouldn't care about anything except my birthdate.

"I'm part of Eighteen Wheel Angels," Ron explains, "truckers who post missing persons flyers at rest stops and businesses."

Shit.

"Who's missing?" I ask.

Two thousand people go missing every day. That's eight hundred and fifty thousand a year. I'm spreading the word about Jessica Foster."

The "J" sound sends my heart lurching. Damn Justine, still tormenting me.

"What do you think the chances of finding her are?" I ask.

"I've been doing this over a decade. I've put up posters of over two hundred people, and not one has been found. Not alive."

"Then why do you continue?"

"Because my daughter was on the first poster I put up."

"I'm sorry."

"Yep," he says, "everybody is. Everybody except the man who . . ." He doesn't finish, which I'm grateful for.

"Does your family know where you are?" he asks. "Or are they putting up 'Missing' posters of you somewhere?"

"I'm not missing. I left."

"My daughter, too. She left, and someone got a hold of her and didn't let her leave again."

Is he a psychopath? Is he taking me to the rest area to kill me? "Well, I'm with you. Am I safe?"

"Yes. You can put away the knife you're hiding beside your right leg."

"It's not a knife. It's a fork."

He doesn't look very worried, and he doesn't look like a psychopath.

I tuck the fork into my backpack. "Why did you pick me up?" I ask.

"I was afraid of who might pick you up if I didn't."

The weight of the lumber doesn't stop us from climbing the incline to the rest area. We put up the poster in the service building, on the bulletin board between the bathrooms. Jessica Foster, forty-two years old. It's so windy that it's impossible to talk until we climb back up into the cab and close our doors, shutting out the howling outside. I turn to him. "Do people really care? People who haven't lost someone?"

"It's too late for me to answer that question. It's been over a decade since I was someone who hadn't lost anyone."

I wonder what he looked like before he lost his daughter. Now his skin looks like it was pulled too tight and then released. Wind, sun, or both have narrowed his eyes and set them deep in his face. "I'm sorry," I say.

"Don't be sorry," he says. "Tell me what happened to you."

"I can't. I'm afraid I'll get in trouble."

"I don't care what your real name is or what you've had to do. I just want to make sure you're okay and that no one else is in danger."

"I may have just killed a man." The words are shocking to my own ears, but Ron doesn't look surprised or fearful. I continue, "I left him drugged in a cabin a couple miles from the highway."

"What did he do to you?" Ron asks.

I tell him everything.

When I finish, Ron has tears in his eyes. He says, "I'm glad you got away. I can't let Alex hurt anyone else." He reaches for his CB radio. "I'm going to call it in."

"No! Please wait until after you drop me off. I need to take care of a couple of things before I talk to the police."

For a moment, his fingers hover over the CB radio. Then he says, "Okay," and puts his hand back on the steering wheel. He looks over at me and tilts his head slightly. "But once I drop you off, I'm not waiting another second."

* * *

Ron takes me as far as he can, then I walk the rest of the way. I stop outside a bar, listening to the noise of drunks and inhaling the smell of beer. A man leans out the door and asks if he can buy me a drink. I'd like a drink, but something about him scares me. I start walking again, faster this time, and I don't stop until I'm all the way to Luke's apartment.

CHAPTER 80

Now

April 30, 2025, Minneapolis

When I knock on Luke's door at 2:00 AM, he doesn't answer right away. I'm afraid he's not alone. My heart aches as the seconds stretch on. My head starts to throb.

I have no money and no place else to go.

Over the throbbing in my head, I hear footsteps. I know he always checks the peephole, so I smooth my windblown hair down and step back. I don't want to look freakishly distorted. I need to appear as normal as possible.

The door opens, and suddenly, there he is. Luke, my knight in shining armor. I notice he's wearing boxers. Only boxers. Maybe by 2:00 AM, he's anyone's knight.

Is waiting tables and bartending what makes his shoulders swell so shamelessly?

"Hannah," he says incredulously. Then, he remembers he's a laid-back guy, and adds, "Nice outfit."

"You too." He's usually clean-shaven, but now a five o'clock shadow darkens his jaw. "Are you alone?"

He scrunches his brow, pretending to think, then smiles. "Not anymore. Welcome back." Even in whatever this situation is, he's exactly as I remember: playful, happy. So unlike Alex. Except he doesn't hug me, and I sense he wants to keep some distance between us.

"Why didn't you bring anyone home tonight?" I ask.

"I wanted to get some sleep."

"Sorry," I say.

"I'm not as much of a man whore as you seem to think." He steps back and gestures for me to come in. "Let me get you some tea."

I sit down at the kitchen table. Everything feels surreal—the past few months with Alex, escaping, and how much life has changed since December. But I don't have the bandwidth to worry about anything other than finding out what happened the night of the party and whether I killed Justine.

When the tea's ready, Luke places it on the table instead of handing it to me. Rather than sitting down, he leans back against the counter.

"Where have you been, Hannah? Why haven't I heard from you?"

"I'll tell you if you'll tell me what I've done."

I brace myself to hear about how I shot Justine. But instead, Luke says, "You disappeared. An anonymous account tagged you in a video of a girl getting shot a few blocks from a party you went to. At least, the caption said it was a few blocks from the party. I was worried it was you who'd been shot."

"What exactly is in the video?"

"It's not great quality. All anyone can say for sure is that the woman who got shot fell to the ground."

"Who was the woman?"

"I have no idea. Her body was never found."

I can't help thinking of the Taylor Swift song, *No Body, No Crime.*

"Is the woman . . . dead?" I ask.

"I don't know. I'm just glad you're alive."

"I'm alive and well. I haven't had a drink in a hundred and eleven days."

He looks at me intensely, like he's going to prod me a little harder, but then he takes a deep breath and tries to keep his tone casual. "I'm glad to hear it. I went dry for a little while myself. I see too many depressing drunks when the bar opens and even more when it closes."

"You were never a sad or angry drunk. You don't mess everything up like I do."

"Nope, I don't," he says. "I go with the flow. You're always fighting something. You're the type who makes the worst drunk."

"Thanks for your opinion."

"I'm a bartender. People usually want my opinion. And I'm just trying to reinforce your decision not to drink."

I stand up and bring my empty teacup to the sink to wash it. "Can I use your internet?" I ask. "I haven't watched television or been online since I left St. Louis."

He hesitates, rubs the back of his neck and looks away for a moment before answering. "If you log into your accounts here, I'm afraid I'll have the police at my door. You need to let them know you're alive and well, ASAP. To them you're still 'missing.'"

I feel tears in my eyes.

He steps forward and wraps his arms around me. I put my head in the crook of his neck. This is where I've longed to be for the last four and a half months.

I don't smell all the products I used to when I hugged him: his aftershave, soap, and deodorant. Instead, I smell his skin, which is slightly musky and makes me feel safe. I can feel the warmth of his bare chest against my body.

Suddenly, I feel guilty. Even though I hate Alex, it still hasn't fully sunk in with my body that we're not together. I release Luke and step back. "Will you put on a shirt so this isn't so awkward?" I ask.

A pained look comes over his face. "Oh, is that why it's awkward?" he asks.

"What do you mean?"

"Do you remember promising to call me once a week when you moved to St. Louis?"

I think back. I'd been so focused on the future that I hadn't been paying much attention to the present, except preparing for graduate school. "No."

"After you moved to St. Louis, the only times I heard from you were when you had a picture you wanted someone to see. And then, when I texted back, you hit the "haha" and just let the conversation drop."

I wish I would have called him. If I'd taken the time to run things past Luke, maybe I wouldn't have ended up stranded in a cabin with Alex, fearing for my life.

"I was a mess in St. Louis. I don't even know how to explain it."

"You pretty much ghosted me even before you moved there. Do you know I called you four times before you left? The two times you answered, you said you didn't have time to hang out. When I saw you at work, you were like one of the zombies from *The Walking Dead*—the latest season, when they were all falling apart. You were so fucked up, and it killed me that I couldn't do anything. You wouldn't let me."

Luke never seemed like the worrying type. I'm surprised by the emotion in his voice.

"You were gone before you were gone," he continues. "What got into you? It seemed like you just stopped giving a fuck about everything around you, including me."

"I'm sorry. You're the last person I should've taken for granted."

"No, *you're* the last person you should take for granted. I deal with people on their way down in life all the time. They're losing their houses, their families, their health. But you? You frustrate me like no one else. Nothing but you is holding you back."

"I won't do anything to worry you again."

"Ah, another promise," he says.

"One I'll keep this time."

"I've been so angry at you, Hannah. You want to be close, then you disappear. Now you want to be close again, but then you pull back."

I don't tell him about Alex—how, despite everything Alex did to me, and how I left him drugged and alone, I still feel like I'm cheating on him. I just say, "I feel guilty about touching you so much when we're just friends. Especially since you're not wearing a shirt."

"I wasn't expecting company."

"I know I've been strange. I'll get myself together and be a better friend."

"Talk is cheap, Hannah, and the last few months have been brutal for me."

I know there's nothing I can say that will help. I just want to hold him again. "Please just go put a shirt on so I can hug you."

He smiles, like the Luke I've known—the laid-back guy who's never serious for more than a couple minutes. "Sure. Any shirt preference?"

"Let's see the options."

He wanders into his bedroom. I follow as far as the hallway and watch as he sifts through his closet. I want to ask him some questions while he's not looking at me. I don't want him to see how uncertain I am about what happened on November 30—and my involvement in it.

"Did the police investigate the gunshots?"

He shrugs. "They probably looked into them as part of the missing persons cases. But all I know is what I read online. Neighbors said they heard five gunshots, though only four bullets were recovered."

"Do they know what kind?"

"I'm sure the police do, but they don't make that information public. Why are you so curious?"

"Wouldn't you be?" I ask.

He doesn't answer. He pulls on a "Back By Popular Demand" shirt and turns to me. "Better?" he asks.

When we hug, I feel Luke's warmth and kindness envelop me, briefly sheltering me from whatever lies ahead. I never want to let go, but I have to keep my head on straight. I have things to do. I pull back and ask, "Where's your laptop?"

"I'll get it, but first, I need you to promise not to log into any sites."

"You're not as laid-back as you pretend to be."

"I'm too cute for prison."

"Can I borrow some money?" I ask. "Cash to get a phone and a ticket home?"

"Cash in exchange for a promise not to go to any site you have to log into," he counters.

Though I wonder what's in my bank account, how many thousands of emails I have, and what's happening on Instagram, Facebook, and TikTok, I suppose that's wise. "Also, a hot breakfast," I say.

He smiles. "I like a woman who knows what she wants."

This is true. Most women want him, and regardless of what he says, he likes most of them. Women find Alex attractive, too, but they don't approach him as openly as I've seen women approach Luke.

Suddenly it occurs to me that maybe I should be thinking of Alex in the past tense. It feels surreal that I don't know if he's alive or dead.

"What's wrong, Hannah? Your face is like one of those Doppler radar maps. Shit's blowing in and out faster than I can track it."

I shake my head. I don't want to talk about Alex.

"What are you thinking about?"

"Isn't it the woman who's supposed to ask that question?"

He doesn't even smile. "Are you thinking about the guy who also went missing from the party the night there were shots?" he asks.

"What?" When he starts to repeat himself, I interrupt. "Why didn't you mention him before?"

"Why didn't *you?* Did this guy hurt you?"

"It's complicated. He was," I search for the right word, one that's truthful but not alarming, "possessive."

"My years as a bartender have taught me that a possessive man rarely goes away willingly."

A handful of Halcion is probably just about as good as being willing.

"Why don't I make you breakfast, and then we'll go to the police station?" he says.

"Is there a reward for me or something?" I ask.

"You can file for a restraining order."

"I don't need a restraining order. The guy is over me."

"If you believe that, then why are you so jumpy?" he asks.

"*I'm* the danger I'm in. It's my own mind I need a restraining order against."

"Is this some sort of Stephen King novel where this guy is actually you? Your dark half?"

"There isn't a light half."

"For fuck's sake, Hannah. Can you drop the act?"

"That's one of the nice things about you. You seem pretty street-smart, but you look at me and see a woman who's incapable of doing anything really wrong."

As he puts his arms around me again, I don't know whether I'm laughing or crying.

* * *

A couple minutes later, I'm sitting at his computer in shock. I Googled my name and November 30. Now I'm on a "Mysterious Disappearances" page that's telling me something I don't believe: *Amelia* is missing. Not Justine. Justine told the police she ran away when I approached Amelia.

What the hell is going on?

Justine's ghost in the cabin felt so real.

The "Mysterious Disappearances" site also tells me what I already know: I went missing, along with a five foot eleven Caucasian male with dark hair and dark eyes.

I'm going back to St. Louis to figure out what happened the night of November 30. I know it's a risk; the police will want to question me about Amelia's disappearance. But I can't go on with my life not knowing if I'm a murderer.

When I'm done looking online, I tell Luke, "If you don't mind another imposition, I could really use a shower."

"A cold shower, I hope. I know you're not completely immune to my charms." He winks and goes to get me a towel.

* * *

Though the sun hasn't risen, when I get out of the shower, Luke makes me a cheese and spinach omelet and some veggie sausages. I'm certain he got the veggie sausages for a woman, or perhaps multiple women. I've seen him eat too much bacon, sausage, and pepperoni to believe he buys a meat substitute for himself.

I'm wearing a robe he pulled out of the closet for me. I try not to wonder how many other women have worn it.

When I'm done, he goes into the bedroom and comes out with a wad of cash. It doesn't look like much, but when he hands it to me, I see it's all hundreds.

"And you once said I was too balanced to fall for," he says. "Now you have no excuse not to call me."

"Thank you, Luke. I'll pay you back as soon as I can."

I never thought I'd want to wear a bra again, but I feel self-conscious walking around without one. I saw one on the neighbor's clothesline out the bathroom window.

"Can you do me one more favor?"

When he comes back inside and hands me the bra, I'm disappointed. It looks too big. But surprisingly, it's actually a little small.

Luke drives me to the Greyhound station. I sit paralyzed in his car for a few breaths, unwilling to get out. The buses rumble, belching exhaust into the air, their fumes mixing with the stench of unwashed bodies

I feel both crowded and lonely at the same time. If I didn't need to find out what happened the night of November 30, I'd tell Luke to turn around and take me home with him.

After a moment, we get out of the car and hug goodbye. It's not foreplay if you're in public, so I hold onto him for a good fifteen seconds.

Then, once again, I'm on my own. As the bus lurches to life, I feel a strange mixture of anxiety and relief.

CHAPTER

81

Now

Afternoon, April 30, 2025, St. Louis

MY CAR IS in it's spot out back. If the police have gone through it, they were at least kind enough not to trash it in the process. Thanks to my out-of-state plates, my renewal tabs haven't been stolen, and thanks to luck, the magnetized key box is still underneath. Best of all, I don't find the gun.

I pull my apartment key out of the magnetized box and return the box to its spot under the car. I dust myself off and turn to my building. Time to check my apartment.

Someone is illegally parked against the stairs leading to the back entrance. I walk around to the front door. My building looks different—bigger somehow. I feel like a child staring up at a castle. The cabin is a hovel in comparison.

Everything is sharper, brighter than I remember: the bricks, the numbers on the apartment doors, even the stairs to my apartment. Stairs! There was only one at the cabin, and it wasn't really a stair—it was more of a stoop. These stairs seem like such a brilliant invention that my heart lifts a little with each step. Because of stairs, no one is stuck on the ground. Maybe the world isn't as harsh as it seems. Maybe everything will be okay.

I don't come across anyone in the hall, but I hear people in their apartments—blaring televisions, doors opening and closing, and a toilet flushing.

My door looks different. Not only different from what I remember, but different from all the other doors. And not just because of the eviction notice, which I tear off and crumple into a ball without a second glance, but because it's darker and newer than the other doors. Yet my key fits in the lock.

I push open the door to my apartment.

Oh my god.

The urn is sitting in the middle of the wood floor, staring up at me expectantly.

What the hell? Who put that here? Is the gun here too?

My drawers have been rifled through, so maybe the police have confiscated the gun. *Did Eli and I stop back here before fleeing to Minnesota?*

I can't focus on the gun now. I have to get rid of the urn.

I find Leroy's business card. When he answers his phone, I tell him it's "little sister."

"I have a job offer for you," I say. "Can you meet me at my building?"

I put on gloves and grab a garbage bag. "I'm sorry, Bill," I say as I lower the urn containing William Gass's ashes into the bag. I don a hat and oversized, Justine-esque sunglasses, then wait outside my building for Leroy. When I spot him approaching, his cane tapping back and forth on the sidewalk in front of him, I step into his path.

"Is that you, Hannah?" he asks.

He's always called me "little sister" before. "How do you know my name?" I ask.

"The whole world knows your name," he replies.

"Is there a reward for information about me?" I ask.

"Sure enough," he says. "One thousand dollars for information leading to your disappearance. I plan on collecting it after we conduct whatever business you have for me."

"Fair enough," I say. "I need you to deliver something for me."

"I don't know. Something in your tone is telling me I might regret it."

"Don't worry. It's just a vase—no real value, just sentimental. I'll give you a hundred dollars."

"Two hundred. I've got to hire a subcontractor, after all."

"Deal. I need your subcontractor to drop this bag with the vase on the front doorstep of a house nearby."

I hold the bag with the urn in it out to Leroy. He takes it with one hand and holds out the other hand. "The money," he says.

I put the bills in his palm.

He laughs, a low, rumbling chuckle. "That's two hundred dollars? I won't believe it unless I can feel two hundred bills. How do I know I didn't just feel two ones?"

"Because I've never done you wrong."

"I haven't given you the chance." He smiles. "But I've always liked you. I won't do you wrong either, Hannah. I've got you."

I tell him the address and ask him to repeat it back to me. "I don't need to," he says. I believe him.

As I return to my building and make my way down the hall toward my apartment, I hear a door creak open. A gasp follows. A woman is staring at me in shock. She doesn't say anything—just pulls out her phone. Before she can snap a picture, I rush into my apartment and slam the door behind me.

With the urn gone, everything in my apartment is normal, except now it also looks like heaven. A couch, a refrigerator, a bathroom. Is this my apartment or a luxury suite? I want to wrap my arms around my unmade bed and hug it. I can hardly believe I have my *own* bed in my own cozy and (most importantly) *warm* apartment.

When I open the drawers in my bedroom, I see that the clothes have been rifled through. I go back out to the counter, and that's when I see the note. My first thought is that it's from Alex, that somehow he's watching me right now. My heart feels wired to explode. I know I can't let myself read the note until I dump out all the alcohol. I don't want an excuse to drink.

After the last of the vodka circles the drain and disappears, I turn back to the note.

Dear Ms. Silver,

The police were here. Instead of contacting us to gain entry, they broke down the door. As you can see, we've replaced it. Please contact the rental office about your overdue rent. Because Washington University listed you as a missing person, we haven't been able to evict you, but if you're reading this note, you're no longer missing and your rent is overdue. Also, you need to call Sergeant Fullerton, who left his card. He wants to talk to you about the evening of November 30th.

Regards,

Alberta Jasper
Parkview Properties, Washington University

I uncrumple what I thought was an eviction notice and see that it's just another copy of the note to call Parkview Properties. I throw it in the trash and then look at the officer's card: *St. Louis Metropolitan Police Department, Sergeant R.J. Fullerton, Detective, Criminal Investigations Unit.*

I have to figure out what I'm going to tell him.

I'll ask Lynette. She'll know what to do. I call her from the phone I got on the way home from the bus station.

CHAPTER

82

Now

"WHAT THE HELL have you gotten yourself into?" she asks. Her voice is the most beautiful sound I've heard in four and a half months. I tell her all about Amelia going missing and Alex keeping me in a cabin up north. I leave out dosing him with Halcion. I ask her what I should tell Sergeant Fullerton.

"The truth."

For a moment I'm speechless. I feel like she's just punched me in the face. If she weren't one of my only two friends in the world, I would hang up and call someone else.

"I don't know what the truth is."

"Find out."

"I tried."

"Try harder. Then write it down. I want to read the book. You'd be proud of me if you saw my bookshelf on Goodreads. I've been doing a lot of reading since you disappeared."

"Reading about what?"

"No, not about anything. I've just been reading. Stories. Novels."

I've noticed that she's more articulate than I remember. I blamed my memory.

"I read one of those Rabbit books by John Updike. I thought you weren't supposed to write long sentences, but I liked most of them. The character's a real ass, though, so none of the other three are going on my TBR list."

"You have a To Be Read list?"

"Yes. One on Goodreads and one on Library Thing. I thought maybe I could figure out where you went if I read some Updike."

She cared where I went. Should I say thank you? I'm afraid if I think about it too long, I'm going to wind up crying, so I quickly ask, "What did you read after that?"

"*Crime and Punishment*."

"Is that why you're telling me to be honest?"

"Nope. But I also read a book that says honesty is the only way to stay sober. Those who aren't honest with themselves have as much chance of staying sober as a camel has of fitting through the eye of a needle."

"I'm pretty sure you're combining two books, both of which I only skimmed." I know I should have read the *Big Book* of Alcoholics Anonymous by now, but I'm not really into nonfiction.

"Might want to give them a little more in-depth reading."

"Well, if I wind up in prison, I'll have plenty of time. Unless I get shivved in the yard."

"Women rarely use shivs. They use nails or teeth. You'll be fine."

"Thanks for the reassurance."

"And I'll accept calls from the penitentiary."

I would have preferred not to be reminded that if I go to prison, every time I make a call, there'll be an operator asking the person at the other end if they'll accept a call from an inmate.

"I could see myself sponsoring someone in prison," Lynette continues, "*if* they landed there by being honest. The one type of person I won't waste my time on is a liar."

"You really think I should risk my life by admitting I don't know what happened the night I went missing?"

"If you're not honest, you're risking your sobriety, which is the same as risking your life."

Her tone is too serious. It's making me anxious. I try to lighten the mood by saying, "I'm a fiction writer. I'm hardwired to be good at lying. I'm sure I can do it safely."

"I didn't say how you were wired, and I don't care what you're good at. Maybe writing fiction is as dangerous as any other sort of lying for an alcoholic. I don't know. What I do know is that if you're not following the simple instructions laid out in the *Big Book* of Alcoholics Anonymous, I can't help you."

"What? Are you threatening to dump me as a sponsee?"

"That's a good idea," she says. "I'm glad you mentioned it. Consider yourself dumped."

I force a laugh, hoping she'll join in and the idea of dumping me will just be a bad joke.

She doesn't laugh. Instead, she continues, "Last fall I was feeling so damn good about myself because I was asked to be someone's sponsor. I listened respectfully while she shared her moral inventory with me so she could get out of treatment as soon as possible. I answered the phone every time she called, even when I didn't feel like it because her problems made me jealous. I wished I could trade my problems for hers. But I kept myself from building a resentment because I cared about her. And despite everything else I was in this life, I was somebody's sponsor—something I never thought I'd be. I was proud to be a sponsor. Then, the girl I'm sponsoring just disappears without a trace and never calls me."

"I would have called you if I could," I say, the words sounding weak even to my own ears.

"Don't interrupt me, I'm not finished."

"Okay. I'm sor—"

"I end up seeing on the news that she went missing after a party. All I can think about is that I should have helped her more, and that I've failed as a sponsor. And you know what that makes me want to do, Hannah?"

"Meth?"

"No. Oxys and alcohol. But I don't give in to that shit because maybe the only thing I can ever really do for another alcoholic is be a good example."

"You've always been a good example."

"I used to be a textbook bad example," she says, "and that's why I thought you had a shot at being sober. I thought that if *I* could get clean, *anyone* could. But I've changed my mind. I think you're incapable of being honest with yourself, and until that changes, you're going to find one way after another to fuck up your life, until you find something that takes you out once and for all.

"Lynette, I know you don't mean what you're saying. Please stop and listen to yourself."

"Oh, believe me, I'm listening. You called me to tell me you're plunging into a moral gray area. You asked me to come with you. Now you listen, Hannah: the answer is no."

I start stuttering, trying to find something to say that won't make her angrier.

"I've gotta go. Watch your back, and your soul," she says, "in whatever order you choose."

CHAPTER

83

Now

I'M STARING AT my phone, wishing Lynette were still at the other end so I could talk her out of dumping me, when there's a loud knock at the door. Through the peephole, I see two people staring at the door with an intensity that feels almost predatory. Neither the man nor the woman is in uniform, but the determination on their faces tells me they're on duty.

When I open the door, the man steps back, pulls out his wallet, and flips it open. He holds his ID at eye level. "Hello, Ms. Silver. I'm Detective Sergeant Fullerton with the St. Louis Metropolitan Police."

The woman steps forward and says, "And I'm Detective Sergeant Hunt." "We'd like to ask you a few questions. Can you come with us?"

"Am I in trouble?"

"No," Hunt says. "We just want to ask you some questions."

I don't want to answer their questions, and I don't want to leave this rediscovered paradise of my modern apartment. But I notice people starting to come out of their apartments. A few have their phones out, probably recording.

"It won't take long," Hunt says.

I let them escort me from my apartment, down the stairs to the front door.

As soon as Detective Fullerton opens the building door, flashes of light explode in the dusk. I flinch from the brightness and the clamor of voices calling out to me. The reporters are even more aggressive and determined than the police. The sliding doors of several vans open, and more cameras take aim at me. A woman rushes toward me with a fat microphone held out, but before she can get close, another reporter steps in front of her and shouts a question that I can't hear in all the noise. Beyond the reporters, I can see people gathering around along the street.

"Hannah, are you okay?" someone shouts, shoving their microphone through the horde. "Where have you been?" another reporter asks, at the same time as a third demands, "Hannah, do you know what happened to Amelia?"

"Keep moving," Detective Hunt says, gripping my elbow.

More cops emerge from police cars idling along the street. They form a perimeter around me, helping the detectives hurry me toward an unmarked car.

Even after I get in, I can hear reporters shouting my name. I look back and see their cameras clicking furiously as we drive away, my name still sounding behind me: *Hannah, Hannah, Hannah . . .*

* * *

At the station, the detectives lead me into a room with nothing but a table, chairs, and a fluorescent light overhead. "Have a seat," Detective Fullerton says. A faint odor of stale coffee lingers. When Fullerton asks me if I want any, I shake my head. "I'll get you some water," he says.

Now it's only Detective Sergeant Hunt and me in the room. Perhaps the police think that's going to make me feel safer, but I know it's dangerous to feel safe when you have a secret to keep.

"Are you okay?" she asks. Her voice is kind, but not *overly* kind.

I nod.

"Can you tell me what happened the night of November thirtieth?" she asks.

I'm not answering her questions until she answers mine. Do they know I drugged Alex? Is he still alive? I know better than to ask her those questions, so instead, I ask, "Is Alex okay?" It's strange being away from him. I wonder where the midpoint between us is. A cornfield in Iowa? Why did he tell me Justine was dead?

"Police went to the cabin, but he wasn't there."

My breath catches in my chest. Where would he go after ingesting a bowl full of Halcion? I've read that police are allowed to lie, and I hope that's what Hunt is doing now. I don't want to ever find him at my door. I realize I want him dead.

"I don't remember the night of November thirtieth," I say. "I used to drink too much."

"What time that day did you start drinking?"

I picture myself in my apartment, drinking and then doing lines with "Eli." I have to know if he's still alive.

"Hannah?" she asks, and repeats her question. "At what time did you start drinking on November thirtieth?"

If she doesn't have any information for me, I don't have any for her. "I don't remember."

"What time did you go to the party?"

"I don't remember."

"How did you get there?"

"Eli—" I stop and correct myself, "*Alex* picked me up."

"How long had you been seeing Alex?"

"A couple of months."

I refuse to answer any more of the questions she asks about my relationship with Alex. I tell her that if she keeps pressing me, I'll get an attorney.

"We can come back to that later," she says. "Where did you go after the party?"

"I don't remember."

"The next day I came to question you. There was no answer at the door, though your car was out back."

"Is that when you broke down my door?"

I know I've said something I shouldn't have by her satisfied look. "No, it isn't. So you weren't home between December first and the day your door was broken down?"

"I don't know."

"Ms. Silver, did you flee November 30th or the morning of December 1?"

"I don't remember."

"Why did you flee so soon after the party that you and Amelia both attended?"

"I don't remember anything."

"You were the last one seen with Amelia, and there were gunshots fired shortly after you two left the party."

I feel like someone just hit me in the chest with a shovel. I was the last one seen with Amelia. Me, not Alex and me. Amelia and I didn't get along, but I've never wanted her dead. Or have I?

"Amelia and I weren't the only ones who left the party."

"We've already questioned Justine. She says she didn't witness the argument you had with Amelia in the street right before the shots were fired. But the other students witnessed you having an argument with Justine before you left the party. They say you stole some jewelry, and Justine was trying to make sure you didn't leave with it. They also say she accused you of having a gun. Do you have a gun, Ms. Silver?"

I press my lips together. I know the best thing I can do for myself right now is shut up.

"The other graduate students say you didn't get along with Justine or Amelia. Justine told us you were jealous of Amelia. You wanted to take Amelia's place as Justine's best friend, didn't you?"

I can't stop myself from saying, "Amelia was never Justine's best friend."

"What was your relationship with Amelia like?" she asks.

I tell her what I should have said right away. "I want an attorney."

* * *

I get a harried-looking public defender who demands that I be taken to the hospital before I answer any more questions.

At the hospital, they tell me what I already know. What I've suspected since putting on the bra at Luke's house and finding it nearly too small. I'm pregnant. I wasn't just pretending to be pregnant at the cabin with Alex; a little life was growing inside me. On the ultrasound, I see a swirl of gray and white shapes. The swirl shifts slightly, as if to greet me. My baby. *My baby.*

Back in my room, the nurse holds my hand and tells me everything is going to be okay. "We're going to keep you overnight to run some tests. Who can I call for you?" she asks.

"Just my lawyer."

"You also have a visitor who doesn't look like press. She says her name is Claire."

Claire! "Please send her in right away."

Claire comes in and gives me a huge hug. I've never seen her hug anyone before. "I'm so glad you came," I tell her. "I know I haven't always been at my best around you. Thank you for not giving up on me."

"Don't feel bad. I would have been stressed out too if I were in your shoes. Justine did everything she could to make you seem crazy, and some people fell for it."

I try to keep the mood from getting too somber. "At least if they try me for shooting Amelia, I can plead insanity."

Claire doesn't reassure me that I won't be tried or that people don't think I'm crazy. She just asks me what happened and what she can do to help. I wonder if I should tell her I'm pregnant. Instead, I ask, "How's Justine?"

"She spent the last quarter in Rome. Since getting back she's been really sick. She just joins the workshop via Zoom. She usually has her camera off. She sounds horrible."

"What do you mean she sounds horrible?"

"She sounds like she has a very unsexy cold."

The nurse comes in with a tray of bland-looking food. Yet I feel my mouth watering. "You must be starving," Claire says.

"And thirsty," I reply, grabbing the little bottle of apple juice from the tray. I unscrew the top and drink it all in just a few gulps.

"I'll let you enjoy your dinner," Claire says. We exchange numbers and I tell her I'll call her later. Hospital food has never tasted so good.

* * *

When the nurse comes back in to take my tray, she tells me, "There's a professor, a patient here, who asked me to send you his regards. Barkley something?"

Newhouse. "He's here? In the hospital?"

"Yes, and he seems like he could use a friend."

"Can you tell him I'll come see him as soon as I've had a chance to talk to my lawyer?"

"Of course," she says. "I'll let him know."

My lawyer bustles in and smiles perfunctorily. "How are you feeling?"

"Pregnant."

He smiles a real smile. "Good! That will help your case."

I hate the thought that I have to have "a case."

"In other good news: Alex was caught on camera selling stolen jewelry at a pawn shop."

It's good news, but still, it hurts to think about. Was Alex just doing what Justine wanted him to? I know Justine wanted to hurt me. But did Alex? And does he still? Will he tell the cops he witnessed me shooting Amelia? Will he give them the notebook?

I can just picture myself in prison, trying to see on all sides of me, turning in circles as I wander down the hall, hands trembling when I pull my prison-issue pants down to sit on the toilet, my bladder too shy to unclench, and me too scared to leave the protective stall, folding in two over my legs, over my life, wondering if there's something sharp—not because I want to hurt another inmate or protect myself from one, but because I need to be done. *Finis.*

But I can't be done. My baby needs me.

"Did Alex really escape the cabin before the police could get to him?"

"Yes, but that's good for our case. Fleeing just makes him look guilty."

"Guilty of everything? Not just kidnapping me but shooting Amelia?"

"Justine told the police you were the last one seen with Amelia. She said she didn't see Alex."

"Yeah, but do you think the police believe her?"

"I don't know yet, and I won't be able to keep the police from questioning you for much longer," my lawyer says.

"Give me an hour."

CHAPTER

84

Now

"HANNAH," PROFESSOR NEWHOUSE says weakly. He's surrounded by monitors, and an IV tube is sticking out of his arm. Without taking his eyes off me, he asks the nurse aide who's hovering beside him, "Can you give us a few moments?" He gestures at the tray of uneaten food in front of him. "And please take this culinary abomination."

"I'll give you some privacy," she says, "but I'm not taking this tray back until you eat something." She squeezes his shoulder and nods at me before leaving the room.

I close the door behind her, then turn back to the professor. "I remember you telling me that if something is free, I like it," I say.

"There's fine print on everything, my dear. If it's free, you like it—except hospital food, which is an exception to every rule."

I laugh before turning serious. "How are you doing?" I ask, watching some fluid moving through the IV tube into his arm.

"Nothing unexpected. I've exhausted my liver and don't qualify for a transplant. I wouldn't take one if they offered it to me, anyway. I'd drown it in scotch. There's no longer any doubt, I'm on my way out of this world. And they won't even let me have a drink to celebrate. They're giving me Ativan instead."

"Does it help?"

"I don't know. It certainly doesn't compare to a drink. A drink is an *experience*." He closes his eyes and smiles. "A drink is romantic, and I love a good romance. Speaking of which," he opens his eyes and looks at me, "how are you taking Amelia's disappearance? Are you happy to have Justine all to yourself?"

"There was never any romance between Justine and me."

"Perhaps not in a traditional sense."

"I was obsessed with her."

"And aren't you still?"

Instead of directly answering his question, I say, "I want to know more about her award-winning story. The story she turned in for workshop was definitely AI. Was her *Atlantic* student fiction writing story also AI? Is that why it's being kept a secret?"

"No," he says, smiling slightly. "I'll tell you, but it's a story best told with a good glass of scotch."

"You're dying because alcohol has destroyed your liver. Do you really want a drink?"

"Yes." He takes a labored breath. "Very much."

I text Claire, and she responds by giving the text a thumbs-up.

"Your drink is on the way," I tell Newhouse. "Tell me about Justine's story before you have your last scotch."

"I didn't get this old by being a fool. I'm going to nap. Wake me up when there's a scotch in my hand."

I'm afraid that if he closes his eyes, he'll be so happy and relaxed he'll go toward the light—all the way, and I'll never find out why Justine's story has been kept so hush-hush. I sit watching the monitors, making sure Professor Newhouse's heart is still beating and that his oxygen level doesn't dip below 90 percent.

I'm relieved when there's a knock on the door. I open it, and Claire hands me the bottle that was originally for my apple juice. *Thanks,* I mouth, and close the door again.

I waft the bottle under the professor's nose. He seems to be asleep but, when I touch the bottle to his hand, he grasps it. He takes a sip, and then another.

"Is there a bigger bottle of this?" he asks, opening his eyes.

"There could be," I say. "Tell me about Justine's story."

He clears his throat, and I say, as if it's just crossed my mind, "Do you mind if I record this?"

He looks pleased as he says, "Must you?" and without waiting for an answer says, "Oh, all right."

He takes another swig from his apple juice bottle, then pauses dramatically before saying, "You can take someone else's talent and put your own name on it. She took the thesis of a University of Iowa nonfiction MFA student, made a few edits so it would read like fiction, and submitted it to *The Atlantic* student fiction writing contest. She also used it to get into ten graduate schools. As you may or may not have noticed, she didn't apply to the University of Iowa."

"I thought that was odd, but I figured she'd rather not be at the top fiction writing school because she might not be the best writer there."

He chuckles. "I'm not sure she writes anything, other than her name at the top of other people's work. She probably thought changing the story genre from nonfiction to fiction would cover her. She must not have looked closely at my biography. And I will admit the picture of me on the Wash U website is from my better years. She thought she'd dug far enough back in time that no one in academia would recognize the piece she stole. Her hands are pretty, but they're not much good for counting."

He looks at me to make sure I'm listening closely. I'm guessing no one has paid much attention to him in a while. No one besides me has even come to visit. "Hannah, when I told you I didn't finish Justine's story, I meant I didn't finish it *recently*. I read every word the first time I saw it, four decades ago, when one of my students turned it in to my class at U of Iowa."

"Why didn't you tell anyone that Justine's story was plagiarism?" I ask, unable to hide my sense of betrayal. He knew Justine had taken the funding that should've gone to me. He saw her mentally torturing me at the parties.

"Because I was too drunk to attend the incoming student selection committee meetings. The committee read the submissions and made the selections without me. By the time I read the story, it was too late. They'd already extended an offer to her. I wasn't going to risk ending my career by drawing attention to my . . . absences. I didn't want anyone to see there were consequences to my drinking."

"I understand," I say, feeling my own shame in response. "I'm really embarrassed about my own drinking."

"No, I didn't say I was embarrassed. I haven't gotten embarrassed in at least a couple decades. I just didn't want to lose my job. I've been teaching for sixty years. What would I have done if I hadn't taught? What will I do if I somehow survive my bad liver?"

"You might consider treatment," I tell him. "I made a really good friend there."

"Good for you." He raises the apple juice bottle like he's toasting me. "I wish you well with it. Just promise me that if you end up in heaven, you'll take my class."

"I'll be there if I can," I say, wondering: *If there's a heaven, will they let me in?*

"Thank you," he says softly, tipping the bottle back. He drains it. "Goodbye, Hannah," he says. "Goodbye for now."

* * *

Before I leave the hospital the next day, the detectives question me with my lawyer present. "Tell them," he urges me. I tell them about being kept prisoner in the cabin and how obsessed Alex was with getting me pregnant.

"And the good news?" my lawyer prompts.

"I'm five weeks pregnant."

Detective Hunt sighs, but Fullerton just nods, as if he knew all along that I was pregnant.

They want me to recount the events of November 30 again. I keep telling them I don't remember. My lawyer points out that they didn't find a gun in my apartment, and no one saw me with one. With no gun and no body, there's no evidence of a crime.

Still, Hunt tells me not to leave St. Louis.

CHAPTER 85

Now

As soon as I get home, I tap into a neighbor's internet connection and check my email.

I'm skimming through a bunch of spam when I see a message with @WUSTL.edu in the return address. The sender is Duncan O'Reilly. The subject line simply reads, "Your Registration."

I double click on it. I start to feel nauseous during the endless minute it takes for it to open.

Dear Ms. Silver,

Our records show that you haven't enrolled in classes or paid your tuition. Please contact the graduate office as soon as possible.

It's dated December 3, 2024, and it smells funny. It reeks of desperation. A director doesn't handle registration issues; his admin does. There's another reason he wants me to come in.

I remind myself I still have the photos and he's weak; he can't hurt me. He didn't need to mask the email as a formal registration inquiry. He could simply have written it as himself, the director of the graduate program in creative writing, asking one of the students to come in to discuss her classes. But he doesn't think like that. What is the inside of his head like? Are his thoughts sluggish, hard to prod into a meaningful direction, or are they like cockroaches in a room where the light has just been turned on, scattering too fast to gather up?

I decide I'll show up unannounced tomorrow.

I turn to my closet. What do I have that will make me look innocent? White would be too obvious, and besides, all the white clothing I have is a couple of sizes too small to look innocent in. At the back of my closet I find dress pants and a light blue shirt that I've never worn.

I lay the clothes out on the counter, like I'm some sort of upstanding nine-to-fiver who has to plan ahead in order to arrange everything for the next day. I can be anyone I can impersonate. Who can I impersonate successfully, though? I need a narrator for my life, someone more together than I am. Someone simple and good and without so many doubts. From now on, I'll live my life as though I'm writing a *Just for Dummies* guide to being normal.

As I walk down the hall to my car to check it out, the narrator says: *The busy professional should always make sure her automobile or other mode of transportation is in good working order so she can get to all her important meetings on time.*

I know there's a god because when I exit my building, I see Lucy. She's across the street, and her tail goes up into a happy *S* shape when she sees me.

In other good news, my car starts as soon as I turn the key. My insurance and registration are still in the glove compartment, and I still have a quarter tank of gas. If Alex shows up and I need to get away, I have the means.

When I get out of my car to go back into my apartment, a couple of reporters emerge out of my blind spot and chase me with microphones. "Hannah—Ms. Silver, is it true you're pregnant?"

I wonder who leaked my pregnancy to the press. My attorney? It doesn't really matter, though. I'll tell my story myself once I figure out what exactly happened the night Amelia went missing.

CHAPTER

86

Now

MY FIRST NIGHT alone in my apartment is torture. Trying to sleep in a bed without Alex is even harder than trying to sleep in a bed *with* him. I used to listen to his breathing when I couldn't sleep. Now, my thoughts parade through my head like a thirty-piece brass band, complete with elephants, crazy clown cars, and Vulcans rushing into the crowd to kiss and scare the pretty girls. Compared to this racket, Eli's breathing was practically a Zen meditation. And it wasn't just his breathing—it was his body, and mine. How they were *ours.*

All those months, I didn't realize how lucky I was to be cold. To have a vital survival task every minute of every day. Here, I don't have to try to stay warm. There's nothing to do at night but try to sleep. No breath to listen to, no body to press against. Only me, and a cacophony of contradictory thoughts: *You have nothing to worry about! Run away! Don't talk to anyone! Write a tell-all memoir! Change your name! Slit your wrists?*

But suicide isn't an option. I put my hand on my stomach. "We're going to be okay," I whisper. "I promise."

* * *

The next morning, I see two police officers parked outside my building, probably waiting to see if Alex comes to find me. I walk over to their window and ask for a ride to campus. "I don't want to hassle with parking," I say, wondering if they know about last fall's incident with my car on the quad. The cop at the wheel tells me to wait while he radios dispatch for another car to take me.

My situation has its perks.

Fifteen minutes later, I enter Duncan Hall and walk into the graduate English offices with my head held high—not so high it's conspicuous, but enough that I don't look like I'm going to confession. I don't check in with the secretary at the desk. I have pictures. I don't need to follow rules.

Duncan is sitting at his desk, squinting at his computer screen as if it might suddenly do something. I imagine him watching porn—something both sadistic and mildly fetishistic.

"Hello, Hannah," he says.

He doesn't sound scared.

"Hey, Duncan," I reply, closing the door and sitting down without being invited.

He smiles. I had attributed the repressed quality of his email to rage, but the gleam in his eyes tells me it was glee. "It's been quite a while since I've seen you," he says.

I wonder why he's engaging in small talk, until he continues, "The last time I saw you was the night Amelia went missing."

This is a much more conversationally aggressive version of Duncan than I'm accustomed to. It's hard to get the upper hand when I don't know why he's so happy to see me. It's like his inner Cheshire cat is about to break out and mark my leg.

"What a coincidence, Duncan. That's the last time I saw you too."

"But did you see me as you threw your gun into the dumpster?"

Did I hear him correctly? I dig my nails into my palms, needing something to focus on besides the alarm that's started to blare in my head. I barely keep from asking: *When? Where? Was anyone with me?*

"What the hell are you talking about?" I ask.

He leans across his desk. "The gun you used to shoot Amelia."

"I don't have a gun," I say, silently adding, *anymore*, "and I've never shot anyone."

He leans back in his chair again and smiles. I had no idea his face was that flexible. "I didn't expect your criminal tendencies to progress so quickly, Hannah. I remember when you went to treatment, and I remember afterward, when so many things went missing from alumni homes that we almost didn't have any more parties. It seems so innocent now, compared to murdering Amelia."

"We've already determined that I didn't take anything from any of their houses," I say, "except, one time, when I took you. Or, I guess, 'was taken' is more accurate." He doesn't look as fearful as I'd like. I continue, "If I'd stolen anything, you would've seen it. You've been to my apartment. Do you remember what you did to me, or do I need to show you the pictures I took to remind you?"

"I have the gun, Hannah."

"Which gun?"

"The .22 with the serial number filed off."

Well, fuck. "Put your phone on the table," I say.

He does. I recognize the iPhone. I have fond memories of it.

"Now you," he says.

I set my phone beside his.

Now that I'm 95 percent sure we're not being recorded, I say, "What's this about you having a gun?"

"I wasn't far behind you when I heard the shots. I watched you go to the dumpster."

"Heard." So he didn't see who shot Amelia. "I would think if you'd heard a shot, your first priority would've been to make sure no one was injured."

He looks a little less like his inner Cheshire cat is about to mark its territory, but then he shrugs, and the terrible calm returns to his eyes.

"This isn't *CSI.* Prints don't last long on a gun," I say with as much confidence as I can fake.

I looked it up at Luke's. According to *Law Enforcement Today*, the colder it is, the less likely police will find prints. Prints are a mixture of dirt and oil from skin, and the less people sweat, the less likely they'll leave prints. The thing is, I'm pretty sure Alex and I were both sweating that night. Not just from anxiety, but from alcohol and cocaine.

Duncan tells me what I once told him, "We can check if you'd like."

I try to look nonchalant, mildly amused.

"I can have you put away," he says.

"I can have you put away too," I say. But the truth is, I don't want those pictures to ever see the light of day. The press might give me the Monica Lewinsky treatment and let Duncan off easy. I'd be seen as a sexual object for the rest of my life. Anything I said or wrote would be merely a footnote in history.

"I can have you put away for life," he says.

He's got me there. But I pretend I don't know it. "Sex offenders don't do so well in prison," I say.

"I'm not going to prison. The most you could hope for is that I'd lose my position here."

"And never get another one for the rest of your life."

"Perhaps if you were someone respectable."

I don't take the bait. He's insulted me much worse before. "If you were going to turn it in to the police, you'd have done it by now," I say. "You're not going to look very innocent turning it in now."

"I don't need to identify myself to turn in the gun. The police could find it on their doorstep and then their forensics department will find your prints on it."

"I want to see it."

"The only way you'll see it is in an evidence bag."

Wow. Did I harden him this much?

I try a different tack, one that's been successful in the past. "If something happened, it wouldn't look good that, prior to the incident, Wash U got me out of a DUI, sent me to an expedited treatment program, then took me back and kept getting me drunk at parties."

"Let me know when you're done," he says.

I've created a monster. I lean back in my chair to signal I've said my piece and I'm not too worried about anything. I didn't escape one terrible man to fall under the thumb of another.

We stare across the desk at each other for so long that I start to feel like I have sandpaper in my eyes. He's not going to back down. He's keeping the gun, using it to hold power over me. He knows I won't report it, not with my prints possibly on it.

"It's been swell," I tell Duncan as I stand up to leave. I turn away and finally let myself blink.

"Hannah," he says.

I slam the door on whatever he's going to say.

He's gotten smarter in the months since I last saw him. Or maybe not. If Duncan truly thinks I'm capable of murder, it's pretty foolish to threaten me.

How could Alex allow me to throw the gun into a dumpster? Or was that part of his plan?

I slip on my sunglasses, pull my hat low, and move quickly through Duncan Hall, slipping into an adjacent corridor. I exit the side door, keeping my head down in case anyone's around. It's time to talk to Justine.

CHAPTER 87

Now

I STAND OUTSIDE JUSTINE'S building, staring at the garden-level apartment in the front corner. The one I know is hers. But from where I'm standing, there's nothing to see.

I glance at the buzzer, knowing better than to press it. I don't want to tip her off that I'm coming. Instead, I wait for someone to exit the building.

When a man comes out, I rush inside before he can ask me anything, such as "Do you live here?"

I walk down the carpeted hallway, stepping as lightly as possible. I feel like an intruder, like I shouldn't be here. But that's how I've always felt around Justine.

I knock gently on number 109, then wait. No answer. I knock again, louder this time. The silence on the other side feels heavy, occupied. I know someone is there. But the door stands unyielding between us.

I step back. I need some sort of plan to get Justine to open the door.

Just as I'm about to leave, a woman enters the building. I pull my hat low and nod to her. She nods back curtly, then slides her little mail key into the mailbox slot near the front door and turns away from me.

"Hey," I say, my voice casual but my pulse quickening. "Do you know anything about 109?"

"Nope. Never see her. Some reporter buzzes me every few days looking for her. I figure if she won't buzz him in, I'm not going to buzz him in to harass her. But I did see a deliveryman at her door last week."

"Oh, thank goodness!" I say. "I've been so worried about her. Do you know what they were delivering?"

"Groceries, I think. They were from Schnucks."

I leave and come back an hour later, bags of groceries in hand. When someone exits the building, I easily slip inside.

At Justine's door, I place the bags just far enough back that she can see them through the peephole. I knock once, then turn and walk quickly down the hall, stomping my feet so she'll hear me retreating. I tiptoe back and wait.

The door creaks open. A hand reaches out for the grocery bags.

"Justine," I say. She tries to close the door, but I slide my foot into the door frame to stop her. "I just want to talk to you."

"Out," she whispers. She's wearing oversized Chanel sunglasses, and she's ghostly pale. Claire was right. She looks sick. Her posture is slumped, and her hair hangs in oily clumps, draped like a tattered curtain around her face.

"I just need to ask you about November thirtieth. Then I'll leave you alone. I swear."

The door to another apartment opens. Justine opens her door wider so she can slam it on me, but my foot stops it. My breath catches, and I swallow back a cry.

I fight through the pain and grab the groceries while she batters my foot. Then I shove my way into the apartment and slam the door behind me.

Justine stares at me a moment, and I stare back. Her forehead isn't right. It's too big, too bulging, to be Justine.

"Amelia!" I exhale the name like a ghost, my voice unsteady. The realization hits me like a lead weight dropped from a thousand feet, landing squarely on my chest. I didn't know how badly I wanted to see Justine until this very moment.

My heart breaks a little as Amelia takes off her Chanel sunglasses and her eyes meet mine. "Yes, but you already knew that."

"Why the hell are you pretending to be Justine?"

"Because I want to be her. The *only* her. Not just a rude imitation like you."

"I don't want to be her."

She laughs again. It strains her face because there's hardly any fat left in her cheeks. I see now why she lost all that weight. She wanted to look like Justine.

"You didn't know how to be her," she says. "But you *wanted* to. Don't you understand, Hannah? You and I are the same."

"What are you talking about?"

"I was a nobody, too. You remember how I was—awkward, uncomfortable. I spent most of my time trying to figure out what to do. I was miserable in my own skin. I shrank inside it. I *cowered*.

"I was humiliated when you stepped in to stop Newhouse from making fun of my unshaved legs, as if I couldn't defend myself. Except that you were right. I *couldn't*, at least not then. Remember when we were in the back of Ben's pickup, and everyone just sat there quietly while Claire told me I don't think like a writer?"

"I'm sorry," I say, and I truly mean it, despite whatever she's about to tell me.

"I decided then to become someone else—Justine. I'm no longer that weak, passive girl who let Newhouse insult her." Her eyes narrow with rage. "But no one treated me differently, even though I changed. Justine, Newhouse, and the rest of you—you put me in a box. Everyone saw me as timid. No one respected me."

She does seem like Justine. Selfish, vindictive, and calculating. She even has teeth marks on the back of her hand.

"I'm better at being Justine than she ever was," Amelia says, her voice rising feverishly. "The last Justine hit a plateau, but there are no limits for me."

The look in her eyes is one I've seen many times in the mirror. She's manic. She's me without meds. I know the energy surging through her body, the tightness in her chest, the shallow breaths. I don't want to be her any longer.

She sees me take a step back and laughs.

"It was Justine who put the cherry pit in your drink," she says. "But it was me who slipped something stronger in. How did you like the GHB?"

"You roofied me?"

She laughs again, a sharp, mocking sound. "You're welcome."

I have a brief flashback to waking up on the campus lawn in my car. My reflection in the officer's sunglasses terrifies me. I look like a lunatic.

"Did you drive my car onto the campus lawn?" I ask her.

"It wasn't me, but it was my idea."

"Then who was it?" I demand.

"It was you."

"No. I was too messed up to drive."

"I helped you. I risked my life to help you." She tilts her head to one side and says, almost fondly, "I loved how hard you fought when I dragged you to the driver's seat of your car." I can't tell if her smile is mocking or seductive now. Both, I decide. Just like Justine's smile when we went to a bar after buying our books. Was Justine already planning then to ruin my life?

"Justine and I only planned for you to get a DUI," Amelia says, "but you must have been going for extra credit. You drove into a No Parking sign and onto the campus lawn. It was exhilarating. I thought I could get you to drive all the way into the English department. But you wouldn't. You put your car in park, handed me the keys, and said, 'Take these.'"

I want to smack the smug look off her face. "Do you have any idea how scared I was that I couldn't remember what happened? I found bruises on my body. I bought a gun."

"I loved it when Justine told me you went and bought a gun."

Even as Alex said he loved me that night I showed him the gun, I now realize he was just excited to have something to report back to Justine. "You, Alex, and Justine are sociopaths," I say.

She laughs. "Okay. But I'm the strongest. I'm the last sociopath standing."

"Really? Where is Justine?" I ask, quickly adding, "Not you—the first one."

"I was the sober cab that night, November thirtieth. I had Ben's keys. After Eli shot Justine, I told him I was taking her to the hospital. Instead, I drove across the Illinois border to East St. Louis and pushed her out of the car."

Alex shot her? *Not me?* I'm hit with a mixture of relief and shock. I'm not a murderer, but I was trapped in a cabin with one for four and a half months. "Where is she?"

Amelia's smile widens. "They don't even have cops in East St. Louis."

"What are you saying?"

"She's dead. A Jane Doe who didn't even make the front page of the *East St Louis Monitor*."

I already knew in my soul that Justine was gone, but the certainty of it still stops my heart for a second. What a sad end for someone who commanded so much attention in real life—just dropped off and left to die.

"If she's dead, who put the urn in my living room?"

"What urn?" Amelia asks.

"The one with Will Gass's ashes."

"It wasn't me," Amelia says. "I would have thrown him in the trash."

"It must have been you if it wasn't Justine."

"I couldn't care less about some urn of ashes. I'm strong and happy. My life has never been better." She takes a step closer, and despite saying she's happy, her smile is strained. "I'll do what I need to keep it that way."

She pushes me so hard I stumble and fall back, crashing onto the floor. "You're weak," she says. "I can do anything to you that I want."

She quickly throws the bolt on the deadlock. I scramble away as she reaches for my ankle. I kick at her arms. "I love that you're putting up a fight," she says. "The medication hasn't completely tamed you."

I scooch away from her and manage to get to my feet. I have to protect my baby.

She pulls out a gun. I recognize it. Did Duncan give it to her?

"Where did you get my gun?" I ask.

"Alex. He gave it to me to get rid of. But why would I get rid of something so beautiful?"

I don't say what I'm thinking: *Justine was more beautiful than the gun, and you had no qualms about leaving her to die.* I wish Duncan hadn't been bluffing when he said he had the gun. Then I wouldn't be staring down the barrel right now.

"It was nice knowing you, Hannah."

I swallow hard. I never imagined that Amelia would be the one holding my life in her hands. "You're really going to shoot me?" The words barely make it out of my throat. If I tell her about the baby, will it make her put the gun down—or push her to pull the trigger?

She giggles. "No, *Justine* is going to shoot you. And then disappear."

She trains the gun on my heart. I know she's not bluffing. She wants to kill me. As soon as she can steady her hands.

I take a deep breath, forcing myself to focus, channeling the energy from the adrenaline coursing through my body. I need to psych her out before her hands stop shaking. "Try to breathe," I say as calmly as I can with my heart jackhammering in my chest. "Relax."

"The pills have made you a complete idiot, Hannah. You think you can talk me out of shooting you?"

"I was just telling you to breathe because you can't aim without breathing."

Her eyes widen. She hadn't considered that she might miss.

I hear footsteps in the hall. I continue, "Before firing the gun, after you've aimed it, you'll need to take a deep breath and exhale slowly."

"Shut up," she snaps.

"When you look through the sights, you'll notice that you're tracing a small figure eight pattern."

"Shut up, you dumb bitch," she screams so loudly the whole room seems to vibrate.

The footsteps halt abruptly. Someone pounds on the door. I hear the lady from earlier—the one who told me Justine got a Schnuck's delivery—asking, "Is everything okay in there?"

Amelia turns, and I lunge forward, shoving her arms up so the gun is no longer aimed at me. A shot rings out, and I feel the jolt in her arms as the recoil throws her off balance. She's at her weakest.

I know enough about fighting to know that timing is everything. You can tell who's going to win before the fight even starts. Her manic energy would terrify me, except that I've had it too. There's no control in manic energy. It's inefficient. It's chaos.

I grip her wrists and slam her against the wall. As I try to wrestle the gun from her, I see a flash of white teeth—her smile, feral and hungry. A jagged, searing pain rips through the side of my neck.

She bit me.

I scream. I can feel the mania bubbling up, trying to take over.

Breathe, I tell myself. *Keep your balance. You have control.*

And I do. I stomp on Amelia's foot. She cries out, and her grip on the gun loosens just enough for me to yank it away.

It fits perfectly in my hands. I point it at her, my voice firm. "Stay where you are."

Her eyes widen, but then she laughs. "You won't shoot me. You didn't even shoot Justine, after everything she did to you. She framed you—had Eli get you high and drag you to the party. Then she narked on you to Duncan." Her face twists in disgust. "And you just took it."

She's right. I couldn't pull the trigger. Not on her. Not on anyone. But I don't need to. I have control now. The Rev app is running, recording this conversation. I opened it before I even knocked on her door.

"Call the police!" I yell to the woman who's banging on the door.

A sense of emptiness invades my chest as I watch Amelia being led out in handcuffs, her eyes frantically darting between me and the officers. I can't help romanticizing her a little; part of me wants her to go free. Still, I don't let myself look away from her wide eyes and twitching mouth. I need to see her megalomania contained. Taken away.

CHAPTER

88

Now

Late spring, 2025

I TRY NOT TO think of Justine. I felt more intensely for Justine than I ever have for anyone, even Alex. I thought she was smart, unbeatable. I thought she had it all. But now, I know it was all a lie.

Where did she get the confidence to pull it off for so long?

Everything must have changed for her when she realized her name meant something. Had a high school English teacher asked about her relation to John, raved about her mediocre research paper, and given her an A? Or maybe, one night, while babysitting, she wandered through the house after putting the kids to bed, admiring the art from the owners' travels, wishing she had a life like theirs. Then, she picked up an old magazine from the coffee table, saw her last name, and thought: *This is how I can live in a beautiful house and travel the world. I won't merely fit into this world. I'll rise above it.*

But it turns out none of these scenarios is true. Other than her last name, she wasn't born lucky. She made her own luck. She'd been a ballerina. Not a great one—at least not great enough for her. And not a great writer. But writing is different from dancing. You can just put your name on anything and claim it's yours.

Except that I won't allow her to get away with it. Armed with the recording I took during my hospital visit to Professor Newhouse, I talk to the *St. Louis Post-Dispatch*, a true crime television show, and then with a vlogger who makes a YouTube video that has been viewed over a million times.

Now the only thing holding me back from writing the story of Justine, Alex, Amelia, and me is my notebook. I wish I hadn't written "Journal" on it. If Alex somehow gets it to the police, the recording of Amelia won't be enough to keep them from questioning me again.

I'm contacted almost every day by agents, reporters, publishers, and producers. They all want a story, one about being trapped in an abusive relationship with a monster who forced me to witness the murder of a beautiful girl, then made me swear upon my life that I'd never tell anyone what happened. The pièce de résistance: being kept as a sex slave in a secluded cabin until I conceived.

I know Amelia is writing a book, too. Her publisher gave her the money to post bond and get a good lawyer. Excerpts have come out. She claims she was having a nervous breakdown when she falsely took credit for dropping Justine off in East St. Louis. She claims it was me who abandoned Justine there. But her lies don't matter. Now, I'm the one with the winning story. I'm just waiting to find out what happened to the notebook before I write it.

CHAPTER

89

Now

I HAVEN'T TALKED TO Lynette in a couple of months, not since she dumped me as a sponsee. But still, one day I decide to call her. When she answers, I don't even bother with small talk. I'm afraid she'll hang up. Instead, I immediately apologize for having taken her for granted. I start to ask what I can do to make an amend, but she interrupts, "Stop, you're boring me. All I want from you is the inside scoop. Boy or girl?"

Apparently, she's still keeping up with news about me. "I decided it would be better not to know," I tell her. I'm afraid it will be a boy, and every time I look at him, I'll think of Alex. I don't need any more reminders that Alex is still out there.

"Now here's what you've gotta do," she says. "Each day, don't drink. Don't get high. And don't become a smoker, at least not until the kid's out."

"I thought you weren't going to sponsor me anymore."

"I wasn't. Women give each other advice all the time."

As soon as it occurs to me, I blurt: "You don't have any other girlfriends either."

"Quality over quantity."

"I guess quantity isn't my thing either. For four and a half months, Alex was my only friend."

"That seems like a quality issue."

"It was complicated."

Silence. I hope she's not worried about me. Well, not too worried. Having someone worry over me and my child, even just a little bit, is nice. It's one of the reasons I like to talk to Luke regularly. After I hang up with Lynette, I call him.

He answers the phone, "Hey, Hannah, what crazy concoction can I bring you two now?"

Thirty minutes later, he's at my door with peanut butter pickle sandwiches and Moose Tracks ice cream. I grab the sandwich from his hands and watch him struggle to rearrange the contents of the freezer so the new ice cream fits.

"Do you like Neapolitan?" he asks.

"Yes, but I don't think I have room for it," I reply around a bite of my sandwich.

"We'll have to combine two or three of these ice creams unless you can finish off two right now." He watches me shove more of the sandwich in my mouth. "How do you feel about cookies and cream chocolate almond fudge malted milk ball?"

I nod and keep chewing.

He brought himself a turkey sandwich and a Snickers bar. He catches me eyeing the Snickers and pulls another from his jacket pocket.

"Thank you," I say, grabbing it from his hand. We knock our Snickers together like we're toasting something.

"What are we toasting?" I ask.

"Friendship."

Suddenly, there's an awkward silence.

Why am I being silent?

Why is he? Why isn't he cracking a joke?

He sets his Snickers on the counter. He looks like he's searching for words, but he gives up and wraps me in his arms. I didn't realize how heavy my head was until I rest it against him. I've always liked hugging him. It makes me feel safe. But now it also makes me feel something else. I don't want to let go, and apparently he doesn't want to either. We don't let go after three seconds like friends do, or five seconds like good friends. Not after ten seconds, fifteen . . . All the things I could say to downplay the emotion and pretend this isn't something real flutter away. Our hug goes on so long there's no way we're going to be able to joke our way out of the feelings between us.

Without letting go, he asks, "Or do you want to toast to new possibilities in life, including between us?"

"What do you mean?" I ask, still holding onto him.

He pulls back and looks me in the eye. "We both have next Monday night off. Would you like to go to dinner?"

"Go out, or have takeout in one of our kitchens as usual?"

"Go out. I was thinking Zelo. They make even better spaghetti than I do."

I meet his gaze. "I don't want to lose you. None of my relationships have worked out, and I'd rather have you in my life as a friend than not have you at all." I place my hand on my stomach. "And there's also the fact that I'm pregnant with another man's child."

"Really?" he teases, looking at my large stomach. "I'd forgotten all about that."

I gently push on his arm. "I'm trying to be serious here for a minute."

"Hannah, I've been putting off telling you how I feel about you for three years. There's always been some reason not to tell you. First, it was because we were coworkers. Then it was because you were leaving for graduate school. Then you weren't responsive except by text. I don't want to put it off any longer. I'm here for you, and that's not going to change. No matter what. Even if things don't work out for us as more than friends."

"What about the baby? Will you be here for the baby too?"

"If you'll let me."

I'm about to say something undercutting, like "I'll try," but instead, I take a deep breath and tell him what I need. "Yes. I would love that. But I need to take things slowly. I was isolated with a man for four and a half months. He was my whole world, even before he took me up north. I can't do that sort of relationship anymore. I need to make sure I don't become dependent on one person ever again. I want my baby to have a healthy mother. Do you think we could take things slow?"

"We'll go as slow as you want. Why rush a good thing?"

Once again, I stop myself from undercutting this moment. Then, I do something I've always waited for a man to do first. I step closer to him and press my lips up to his. Without realizing it, I've been waiting to do this since we first met.

* * *

After Luke leaves for work, I call Lynette. I'm determined not to narrow my world down to one person. I love Luke, but I need Lynette too. I have a favor to ask of her.

"I'm calling because I was wondering . . . will you . . ." I almost can't bring myself to ask. "Will you come to the hospital with me when it's time?"

I'd assumed she'd need to think about it. But she immediately says, "Sure. I suppose I could. Sounds more important than anything else I have going on."

"Thank you, Lynette. Thank you for putting up with me and being here for me again."

"Who says I'm being here for you? Maybe I just really want to meet the kid."

"Okay, I'll take that. Thank you."

"You're welcome," she says. "I'm glad you called. I saw a picture of you a couple days ago. In one of those online groups that tries to figure out what happened and where the creep is."

I try not to look at those things. A few times someone posted a photo of a man who looks vaguely like Alex, and I started to feel the edges of my heart digging into my chest.

Now, I'm pretty happy if I just focus on what's in front of me. I drink herbal tea, go on walks, read, binge-watch as many shows as I can, and work lunch and/or dinner shifts. Being pregnant has helped keep me from raiding the liquor stash at work.

I said I'd never be like my mom, and I meant it.

When I don't react to Lynette's news about seeing my photo, she continues, "I stared at the picture for a while. You were walking into a store or something, and you looked different from how I remembered. I didn't believe it was you at first. You looked good. Happy."

My body feels foreign and cumbersome, and I'm overwhelmed by strange cravings and occasional loneliness. But I'm not stuck in a cabin with a man who might kill me.

"You know," I tell Lynette, "as strange as it is, I'm more content than I can ever remember being before."

"Considering your memory, that's not much of an accomplishment. You did look pretty damn cheerful in the picture though."

"I like putting one foot in front of the other. I like my cat. I like you."

"I don't mind you either," she says. "But now I need to get back to dinner. This oatmeal isn't going to microwave itself. Keep up the good work."

"Thanks, Lynette. I plan to."

And I do. My life is good. I'm grateful for all the things I used to take for granted—my car, my microwave, Lucy, "room temperature." I take my medication every night, and contrary to what I used to think, it doesn't keep me from writing. People talk about me online and sometimes in real life, in whispers as I pass by, but I no longer let their opinion of me change my own. Gossip, my diagnosis, and my scar aren't telling my story for me anymore. I'm telling it myself, one chapter at a time.

CHAPTER

90

Now: My Story

On a sweltering morning in early June, Claire texts me a link to People.com. I click on it, and a picture of Alex, alongside one of me, appear above the headline "Alex Bazin, Suspect in Kidnapping of Twenty-Seven-Year-Old Hannah Silver, Found Dead." My heart nearly stops as I read further. Alex's remains were found in the woods near the cabin he kept me in for four and a half months.

His "remains." He's really gone.

The cabin was burned to the ground. This is the best news I've ever read. My prison cell has been reduced to ashes; I never have to go back there. I scour the internet for more information and find various crime analysts' opinions. A retired detective thinks Alex set the fire to destroy evidence of the kidnapping.

I'm shocked and sad, but more than anything, I'm relieved. My baby and I are safe. Alex is gone forever.

Now I can write whatever I want without worrying he'll come out with the notebook. An accompanying picture showing the charred remains of the cabin gives me confidence that the notebook has been reduced to ashes. I'm ready to sign a publishing contract.

I Google the agents who've emailed me until I find one who looks like a Manhattan edition of Lynette, complete with a full set of bright white teeth and oversized glasses.

"I'm going to make you so much money," she tells me over the phone, "that you'll be bathing in it for the rest of your life."

I don't tell her that telling my story matters more to me than making money; now that she's painted such a vivid picture of how rich I'll be, it sounds rather lovely.

She's true to her word. My memoir sells at auction for $500,000.

Now I just have to write it.

One bad guy down, one to go.

Alex is dead. And Amelia—she isn't a bad guy, she's just an unmedicated version of me. Now that I'm all the way back on my mood stabilizer, I'm not worried about her.

There's only one person left to deal with.

I make some decaf coffee and sit down to write my tell-all memoir. I hear my own voice in my head: *Nonfiction is plagiarism. Don't plagiarize reality. Write your own story.*

I put my hands on the keyboard and start to type.

There are three people I suspect of killing Justine.

Duncan, the director of the graduate writing program, is first on my list of suspects.

ACKNOWLEDGMENTS

I'm so grateful for all the support I've received. Thank you to my tireless agent Terrie Wolf, and the members of our wolf pack. Huge thanks to gifted editor Rebecca Nelson and all the talented people at Crooked Lane Books. I'm eternally grateful to the members of my writers' group, Sandy Steffenson and Richard Thompson, who've been meeting with me every other week since 2009. Thank you to Terri Bischoff for the countless hours we spent in conversation, moving from Bob's Java Hut to the stock room at Once Upon a Crime in Minneapolis, where we explored both the twists and turns of novels and life. Thank you to my mom for giving me a love of reading and novels. I'm lucky to have a father and brother who attend every reading they can to cheer me on, and to have friends who serve as personal cheerleaders and confidants, especially Lynn Nelvik and Holly McVoy. I'm grateful for the love and support of John Weber.

Thank you to the readers whose enthusiasm makes writing so rewarding.

This book is dedicated to the ever-enduring Sarah Rudolph, my aunt and second mother.